# Second Chance

*Siân James*

PIATKUS

Copyright © 2000 by Siân James

First published in Great Britain in 2000 by
Judy Piatkus (Publishers) Ltd of
5 Windmill Street, London W1T 2JA
email: info@piatkus.co.uk

This edition published 2000

**The moral right of the author has been asserted**

*A catalogue record for this book is available from the British Library*

ISBN 0 7499 3208 2

Set in Times by
Phoenix Photosetting, Chatham, Kent
Printed and bound in Great Britain by
Cox & Wyman Ltd, Reading, Berkshire

To dear darling Anna
Last, but not least.

# Chapter One

It was ten o'clock, a Tuesday morning in late September. I was standing outside my mother's cottage, savouring the weak sunshine and remembering my childhood, the first days at school, walking reluctantly down the track, turning every few steps to wave to my mother standing where I now stood, the smell of autumn, the nip in the air, the blood-red berries, hips and haws, in the thinning hedges, a gulp of fear as I rounded the bend and could no longer see her. There'd been a strong bond between us, not surprising, really: an only child, an absent father.

About to turn back into the house, I saw someone coming up the lane towards me and waving – a postman pushing a bike, no, a postwoman. I stayed at the door.

'Hello,' the woman said. 'Kate, is it? We were all so sorry to hear about your poor mother. When is the funeral? We'll all be there. Everyone had a good word for your poor mother, and she seemed so well at the moment. I'm Lorna Davies, by the way. I feel I've known you for years, your mother told me so much about you. Whenever I had a letter for her she used to make me come in and listen to your latest exploits. You and I are the same age, it seems. Forty-three last spring, is it? Is that right?'

'Come in and have a cup with me,' I said, smiling a little wanly. I hadn't yet found it necessary to lie about my age, but realised that I still thought of myself as thirty-something.

1

Forty-three last spring, I told myself firmly. It seemed a time for facing all sorts of unpalatable truths.

'No, please, I was about to put the kettle on. I haven't had breakfast yet. Had a bad night and slept late.'

'No need to make excuses. I know about you actresses. Parties all night and up at midday. Well, I won't say no. The tea is in that tin on the mantelpiece. No, the blue one with peacocks. Shall I make up the fire while you get yourself some toast? No, I won't have any, thank you. A digestive biscuit, I usually have. The square tin with the Queen Mother. I can't stay long at the moment, but my mother-in-law would come up and help a bit, you know, a bit of baking and so on. A cup of tea and some cake in the vestry is all people expect these days, perhaps some sausage rolls and slices of quiche, no need for any fuss. My mother-in-law would be glad to see to it all if you don't feel up to it.'

'No, I don't feel up to it,' I said, sitting at the table and frowning at the toast I'd made which was too crisp, and black and frilly at the edges.

'The marmalade is in that little cupboard, look. And margarine in the fridge, the butter'll be too hard. How long can you stay? Have you fed Arthur this morning? The cat, girl. He hasn't been in? Oh, he's grieving. They do, you know. He might be down Tan-y-Bryn way. Gwenda Rees will feed him with hers. Lovely cup of tea – I like it good and strong. But don't let him stay there too long. He's an indoor cat, Arthur, and the farm cats will torment him. I must go now. My mother-in-law will be up this afternoon. Maggie Davies, she is, Mrs Tudor Davies when she's trying to impress. Only a little word: don't let her take over. You say exactly what you want. She'll do what you tell her as long as you're firm. Look, why don't you phone Gwenda and ask her to fetch Arthur up? No trouble for her, she's got a car of her own, and he'll be company for you. Nice cat. I'll tell you what, I'll call in on Gwenda, she's a friend of mine, and tell her you're a bit moithered at the moment. No, don't come to the door, I'll let myself out.'

She's gone. A good, wholesome woman with a square jaw and big hips. The salt of the earth. And a voice to fill the Albert Hall. It's the great open spaces that gives you a voice like that. Mine used to be as good, but I've become cityfied and refined.

Oh God, this is going to be even worse than I thought. Grief is one thing, but I hadn't reckoned on funeral bake-meats. I've been away too long. Oh God, I've got to pull myself together and see the minister this afternoon to choose hymns and so on. Which were her favourite hymns? I've no idea. Was she religious? Not as far as I know, though she never liked it when I spoke up for the devil.

I didn't have an easy childhood. Easy? What am I talking about? We're facing the truth, here. It was hell.

The earliest memories. Going back and back.

My mother screaming and throwing herself about even as my Auntie Jane held her. 'Don't you worry, bach. Your mummy's got a nasty pain, but she'll soon be better. You go back to bed, bach. I'll come up in a minute to tuck you in again. As soon as she's better.'

Screaming, screaming, screaming. Because my father had left her. 'Your daddy's had to go away, bach.' And because of the thing in the chamber-pot. The thing Auntie Jane poured into the enamel bucket and tried to hide. 'Only blood clots, bach. Because your mummy's had a very bad stomach-ache and that happens sometimes. Now, don't go and worry your mummy about it because she's having a little sleep now and it will do her good. Oh, she'll be better in no time at all. I'll make you some chips for your dinner. All right? Yes, you'd like that, I know, and *Listen with Mother* on the wireless after.'

Auntie Jane was my great-aunt, my mother's aunt, though only about ten or twelve years older. Life was bearable when she was with us, but she couldn't come too often because she

3

had a farm and children of her own – big rough children who swooped about on bikes – and a demanding husband. I remember that word, 'Ted is so demanding,' she'd tell my mother. 'Ted wants more than I've got. And he's getting mean as well in his old age. He begrudges me every shilling.'

'You bring too much up here,' my mother would say, suddenly calm and wise. 'He can't support two families.'

'Don't you stick up for him. Never stick up for a man, Miri. He's mean to the bone. If he won't be able to do someone down in the mart tomorrow, he'll take it out on us. I have to tell the lads to keep out of his way. Don't you marry a farmer, Kate, whatever you do. Remember what I say. Now, you're not to fret, Kate, because I've got to go. Your mummy's going to be much better soon. She cries because your daddy had to go away, bach. But it's not your fault, Kate. You keep telling yourself that. And remember, if you say you want a cup of tea and some bread and butter, then your mummy'll have some as well. You take care of her, bach, because she's had a hard time. But she's getting better every day. And I'll be up again next week.'

Why had my father left us? Forty years on – yes, forty years – and I'm still not absolutely sure. Even now, I know very little about him, hardly anything. There was once a photograph on the dresser, a wedding photograph, but it was taken away. I suppose Auntie Jane took it away.

When I was sixteen, full of self-confidence, my life opening up, I pressed my mother for any information she might have. I only knew his name, Philip Rivers, and that he'd worked in a bank in the nearby town. Was he English, as his name suggested? Where had he come from? Was he still alive? Did he have a family? I wasn't sure I wanted to find him, he'd caused us too much anguish, but I wouldn't have minded grandparents, cultured people perhaps, with a house called 'The Old Rectory' or 'The Malt House' with a library and a garden with a stream. Like the people in the books I read.

4

'Why are you interested in him?' she asked harshly. 'He's never sent us any money, he's never been in touch, never shown a moment's interest in either of us. Let him go.'

'Perhaps he cheated the bank. Perhaps he had to disappear.'

'Yes, your Auntie Jane thought of that. She got Haydn Williams, your Uncle Ted's solicitor, to make enquiries, but there was no sort of trouble. He'd even given them a month's notice, saying he'd got a job in an accountant's office in North Wales. The staff had collected for a leaving present, a glass biscuit barrel, the manager said it was.'

'Did the solicitor contact the accountant's office?'

'He hadn't given them an address. But Haydn Williams put adverts in all the North Wales papers asking for information about him – it cost your Uncle Ted plenty – but there was no reply. No clues to follow. Nothing.'

I lowered my voice. 'Did you quarrel much?'

'We never had a quarrel. Not once.'

'But you must have suspected that things were . . . well, not as they should be between you.'

'I didn't suspect anything. No one did. There wasn't any gossip about him and some other woman, either. Not as far as your Auntie Jane could discover and she talked to everyone, the girls at the bank and the women at the Gwalia where he sometimes had his lunch. No one had anything to say about him. Only that he was always polite, always quiet.'

'You must have contacted his parents?'

'He didn't have any parents. He was a Barnardo's boy from up Wrexham way. I thought you knew that – I thought your Auntie Jane would have told you that. Rivers was a name they gave him at Barnardo's. That's why I wanted you to go back to Williams when you went to big school, but you didn't choose to.'

'I'd got used to Kate Rivers by that time.'

'They gave them tidy names at Barnardo's, I will say that.

5

Hill and Field, Bridges and Forest. Nature names. Anyway, you'll change your name when you get married and that will be soon enough, I daresay.'

'Why should I get married? It didn't do much for you.'

'No.'

I was hard when I was sixteen, resenting all the hardship I'd suffered.

I can't ever forget the screaming; that was the worst part. The way she flung herself from side to side even when Auntie Jane was holding her. I've used that scream in so many parts – Hester in *The Deep Blue Sea*, Bertha in *Jane Eyre*, Constance in *King John*. It seems callous, I know, but you have to make use of everything. I'll even be watching people at the funeral, I know I will, noting their backs, straight or slumped, the little furtive glances in my direction, and who's that man at my side, the chapel clothes, not necessarily black, these days, but dauntingly respectable, the lace handkerchiefs dabbing at the eyes and the corners of the mouths.

'Try not to worry, bach. Your mummy's getting better every day.'

Better? God, it must have been all of five years before she was even moderately sane. I was doing the housework and the cooking before I'd started school. Well, not cooking exactly, but cups of tea and bread and butter and tinned soup and boiled eggs, with no one to worry if I cut my hand or scalded myself. I suppose I'd have been taken into care if it wasn't for Auntie Jane who did our shopping once a week; four large sliced loaves, tea, margarine, sugar, baked beans, vegetable soup, processed cheese and bananas, always the same items, and eggs from the farm; far too many eggs. 'Now, don't worry, bach. Your mummy's getting better, I notice it every time I come. You look after her nicely, Kate, and see that she gets dressed every day. You tell her, "Mummy, I won't get dressed unless you do." You're a little champion, you are, there's no one like you in the world. Now, you eat a slice of my fruit cake every day and see that your mummy does too. It's very nourishing, my fruit cake, and it will keep you regular as well.'

It was Auntie Jane who took me to school that first day. The other new children, two girls and a boy, were crying at being left, but I had grown-up worries. Who'd give my mother her dinner? Who'd remind her to eat when I wasn't there?

My teacher is Mrs Evans. She's big and fluffy as a bear and she smells of lavender soap and some darker smell as well, like beds. She's always surprised by my work. 'I'm astonished,' she says every time she comes round the tables. 'Absolutely astonished.' She tells the headmaster how astonished she is and he nods his head so hard and long that I'm afraid it will fall off. When the other children have gone out to play, she cuddles me, and I tell her about my daddy leaving and my mummy crying and she says it's very sad. 'Lucky your mummy's got you,' she says. 'You're as smart as paint, you are. The cleverest little girl in the school.'

'I wonder if her mother's getting all the benefits she's entitled to,' she whispers to the headmaster when he comes round for the register. 'I think I'll call and see her next Saturday.'

'Mrs Evans is coming up here on Saturday,' I tell my mother the very moment I get home. 'It's about money, I think. She whispered something to Mr Adams. About helping us, I think.' I'd been uneasy about it all day – my mother was frightened of strangers – but as there's no sort of response from her, I stop worrying.

On Saturday morning, though, she's taken up a position by the window even before I come downstairs, and she's standing there still as a post. 'Waiting,' she says in a voice which makes me shiver. I make her a cup of tea with two sugars, but she won't have it. She won't sit down either.

It's well into the morning before she sees Mrs Evans's little blue car coming up the track. As soon as she does, she turns and pulls me with her into the cupboard under the stairs and closes the door on us. The cupboard is dark and smells of firewood and wet earth. I know my mother is frightened because her arms round my shoulders are shaking and shaking.

We hear Mrs Evans knocking on the front door and then the back. She isn't going away. 'We're here, Mrs Evans,' I want to shout. 'We're in the cwtsh under the stairs,' but I don't, because I know my mother is even more frightened than I am. Mrs Evans knocks again on the back door then goes round to the front and shouts through the letter-box. 'Mrs Rivers. Mrs Rivers. It's Christine Evans, Katie's teacher. I'd like to talk to you, Mrs Rivers.' We strain to listen, but we don't hear any footsteps; she isn't going away. Suddenly there's a sound like a tap running and something splashes over my feet. It's my mother doing pi-pi. 'Don't cry,' my mother whispers and she hugs me tight.

At last we shuffle out. My mother smiles for a moment because Mrs Evans has gone away. I haven't seen her smile before. She smells of pi-pi and there's a big dark patch on her grey skirt, but I don't say anything. When Gethyn Owen wet himself in class, Mrs Evans picked him up and carried him off to the cloakroom and when he came back he had different trousers on, but Mrs Evans said no one was to mention it. I think my mother is wet and cold, but I don't mention it and she goes to sit close to the fire and after a while she stops shivering and I make her a big mug of tea and to my surprise she smiles again. Perhaps she is getting better. She smells of pi-pi though, and so does the cupboard under the stairs, but I don't do anything about it. Things sometimes get better if you just leave them alone.

There's a knock on the door. It's an effort to get back to the present.

8

It's Gwenda Rees, a pretty, dark-haired woman, with a cat in a basket: Arthur. He looks around him but doesn't bother to get out, not at all sure, it seems, whether he intends to stay. I stroke his head and smile at Gwenda Rees. 'Do sit down. How kind of you to bring him back. No, we've never met before. Hello, Arthur. I wonder if he'd like to come back to London with me. Do you know how old he is?'

'I don't think your mother knew. He arrived here one day fully grown and determined to stay. But I think she must have had him two or three years. One of my lads used to come up and leave him a bowl of milk out the back when she was away visiting you. Yes, I've got two boys, Gareth and Dafydd. Two villains ... You never came home much lately, did you? Well, you were always busy, that was it. Your mother was always telling us how busy you were. Not your fault.'

'It was easier for her to visit me, Mrs Rees. She liked London. Liked the shops.'

'Oh, I know. We heard all about it, girl. Harrods' Food Hall. No such place in the world, according to her ... And Gwenda I am, by the way. No one round here calls me Mrs Rees. But your mother, now, was always Mrs Rivers, never Miriam. She didn't like anyone being too familiar. Her age, I suppose. When you're older, you gather these shreds of dignity around you. What else have you got? Well, she had London, fair play. Not an easy life, by all accounts, but a daughter doing well and showing her the sights. And buying her smart clothes too. A hundred and sixty pounds that last navy-blue suit was, according to her, all except a penny. You've got nothing to blame yourself for, nothing at all.'

We were both fully aware of how guilty I felt. 'I had her to stay for a week twice a year, spring and autumn. If I happened to be rehearsing, Mrs Heathfield, my help, used to call and take her to Oxford Street by taxi.'

'There you are. You did your best. Hamper every

Christmas. Bottle of French brandy. I always called for my Christmas drink.'

We fell silent. Arthur yawned delicately. And then, with a minimum of effort, obviously unwilling to show any trace of eagerness, got out of the basket.

'She didn't even tell me about Arthur. Not a word.'

'What is there to say about Arthur? Black and white cat, bit of a thief. What else can you say about Arthur?'

'He's a fine cat.'

'Oh yes. Handsome enough. Keep him in for a few days to make him settle again. He wouldn't take to London, though. He likes a bit of hunting, does Arthur.'

'I've got a big garden.'

'Oh, I know that, girl. Patio. Floodlights. Landscaped garden, 170 feet long. And your friend going out at midnight with a torch to examine the strawberries. Will he be coming to the funeral, say?'

'I think so. He was away when I got the news, but I'll be talking to him as soon as he gets back.'

'Will you keep this house, or sell it? There's young folk in the village would be very eager to have it, but I daresay it would make more money as a holiday home.'

'I haven't thought about it yet. Perhaps I'll keep it for my retirement.'

'You won't retire for many years yet, girl. You look very young on the telly. Though I know you're older than I am – you were already in the Juniors when I started in the Infants. Gwenda Parry I was then. No, why should you remember the small fry? Only I always tell people, "Kate Rivers? I was in school with her." Oh, your mother always let us know when you were on.'

There was another silence, both of us concentrating our attention on Arthur who was sitting hunched up on the hearthrug, his body language making it clear that he was there under protest and wouldn't be staying.

'She never liked it when I was "the other woman",' I said,

making another effort to be sociable. ' "Where did it come from?" she used to ask me. "All that wickedness?" "Wickedness is easy," I'd say. "It's goodness I can't get hold of. No experience of that." Will you have a cup of tea?'

'No thank you, love, I mustn't stay any longer. And you've got masses to do, I'm sure. Maggie Davies will be up here after dinner, that's Lorna's mother-in-law. She'll do everything you want, but she'll charge, mind. Five pounds an hour she charges visitors. But you tell her you're not a visitor and four pounds is all you're prepared to pay. Get it straight from the start. I was a friend of your mother's, anyone would tell you that, I always did what I could for her, but Maggie was usually ready to run her down. Well, people aren't perfect, and we wouldn't like them if they were, but it's just as well to know where you stand, isn't it? Maggie likes things her own way, Lorna would tell you the same, and you have to stand up to her. No, don't get up. I'll let myself out. You keep an eye on Arthur . . . What did you say your manfriend was called? Paul. Oh yes, I remember your poor mother mentioning him. Paul Farringdon. A photographer, if I remember right. Nature programmes on BBC 2 if I remember right.'

# Chapter Two

I phoned home two or three times that evening, but there was no reply. Paul was due back from Spain sometime during the afternoon; perhaps his flight had been delayed, perhaps he'd gone out for a meal, thinking I'd forgotten him. Of course, I should have left him a note. Belatedly, I decided to leave a message on the answerphone. 'Paul, I'm at my mother's. Please ring as soon as you can.' I fully intended to tell him about her sudden death, but found I couldn't. After putting the phone down, I rehearsed the words several times. 'My mother's dead. My mother's dead. My mother's dead.' I still couldn't quite believe it. On Sunday morning when I'd last spoken to her, she'd seemed her usual self, talking about her next visit to me, wondering whether she'd get the coach all the way, or take the train from Shrewsbury as she usually did, and wanting me to find out which would be cheaper. Even though I paid her fare, she was always intent on finding bargains.

My mother liked Paul. She thought he was steady and reliable and advocated marriage. 'He's done that,' I used to tell her, 'and it didn't suit him too well.'

'Perhaps he married the wrong woman. Why don't you propose to him? There's no shame in it nowadays.'

She prided herself on her knowledge of modern manners, gleaned from television plays and *The Mail on Sunday*.

At one time I wanted marriage and children, but the right

time and the right man never coincided. And now that it seems too late to have children, there doesn't seem much point in it. Paul has two daughters, Selena and Annabel, whom I try to like. They're both at Cambridge, but too wild to get much out of it. When I was at university I worked like a maniac; I had to get a good degree and a grant to go to drama school afterwards. Selena and Annabel don't have to put themselves out in any way; they'll have wonderfully rewarding lives however little they do. Their mother, Francesca Bird, is very rich and owns an art gallery in the West End and their father is a moderately prosperous photographer who adores them.

As for me, I've worked hard and played hard and my life has been fairly succesful and fairly happy. I've had many disappointments, some of which still rankle, but I've always done my best not to get into any situation which might end in tragedy. For instance, I've always steered clear of the known heart-breakers, the dangerously attractive men who make you feel sorry for every woman they've ever had dealings with. I've known several of those, but so far I've managed to remain relatively unscathed.

I was introduced to Paul at a party almost exactly ten years ago at a time when he was struggling to get over a divorce. I didn't know why he was looking so dejected and said something completely banal, 'Cheer up, it may never happen,' at which he turned to me and said, 'Darling, it already has.'

We found a quiet corner and he told me about the beautiful woman he'd married and cherished, about their twin daughters and about the man who'd stolen her away. It certainly wasn't the usual party chit-chat, perhaps I'd got tired of that, because I found myself strangely moved by what was, after all, a fairly commonplace story. But what made me tell him, on that first meeting, about my childhood, my father's desertion and my mother's breakdown? I'd never mentioned it to anyone before. And I went into the minutest details too, dismayed that I remembered so much

14

that I'd been trying for many years to forget. I was dressed in a tight strapless black dress, I remember, I'd had my hair highlighted with something called Titian Glow, I had scarlet lips and gold eyeshadow and I sat in the roof garden of that Kensington penthouse and sobbed.

When I'd finished patting my eyes and blowing my nose, I caught him giving me a long, cool appraisal. 'Ah, Kate Rivers,' he seemed to be thinking, 'doing her probably fairly regular party piece.' I picked up my evening bag and fled.

When I rang my hosts the next morning to say, thank you, great party and sorry I had to rush off, I was told that Paul Farringdon had stayed on searching for me when everyone else had left, that to get rid of him, they'd had to give him my telephone number and hoped I didn't mind.

For a few days I waited to hear from him and had to admit to feeling disappointed, even aggrieved, when he didn't ring.

A month or so later I happened to run into him at a local estate agent's. We both seemed embarrassed, but all the same decided to have lunch together, during which we didn't refer to the party or my sudden disappearance, but talked of property prices, the merits of various districts and the horrors of negative equity. We were both looking for a flat, he because he had had to move out of the marital home which was his wife's, and I because the lease on my present flat was running out.

We looked through lists together. We seemed to have the same priorities; a fairly quiet road with no pub or takeaway within fifty yards, and no more than ten minutes walk from the tube or a good bus-route.

It was early June, I remember, and sunny. We ate pasta and tomato salad and drank a very rough Chianti. I liked the thorough way he mopped up his salad dressing; I find something reassuring about a man who's fond of bread.

'What happened to your mother?' he asked when he'd finished eating. 'Did she recover?' He'd remembered our

15

conversation. He looked over at me as though really anxious to know.

'She did recover. Eventually. More or less.'

'Is she still alive?'

'Yes.'

He leaned back in his chair and looked at me for a moment. And I felt that something had been decided. This man was interested in me and I in him. The sun was suddenly white and dazzling and I put on a pair of rather glamorous sunglasses and waited for him to make the next move.

He invited himself to the theatre in Greenwich where I was playing that night. I wished he was seeing me in a leading role, or at least one I was proud of, rather than in a small part in a fairly worthless play which I'd taken because it slotted in rather nicely between two tellys. Anyway, I was pleased when he dismissed the play as sexist rubbish, said he'd decide what sort of actor I was when he saw me in something better, and then drove me to an interesting but unassuming restaurant in Blackheath. I was not so pleased, though, when he dropped me off outside my flat about an hour later, without even a perfunctory kiss; a brief squeeze of the hand only.

I'd summed him up as straightforward and unaffected; mature, in fact, but felt, all the same, that there was a subtle difference between maturity and advanced middle age. He was interested in me, I knew that, but didn't seem prepared to make any definite move. Perhaps it would be another month before I saw him again. He hadn't even given me his telephone number.

I was annoyed with myself for feeling so let-down. My last affair, which had lasted about three years, had ended six months earlier, and though it was I who'd finally decided on the break-up, I was still finding the nights long and lonely. I knew I was ready to start again. I wanted another affair, but more loving than the last and less destructive. Why had I

16

decided on this man whom I hardly knew? He wasn't exactly handsome, but easy on the eye for all that; good bones, lines around the eyes, a smile that seemed tender rather than clever or malicious.

I went over our conversation in the car and the restaurant. Had I said something to shock him? People sometimes accuse me of being outspoken and tactless, but I'd had no occasion for it; we hadn't argued or disagreed about anything. Had I seemed too eager, asked too many questions about his work and his family? If that was it, I had to accept defeat. I always ask too many questions.

All the same, I would have liked to show him my flat, all my pretty things; three antique rugs, some Meissen cups and saucers, my French bed with the heavy lace bedcover I'd recently dyed with china tea. I'd spent over an hour tidying up: I'd have a wretched time finding my clothes the next day.

I got myself to bed, but couldn't sleep, disappointment eating into me. I was thirty-three, I told myself, perhaps too old for easy conquests. But he's a lot older, I said the next minute, at least ten years older. Who does he think he is? He asks for my phone number at a party and doesn't ring me, then takes me out for a meal late at night and doesn't proposition me. I went over the time we'd spent together, minute by minute. I liked the way he'd taken care of me without being officious, the way he'd chatted to the waiter, asking his opinion about what to order. I hate men who're haughty with waiters – and it's always men – I realise it's only a lack of self-esteem, but I still hate it. And men who pretend they know absolutely everything there is to know about wine. How can they know anything at all about poetry and music and art, the things that really matter, if they spend all their time learning absolutely everything there is to know about wine. For about an hour I thought about all the foolish and pompous men I'd had dealings with in my life. But at the end of it I found myself even more convinced that Paul Farringdon was different; caring and kind.

I felt too disappointed, too cheated, to sleep. I grieved and fretted and tossed and turned in my king-sized bed and at eight o'clock, still wide awake, I got up and went to my tiny guest room and tried again in a cool, fresh bed with only a sheet and a thin weave blanket over me. And this time I slept. And because I was in a different room, didn't hear the phone.

I slept until three. It was a beautiful fresh day, the light, coming in from the garden instead of the street, apple green. I thought of iced water and coffee, but was in no hurry to get either. I was pleased I'd slept through half the day. I knew I'd start feeling hurt and aggrieved again as soon as I was fully awake.

This time I heard the phone. It was Paul. 'You were out early,' he said. 'I phoned, hoping we could lunch together.'

A sob came up from my throat. 'Did you say lunch?'

'Yes, but I suppose you've had some by this time.'

I didn't answer. Why couldn't he have suggested lunch last night so that I could have had a decent night's sleep? 'I've only now woken up,' I said. 'I was awake all night.'

'Why couldn't you sleep? I thought you'd be exhausted after your performance last night. That's why I didn't suggest coming in.'

'I thought you didn't want to. And that's why I couldn't sleep.'

It was his turn to be silent. 'You're very direct, aren't you,' he said at last. 'I've never met anyone before who says exactly what they mean. I'm not used to it.'

'Are you complaining about me already?'

'Kate, I simply can't believe my luck. I simply can't believe you wanted me last night. It stuns me.'

I counted to ten. 'I want you now, too.'

Another silence. 'I'll be with you in half an hour.'

'Half an hour? There's no traffic here on Sunday afternoon. It'll only take you ten minutes if you hurry.'

\*

18

So lovely, that first time together. Even though the flat was on the first floor, we could smell the roses and honeysuckle in the garden.

Perhaps it was my fault, after that beginning, that things moved so fast. Within three days Paul had suggested that we buy a house between us rather than a flat each. But I was wary, knowing from experience that when two hardworking people share a house it turns out exactly like marriage but without the wedding presents and the party. And when they separate they still have all the books and tapes to sort out.

I held out for a few weeks. During that time he spent most of the time in my flat and I found I liked him more and more. He was domesticated without being faddy and good-humoured without being tiresomely cheerful at all times. Could I ever, I asked myself, find a more loving or more civilised partner? Definitely not. There might be something missing – that frisson of danger, perhaps – but it was surely something I was now mature enough to do without.

What small events govern our lives. I can't now escape the thought that I was feeling ready to settle down at that time because I'd recently lost a television part I'd been up for. My agent had been convinced I'd get it; it was the juvenile lead in a fairly lightweight domestic comedy; I'd been full of confidence as I went to the audition. But the director dismissed me as being 'just the teeniest bit too old'. I must have looked stunned because he hastened to add, 'Of course, in the stage version with the right make-up and lighting, you'd have been quite marvellous. But perhaps not on the box, darling.' I took a taxi home, feeling too old to face the Tube. Something hardened inside me. I felt fifty – and over the hill.

Was it in this mood of near-desperation that I decided that Paul was the perfect candidate for a long-term partner and the father of my children? Certainly, I soon became as enthusiastic as he about buying a family house. Whenever I had time off work, I'd be out looking at yet another 'highly desirable' property, 'surprisingly spacious', 'recently restored to the highest standards', and always in 'a sought-after residential area'. I looked at a dozen or more before finding one that was even moderately acceptable, with, at least, a large kitchen and a garden with a tree.

After an exhausting few months when everything that could possibly go wrong, went wrong, we moved in; by this time too poor and too shell-shocked even to have a house-warming party.

A few weeks later I wrote telling my mother about Paul; that we were thinking of settling down together and perhaps having a family and suggesting that she came up to meet him. The next morning I got a postcard – a picture postcard – from her. *No, you bring him here and let me know when.*

I'd never taken any previous boyfriend home, but somehow knew that Paul, though having middle-class written all over him, would manage to fit in.

It gave me pleasure to think of how excited my mother would be, about the preparations she'd be making, cooking and cleaning. She'd lately become extremely house-proud: I think it dated back to the time I'd bought her the three-piece suite.

It was about three years ago when I'd had a sizeable cheque from a film. I was delighted, of course, to be able to give her the money, but less than enchanted to find that she expected me to go to Shrewsbury with her to choose it; to an out-of-town discount warehouse. 'The furniture they have is not cheap,' she was at pains to point out, 'but they have a huge choice at very reasonable prices.'

It was an immense place like an aircraft hangar, packed tightly with voluptuous, marshmallow-soft sofas and chairs of every conceivable colour, shape and size.

A three-piece suite is a comfortable and not completely unaesthetic seating arrangement, but hundreds of them displayed together seemed like a vision of out-of-control consumerist hell. I'd decided on the set of the first film I one day hoped to direct, its title, *Murder in Comfort*, the background music and all the cast, while my mother walked round the warehouse's entire stock three times and a smaller selection at the back eleven or twelve times. After I'd been summoned to approve her final choice – I did, it was comfortable and relatively plain with no scrolls or braid – she sat on the chosen sofa and fainted. From excitement and extreme exhaustion, I suppose. I loosened her jacket and fanned her with my newspaper, while the salesman rushed for a glass of water. Though I suspect he was close to fainting as well by that time.

'My mother would like me to take you home to see her three-piece suite,' I told Paul when he came in that night.

'Goody,' he said.

# Chapter Three

I used to sleep with her in the lumpy double bed heavy with blankets and quilts. She was often very restless, plunging about like an animal in a trap. Sometimes I dreamed that there were horses running up the lane after me, but it was only my mother tossing and turning. At other times, she'd moan in her sleep and call out to my father: 'Philip. Philip.' Her voice would take on a high, thin note so that the name sounded like a whiplash. I've never been able to like that name.

'Do you like the name Philip?' I asked Auntie Jane on one occasion. I was probably seven or eight at the time.

'Haven't thought about it. It's better than Jeremiah, I suppose. Or Theophilus. There were lots of those around here years ago. My grandfather was called Jubilee because he was born on the day of Victoria's in 1887. Jubilee Morgan. That seems a bit cruel to me, but he seemed to rejoice in it. His farm failed, mind, but he became a lay-preacher and a bit of a poet after. A name does affect your nature, for sure. Now, if your Uncle Ted went bankrupt, he wouldn't find anything to turn his hand to. There's no point in thinking of being a lay-preacher, for instance, if you've got a name like Ted Jones because nobody would take you seriously. Isabel Kingdom Brunel is a fine name. With a name like that you'd have no difficulty building Paddington Station.'

'Is Isabel a name for a man?' I asked. But not wanting to doubt her, added, 'Perhaps there's a different spelling, like Francis?'

'Oh, you've lost me now. You're too clever, altogether.'

'Are your boys clever?' I asked her. I couldn't help being interested in her sons though they were so rough and ugly. She'd given the three of them old-fashioned Welsh names; Iestyn, Bleddyn and Rhydian. I couldn't tell which was which because I was always too nervous to look at them properly.

'Their teacher says they've got good brains, but I can't judge because they never say anything in the house except "What's for dinner?" and, "Any more?" And they're not in the house much, to tell you the truth. No, always haring out and leaving doors open. It would have been so nice to have had a little girl.' She sighed deeply and gave me a hug, but I knew it was only politeness; she was very proud of her boys who ate like horses, ganged up against their father and hadn't had a day's illness in their lives.

When I got to the grammar school in town I discovered that my cousins, or cousins-once-removed, were the most popular boys there. It still surprises me because country boys, and especially farm boys, were usually either disparaged or ignored. Those three certainly couldn't have been ignored; they were very tall and dark with beak noses and riotously untidy black hair. They wore only very few items of school uniform along with their farm-workers' clothes and seemed to get away with it, though the Head was strict with other boys, insisting on the full regalia; ties, white shirts, navy-blue blazers, grey trousers, black socks. Perhaps he realised that there was nothing rebellious in the way they dressed, that they simply led their own lives, made their own rules. Anyway, he'd never have dared expel them or where would the cricket team be, the rugby team, the athletics?

They weren't keen participants, in any case, always having to be persuaded to turn up to any match taking place

24

in out-of-school hours, so I think he made it clear that no one was to cross them in any way. Rhydian, the eldest, had broken the school record for the 1500 metres, but when the games master put him up for the All-Wales championship, there was no sign of him on the Saturday morning when the coach was due to start. The Head had to drive out the nine miles to the farm to fetch him. 'Aren't you interested in the honour of the school?' he asked him. 'No, sir,' he said.

When I started school at eleven, they were sixteen, seventeen, eighteen. I think I was more nervous of them than I was of any of my teachers, terrified that they might tease me as they had when I was five or six. My hope was that they'd no longer recognise me, but I noticed the youngest of them, Iestyn, glancing at me once or twice and while not exactly smiling, his scowl seeming less pronounced than usual.

The three boys were academic, it seems, as well as athletic, but Bleddyn turned out to be a mathematical genius. It hadn't been noticed until he was in the Sixth; he'd done very little work until then. But in the Lower Sixth, when Rhydian and other older boys began to solicit his help, it became apparent that he could see numbers whirring about and sorting themselves out in his head, that he was able to come up with the correct answer to any problem without showing any working and without being able to explain his method. He seemed surprised that the other boys, some of whom seemed sophisticated and urbane, able to argue fluently in the debating society, for instance, even talk to girls, found difficulty in something which seemed straightforward and obvious to him.

Rhydian got a couple of A-levels and much to Uncle Ted's annoyance – and derision – decided on a local farming college, but the following year, Bleddyn was put in for a scholarship to Oxford. 'Did they say you were an exceptional candidate?' the Head wanted to know when he got back from his interview. 'No, sir. It was only my fingernails they seemed to notice. I don't suppose any of them have done much in the way of farm work, sir.'

As soon as any of the younger teachers discovered that I was related to 'the Gorsgoch boys', they'd repeat those stories and many, many more. They were heroes, it seemed, particularly when they'd left school and were no longer a threat to discipline.

When the two older brothers had left, with Iestyn still in the Upper Sixth, a fiercely unambitious student, an untidy lounging prefect who avoided his duties and argued with the Head, I was astonished and thrilled to get a note from him. *Dear baby cousin, I've been wondering whether you'd like to come to the pictures with me on Saturday night. I'll put you on the nine o'clock bus after, so no worries. People may tell you that I'm a terror but don't believe them. Yours Sincerely, Iestyn Jones. P.S. I think you're very pretty.*

I wasn't quite fourteen at the time and though tall for my age and well-developed, didn't have the courage to go. I wanted to very badly and spent a miserable few days, desperately annoyed with myself for being so cowardly. I think it was at that point that I decided to come out of my shell; when I started school the next year I was loud and noisy and up for anything. But Iestyn was at Cardiff University by that time, playing rugby and drinking – and fancying other girls, no doubt. I kept the note he sent me for a long time, two or three years at least. *I think you're very pretty.*

'How are your cousins getting on?' the Head would ask me from time to time after they'd all left. 'Still savages, I suppose?'

I didn't know. They rarely wrote home; I think Auntie Jane would have been worried if they did. She was suspicious of letters, holding them at arm's length for a minute or so before daring to open them.

After Auntie Jane's death, I didn't hear much about them and when they left school, didn't see them again. Except on one occasion when, by chance, I met my eldest cousin, Rhydian.

I was in the Sixth, the Lower Sixth I think, when I was invited on one hot Saturday afternoon to Isabel Langford's house to play tennis, followed by afternoon tea. I was surprised to be asked; she and I weren't particularly friendly and, besides, I wasn't a very good player. I agreed to go willingly enough, though, because her family had their own tennis court at the back of their large detached house, so there'd be no hanging about waiting for one of the town courts. Also, never having had much to do with middle-class life, I was interested to see how the other half lived: Isabel's father owned a factory in Liverpool.

I turned up, I remember, in my school uniform shorts and shirt with a school racquet I'd managed to borrow. The house was even more impressive at close quarters, built of a mellow grey stone, a turret at one corner, French windows, climbing roses and clematis; my carefully nurtured self-assurance plummeted as I walked up the drive. I'd been expecting some sort of party, but to my surprise the only other people there were Isabel's brother, Edward, who was at Leeds University, and my cousin, Rhydian. Isabel introduced us, but neither Rhydian nor I mentioned our relationship, I had the excuse of being gauche and embarrassed; he seemed completely at ease so I assumed he was ashamed of me and glared at him. 'He's my brother's oldest friend,' Isabel said, making it clear as she looked at him that he was the sole reason for the afternoon. I cast my eyes over him. Yes, I could understand her infatuation.

'I'm not much good at this game, I'm afraid,' I said.

'Don't worry, I'm going to be your partner and I'm hot stuff,' Edward said. He was tall and fair and English-looking, smiling a lot.

Edward was a good player, but Rhydian was even better and far more aggressive. I was pleased I wasn't his partner; when Isabel failed to return a shot he scowled at her whereas

Edward smiled forgivingly at my frequent mistakes. We only played for an hour or so. For a long time, though, I remembered the way Rhydian looked up at me before smashing the ball in my direction – the way his shoulders turned, the way his eyes blazed.

He and Edward didn't stay for tea. 'Rhydian is gorgeous, isn't he,' Isabel said after they'd rushed off somewhere. 'He's not too bad,' I replied, tossing my hair back, a gesture I'd been practising in my bedroom mirror.

I wondered if any of them would be at my mother's funeral. Rhydian had been running Gorsgoch Farm for years; his wife, Grace, had been to see my mother several times; I couldn't remember whether they had two children or three. Iestyn was a geography teacher somewhere and Bleddyn had stayed on at Oxford, still being brilliant, it seemed.

Perhaps my mother had some photographs of them at graduation or wedding. I'd rarely thought of them over the years, but now they were back in my mind – 'the dark cloud' as the Head had once called them.

I took several boxes, chocolate boxes tied with Christmas ribbon, out of the cupboard by the fireplace, but found I wasn't, after all, ready to open them. I was sure my mother wouldn't have many secrets, all the same, it seemed too soon to be going through her things. I put them back. Then I got myself another coffee and sat down to make a list of things I had to do. But suddenly I didn't seem to have the energy or the will to do anything. For the first time since I got the news I was overtaken by grief, not so much for my mother's death as for all the sadness of her life.

Once, for all too brief a time, she'd been happy. She used to tell me over and over again about the time she'd first met my father and fallen in love with him. I could hear her voice, her young voice, in my head. 'He was different from every other boy I'd ever met. He used to dress like a toff. I didn't want to marry a farmer's lad, and who else was there up here? I was only a shop girl, but your father worked in a bank. He had lovely fingernails, long and shiny as a girl's. I stopped biting mine when he started to take me out. In those days, when boys took girls out, it was always to the pictures, to the back row of the one-and-nines, but he took me to the Rendezvous Restaurant in St David's Road and we used to have mixed grills and chocolate ice cream after. It was ever so expensive because it was such a swanky place with candles on the tables and little vases of flowers. And he always left sixpence under the plate for the waitress, too. Oh, I was proud to be with him.'

Her voice would become more and more dreamy. 'I bought an angora-wool dress – eau de nil, the lady in D.C. Lewis said it was, a sort of pale green – with a tight navy-blue leather belt. It cost me a month's wages, that dress, but it was worth every penny, because the very first time I wore it he asked me to be engaged to him. That was the best evening of my life. When I went home on the bus after, I was still in a daze. I offered the conductor my fare twice over and I remember him saying, "You don't have to pay every time I come round, love." That was the state I was in, my mind in some sort of shimmering, like getting up at first light on a snowy day. He didn't buy me a ring because he wanted to save to get married, but I didn't mind because Ted had bought Jane a diamond solitaire and she used to let me take it to show the girls at work, because she couldn't wear it on the farm. Jane was always a good friend to me.'

I could hear her voice, all the hope and disappointment in it. I found myself crying – I very seldom cry – and was soon sobbing hard. And then Arthur jumped up on my lap and the shock stopped me. I sat there, his hot weight pressing on my knees while I stroked his head and gulped for breath. 'I don't want you, Arthur,' I said in a clear, loud voice. 'There isn't room in my life for a cat. I don't like cats. And if I was having one it would be a small, elegant female, probably a mushroom-coloured Siamese with gentian blue eyes.' He

29

rubbed his head against my arm. The tips of his ears were transparent and very cold.

The phone rang. Arthur jumped down and I blew my nose. It was Paul, sounding tired and upset. 'I have to go to Cambridge,' he said. 'Annabel is in trouble and I've got to bail her out. Listen, darling, I'll ring you tonight. I haven't a moment now. Bye.'

'Bye,' I said, but he'd already put the phone down. I started to cry again, angry with Annabel and with him. He hadn't even given me time to tell him about my mother's death. Annabel was a stupid girl who'd do anything to be noticed. What had she done this time? As though I cared.

Selena and Annabel were eleven years old and at boarding school when Paul and I started living together. I saw snapshots of them, little blonde girls, slender as flowers, and looked forward to meeting them. I imagined having them to stay, taking them shopping, being their confidante and friend. It didn't work out quite like that.

Paul hinted that they could be difficult. 'Their headmistress says they're typical of children from broken homes, needing to test everyone's love and loyalty. And of course, identical twins are always a law unto themselves, so absorbed in each other they don't need to seek other people's approval. You mustn't be upset, Kate, if they seem to reject you at first. I'm quite sure they won't mean it, but they can certainly be hurtful. I realise that all too well.'

I was pleased that he was being honest with me, but of course, I was determined to succeed where others might have failed. I'd make no demands on them. I had no intention of being a mother-figure so they wouldn't resent me. I'd play it very cool, treating them as guests rather than as children. They'd be allowed to come and go as they pleased, choose when to get up, when to go to bed and what they wanted to eat. If there were rules, that would be Paul's province.

I read all the recent research on identical twins and found it fascinating. The embryo meant for one person splits in two in the first week after conception. Most of the resulting pairs didn't survive. Those that did were stronger and tougher and more resilient than other foetuses; they needed to be because they were competing for the mother's nourishment. The notion of two people evolving in this way seemed bizarre. How strange that there weren't more twins in myths and folklore; there was surely something pretty near to magic in their conception.

'There probably wouldn't have been many twins in the ancient world,' Paul said. 'Even today they need specialised medical care. Annabel and Selena had to be induced two months early, because the scans showed that one was taking the lion's share of the nourishment and the other was left very small and weak; in effect, one was killing the other. People talk about identical twins' closeness and their special bond, but they begin with a fight for survival and I often think that remains somewhere in their make-up.'

I felt that someone was scoring my back with the tip of a knife. 'Go on,' I said.

'Selena was small as a kitten when she was born, less than two pounds in weight, and though Annabel was quite a lot bigger, we had to leave both of them in the hospital for six weeks. It was a harrowing time. I don't think Francesca ever quite got over it.'

He sighed and didn't seem to want to say any more. But I couldn't stop thinking about the little girls and looking at their photographs.

The first thing that went wrong was the timing of their first visit. Francesca phoned Paul to say she couldn't have them for Easter as she'd intended, because she had to fly to Mexico for her work. She was sure he'd be able to collect them from school and take care of them until she came back in ten days' time.

31

'Didn't you tell her how inconvenient it would be?' I asked him. There were still workmen in the house, not one room was ready; the kitchen had nothing in it but a kettle and a toaster, the bathroom had no floorboards, there was a downstairs cloakroom with lavatory and washbasin, but the shower didn't work: we were virtually camping in the house. How could we have anyone to stay? It was impossible. I thought Paul would accept that.

But he looked stricken. He was thrilled at the prospect of seeing the girls when he'd thought they'd be flying out to Crete with Francesca and the young poet she was currently living with. And though I could have argued, I didn't. I can't bear to be responsible for anyone's unhappiness. My childhood has had that effect on me. I'll put up with almost anything, rather than cause conflict.

So they came to us. And from the beginning I was tense and tired, unable to relax properly because of the chaos in the house. And they seemed to take advantage of my unease; demanding all Paul's attention, wanting all their usual holiday treats – skating rinks, shopping trips and gigs – not prepared to make any allowances. They were volatile, temperamental and merciless. I couldn't find any resemblance between them and Paul, who was kind and down-to-earth. They were thistledown. When they moved they gave the impression of floating. They were as decorative as the high-born children in paintings by Laurence or Sargent, Titania's fairies by Schiele. When they talked and giggled together it sounded like goldfinches or a fall of windbells.

But I eventually became convinced that all their childish patter was carefully rehearsed for the maximum shock value. They played the part of innocent children, but they weren't children and they certainly weren't innocent.

As soon as they arrived I felt older and more staid. I'd always considered myself smart and sophisticated, not exactly beautiful, but the next best thing; stylish and

32

attractive. But at their arrival I was suddenly 'mumsie'. They considered me middle-aged and took pleasure in letting me know it.

'We've worried and worried about Daddy. You've no idea what a trial it is to have a father who knows nothing about the ways of the world. We used to introduce him to all the beautiful girls, didn't we, Selena? Do you remember the Constantines' Swedish au pair – I can't remember her name, probably Frida – but he didn't try anything on with her, did he? When Mummy slipped away somewhere with one of her conquests, all Daddy would ever do was mope and sigh. Of course, we never thought of anyone old, I mean older, I mean mature. We only thought of beautiful young girls.'

They were so pretty, so innocent-seeming and tender, their hair as soft and fair as a baby's, their hand-span waists, their little pink tongues like cats' tongues poking out between their lips as they waited their turn to speak.

'Men are always nice to us, aren't they, Selena? They give us masses of things – well, money and presents – and take us out in their yachts. This is in Crete, Kate. Did you used to go to Crete on holiday when you were young, Kate? Don't look like that, Daddy, we never let any men touch us, do we, Selena? We wouldn't like it at all, their skin is far too rough. But we sometimes let them take photographs of us; they're always wanting to do that. We'll probably be famous models in a year or two. Identical twins are particularly sought after, aren't they, Selena? We're longing to leave school.'

'Sometimes we paint our bodies with henna, don't we, Annabel? Snakes around our waists and sun-burst patterns on our chests. Are you shocked, Daddy? You and Mummy used to do things in the garden in Crete which shocked us. We used to stand on the veranda and watch you when you thought we were in bed. Now I suppose you do them with Kate. Or is Kate too old for flying? We call it flying, don't we, Annabel, because we think the other word is too gross. Oh, don't look like that, Daddy. You're an old frump.

33

Mummy doesn't mind what we say. She says we're Nature's children, doesn't she, Annabel? Mummy's a free spirit and she wants us to be the same, but she warned us that you'd want us to be well-behaved. I expect Kate is very well-behaved like you are. Were you brought up to be a well-behaved young lady, Kate?'

'I can't remember. It was so long ago.'

Paul smiled at me, but they accepted my answer with perfect gravity. And disdain.

I was out of work for several weeks at the time, and with all the hassle in the house, workmen not turning up or turning up with fittings of the wrong size or colour, carpets we hadn't ordered, the self-confidence I'd managed to build up since my twenties almost deserted me. I began to feel only a substitute for the dazzling Francesca.

'Do you still love Francesca?' I asked Paul one night when we were on our own. It was the last thing I'd intended to say.

'I love *you*, Kate. Are those girls getting to you?' (Did he understand?) 'All that silly jabbering. They've always done it. I've never taken any notice of them and neither must you. They read too much and watch too much TV. They invent stories. Their lives are all make-believe. They don't do any of the outrageous things they talk about. Surely you realise that? They're really very shy backward little girls who live in their imagination. Their headmistress would tell you that. They're desperate for the sort of adventures they think grown-ups have, so they invent them. They're longing to grow up, that's all.'

I was pleased that Paul was able to treat their bizarre conversation so lightly, but I couldn't. To my mind there was definitely something sinister about it. The way they lowered their voices when they came to certain of the more preposterous details, hurrying over them as though they hardly wanted them heard, seemed to indicate fact not fiction, possibly events they weren't entirely happy about.

'We let the gardener's boy sit on the wall and watch us, don't we, Selena? And once we let him . . . decorate us with flowers, but that was about all . . . . That was almost all, anyway – all we want to think about.' Perhaps they wanted to be questioned, even reproved. Perhaps I should have stepped in and tried to suggest what was acceptable behaviour, what unacceptable. But I was too much of a coward. Already feeling despised, I didn't want to be totally rejected. I'd decided on my role – as onlooker – and was determined not to change it.

Paul must have realised that I wasn't completely convinced by his defence of the girls. 'Though I suppose they've been damaged to some extent, by Francesca leaving me,' he added. With too much sadness in his voice.

'You still love her, don't you?'

'I haven't completely got her out of my system, but I don't love her. I love you, Kate.'

It was at the end of this traumatic week that Paul got his first call for help from Francesca. The deal she'd made with some well-established American artist working in Mexico had somehow fallen through and left her heavily in debt. As far as I could understand, she'd already been living off the huge sums of money she was expecting to make from some paintings and drawings this 'almost famous' artist was letting her have at sacrificial prices, and since the poet she was living with was penniless – though undoubtedly a genius – it meant that she'd no longer be able to hang on to the house her father had given her in Holland Park when she'd got married, so that she and the children would be homeless.

In those early days I was trying hard to be sympathetic, so I didn't like to suggest that she sell the large Holland Park house and buy a smaller house or even a flat in some less desirable area. No, I agreed with Paul that he could do nothing else but pay off her debts, even though it meant that

35

he could contribute little or nothing – it turned out to be nothing – to the full-scale alterations we were having done in our very modest house.

That was the first time I was thwarted by Francesca. Eventually I got used to it and didn't feel so bruised.

# Chapter Four

Auntie Jane had come to see us every week as long as I could remember. Then, one week, she failed to come. I arrived home from school to find my mother terribly agitated. It was Thursday, the paraffin van had been as usual, but there'd been no sign of Auntie Jane. And we had practically no food left, only a scrape of margarine, a few slices of bread and a small tin of beans. And no money because Auntie Jane drew her pension, bought our food and paid our bills. We'd starve, for sure, and our electric would be turned off.

'She'll come tomorrow,' I said.

It was only as my mother was crying that I realised that she no longer cried as she used to; she was getting better. I looked at her with pride. 'I'll go down the village and get some more bread and some cheese. I'll tell them Auntie Jane will pay tomorrow.'

Auntie Jane didn't arrive the next day either, but in the evening Uncle Ted arrived with our groceries. Usually we only saw him on Christmas Day when he came to fetch us for our annual visit to the farm, I hardly recognised him in his working clothes. He brought bad news: Auntie Jane was in hospital and having an operation the next day. 'A hysterectomy,' he said, in such grave tones that I've never been able to hear the word since without quailing. She would be three weeks in hospital and wouldn't be able to do any work on the farm for three months.

'Poor Jane,' my mother said, 'and oh Ted, whatever shall we do up here on our own?'

He studied her for a long time. 'I'll have to take Jane's place, I suppose,' he said at last. 'Though God knows how I'm going to find the time.'

I unpacked the cardboard box of groceries he'd brought. Auntie Jane, in hospital and awaiting her operation, had remembered to make Uncle Ted a list; four large sliced loaves, margarine, tea, sugar, cheese, baked beans, eggs and bananas, all as usual except for the large home-made fruit-cake. She must have been too ill for baking, I thought, tears filling my eyes; both for her and for the loss of the cake. I made a pot of tea.

Uncle Ted sat down and watched me setting out three cups and saucers. 'You're looking very well, Miriam,' he told my mother. 'My dear, you don't look a day over twenty-one. You should start going around a bit to get yourself another husband. A farmer this time, somebody solid.'

'Oh Ted,' my mother said, smiling weakly. 'My heart is broken, you know that.'

'They mend,' he said. 'Hearts do mend. "A time to mourn and a time to give up mourning." That's from the Bible, Katie, and a good piece of advice for your mother.'

He looked at her again. 'Time now to find a little job, Miriam. Time now to try to do without poor Jane's help.' He drank his tea noisily and got to his feet.

He patted my hair before he left and said I was a good girl. I wanted to bite his hand. Auntie Jane always said he was a mean bugger so he had no right to pretend to be nice. He put some money on the table. 'Here's what was left from your pension, Miriam. Jane says you need to keep that to pay the milk and Katie's school dinners.'

'Thank you, Ted,' my mother said meekly. But I could see it was much less than Auntie Jane left us.

'This isn't enough,' I said when he'd left.

'Jane lets us have some of her housekeeping,' my mother

38

said. 'We'd never manage on my pension. And she buys all your clothes as well. She never lets you go short of anything, does she?'

I'd always loved Auntie Jane but had never realised quite how much we owed her.

Up until then, not wanting to be too much of a burden on the Lord Jesus, my prayers had been only for my mother's recovery; from that evening, I added Auntie Jane, with a postscript that Uncle Ted should bring us our groceries until her complete recovery, but please, please, let it be soon.

Uncle Ted, big, loud and handsome, came the following week as well, but not until seven o'clock. He'd already been to see Auntie Jane in the hospital. He was annoyed that she was taking tea round to the other patients instead of resting.

'Jane is always kind,' my mother said, tears in her eyes.

'Jane is always a fool,' he retorted. 'She must learn to put first things first. And the first things are her husband and the farm.' He glared at my mother and me so that we realised what a burden we were.

I unpacked the groceries, refusing to meet his eyes. But when I'd finished putting everything away, I was astonished to see that he was holding my mother's hand and smiling at her. 'You get off to bed,' he told me. 'I've brought along a pack of cards to teach your mother to play whist. It'll do her good to have some company, won't it?' His voice was sickly sweet.

After a while he followed me out to the back-kitchen where I was washing my face and hands before going to bed. 'I'm going to try to persuade your mother to try for a little job I saw advertised in the *Cambrian News* last week. It's the woman from that big house, red brick with a double garage, next to the surgery in Meadow Lane, who's wanting part-time help. Not too far to walk. Suit your mother down to the ground. You talk to her about it tomorrow. Get her used to the idea. She's looking very well these days. She'll manage fine.' His voice was ordinary again, loud and harsh, and I preferred it like that.

'I know she's better,' I said. 'She brushes the floor now and washes the dishes, but I don't think she'd like anyone telling her what to do. And what if the woman started shouting at her? She'd cry and come home. That's what happened when she went down the shop last week and she was still crying when I came home from school.'

'You leave her to me,' Uncle Ted said, smiling again.

It was the last thing I wanted to do. I went to bed but couldn't sleep until I heard his car driving away and my mother coming upstairs. What had he been saying to her? Why was she humming under her breath? I was disturbed without quite knowing why. I think you almost understand a whole lot of things when you're a child; there's one step missing, but you're almost there.

In the morning I asked her why he'd stayed so long. 'He's lonely without Jane, I suppose. He was always fond of me, always wanting to hold my hand when he could.'

Was that all he did? Even now, I'm not sure. But he carried on bringing us our groceries and always stayed for an hour or two after I'd gone to bed, and though I wasn't happy about it, had to admit that his visits, all his flirting and sweet talk and possibly more, were doing my mother a great deal of good. She started going to the mobile hairdresser in the village to have her hair cut and set, and began ironing her dresses and finding different things to wear from a chest in the small bedroom where we didn't usually go because of the mice. One day she came to meet me from school in a long silky dress, a lace scarf round her neck and pointy silver shoes on her feet. 'Was that your mother?' Elinor Rees asked me the next day. 'She did look a sketch.'

'She used to be a famous singer,' I said. I think it was about this time, when I was eight or nine, that I started living a second life surrounded by riches and luxury, my parents famous celebrities as in the library book *Alone For the Summer*, which I'd recently been reading and re-reading.

'You mustn't wear your best clothes to meet me from school,' I told my mother. 'When shall I wear them, then?' 'On Saturday evening. I'll put a candle on the table and we'll be two rich ladies and we'll drink some of Auntie Jane's rhubarb wine.' (The rhubarb wine was for emergencies only, but I gave her an eggcupful sometimes. And sometimes a cupful. It made her happy.)

Uncle Ted brought us chocolate every week; a bar of Cadbury's milk for my mother and a Mars Bar for me. I always intended to refuse mine, but when he put it down on the table, I never could.

There are several ways you can eat a Mars Bar. You can cut it into fifteen neat slices and have two every day and three on Sunday, you can eat the two end pieces, thickly coated with ridges of creamy chocolate, and hide the middle part in a cupboard for Saturday – only sometimes your mother finds it first – or if you're in a bad mood and feeling particularly sorry for yourself, you can gobble it all down like a dog with its dinner, hardly stopping to breathe. But you try not to succumb to that because it leaves you feeling greedy and sick.

A knock at the door. God help us, I was crying again. I wiped my eyes and went to answer it. 'Hello, my dear. Have I come at a bad time? I'm Mrs Tudor Davies, Top Villa. Lorna told me that you wanted a bit of help for the funeral, but I can easily come back when you're more yourself.'

'No, I'm fine. And I'll be glad to get it all settled – the food arrangements, I mean. I'll be very grateful if you can see to it for me.'

'Your mother seemed very well when I saw her recently. It must have been a shock for you. When did you see her last?'

'She came up to stay with me over Easter.'

41

'I remember her mentioning it. I used to see her on a Wednesday afternoon sometimes. You know, the meetings in the village hall, second Wednesday in the month, Merched y Wawr, only sometimes she forgot about them, you know. Her memory, you know.'

I didn't particularly want to discuss my mother with this woman who, according to my new friend, Gwenda Rees, was 'always ready to run her down'. I sniffed and dried my eyes.

'You cry, bach, don't mind me. Losing a mother is a terrible blow. "Cledd a min yw claddu mam." You know that line, I suppose. Lovely piece of cynghanedd, that. And what do you think, Ifor Edwards, Maes yr Haf, had it put down wrong on his mother's grave, beautiful gold lettering on white marble, and the wrong words. "Cledd a min yw *marw* mam". The sense is the same, perhaps, but where's the poetry? What a shame, and him a solicitor too. Well, half a dozen eight-inch quiches, I was thinking, two dozen small sausage rolls, two large loaves, one white, one brown, for ham sandwiches, a pound and a half of sliced ham and two pounds of cheddar, best tasty, with assorted cheese biscuits. Would that suit you?'

'That would be fine, I'm sure.'

'I'll keep you the bills for everything, don't worry.'

'I won't worry at all about the food. Or the bills.'

'Or the serving. Lorna and Ceri, my two daughters-in-law, will help with that.'

'Excellent.'

'I suppose some of your relatives from Gorsgoch will be there and poor old George Williams as well.'

'I suppose so.'

'Because he was very friendly, you know, with your mother in these latter years.'

'Oh yes. I'll be very pleased to meet poor George Williams.'

'You know about him then?'

'Oh yes.'

*

At last she goes, leaving me with only the order of the service and the hymns to worry about. And what to do with the house and all my mother's clothes. And the fine cat, Arthur, who's at the door demanding to go out. And poor old George Williams, whoever he is.

And where is Paul Farringdon, now that I need him?

Is he ever around when I particularly need him? No, it's his ex-wife, the irresistible Francesca and his beautiful wild daughters who have first claim on his time and attention. Always.

When I'm fairly composed again, I walk down to the village to speak to the Reverend Lewis Owen, my mother's minister, who lives in the manse next door to the redbrick chapel. I'm in no hurry, so for a while I stand on the road opposite the little chapel and examine it. It seems to me beautiful; two nicely proportioned arched windows and an arched door on the ground floor, with exquisitely elaborate brickwork around them and under the steeply pitched roof. The men who built it may not have had many resources, but they certainly made the most of different coloured bricks, cream, yellow and rose-red. I don't think I'd ever looked at it before.

Slowly and reluctantly I cross the road to the manse and raise the knocker on the door, but it's opened before I let it fall. The man at the door is in pullover and jeans and looks like a young student, but before I can ask for his father, he shoots out his hand and tells me he is Lewis Owen, minister of Horeb, and that he's very sorry to hear of my mother's death. 'Come in,' he says, 'and you can tell me what to say about her. I know you, of course, from the television, but I didn't know your mother very well. I'm new here, you see.'

I'm shocked by his youth. Does this boy preach sermons about the love and the wrath of God? Does he expect people to listen to him? Doesn't he realise that he should wear a black suit and white dog-collar to lend him some dignity? If he was on stage he'd be properly dressed and warned not to run his fingers through his red hair too.

'Please sit down,' he says, moving copies of the *New Statesman* and *Private Eye* from the largest and most comfortable chair. 'I'll get you a cup of tea and then we'll have a chat.'

A chat? When I was a child, the minister of Horeb, the Reverend William Pierce, wouldn't have known how to chat. He intoned in a solemn, mellifluous voice; no one else expected to say anything.

Lewis Owen, latterday saint, came back with some tea things on a tray.

'How old was your mother?' he asked as he poured out a cup of very dark tea and handed it to me. I looked at him coldly. Surely he should have referred to her as 'your dear mother'. After all, she'd only been dead two days.

'Sixty-five,' I said.

At this point, he should have tutted and said, 'Sixty-five! That's no age, is it.' But all he did was look out of the window trying to suppress a yawn.

'A stroke,' he said at last. 'Yes, I heard that from Lorna yesterday. She warned me that you were expected. I hope you didn't have to leave London in the middle of some television play?'

'I'm here to talk about my mother.'

'Of course.'

'Miriam Rivers.' I stopped as soon as I'd begun. What was there to say about my mother? Lewis Owen was looking at me intently so I struggled on. 'She wasn't anything of a "character", not really, just an ordinary woman who'd had a lot of trouble in her life, poverty and so on. Like most women, I suppose – most women around here, anyway. She had a nervous breakdown when I was small and I used to look after her, rather devotedly, I think . . .. But I've neglected her in the last years. Of course, you probably won't want to mention that in your address.'

44

'Probably not.'

'I don't know which her favourite hymns were, but I like the very sad ones, "Hyder" and so on. And "Mor hyfryd yw y rhai drwy ffydd" to finish off.'

'A real old dirge, that one.'

'I suppose you like the happy, clappy things that put bums on seats.'

'Miss Rivers, don't take it out on me. Everyone feels guilty at the death of someone close to them. No one ever feels they've done as much as they should. Except the hypocrites. And I suppose you remember that Jesus Christ forgave the sinners, but chastised the hypocrites.'

I finished my tea and stumbled to my feet. 'Thank you, Mr Owen. I'll see you on Friday.'

I felt my mother was in good hands.

# Chapter Five

At one time, Paul and I intended to get married. I don't remember much about our plans for the wedding except that it was to be very low-key; Brixton Register Office and a few friends back to lunch at our new house afterwards. I went as far as buying a very dashing suit, the colour 'winter white', the fashionable shade that year, and though it was no different from 'white' or even 'summer white', it sounded appropriate for January. We were going to fly to Scotland for our honeymoon; Paul had promised deep snow, log fires, rugs, grand opera on video and huge meals.

I shouldn't let myself think of those thwarted plans on such a desolate day as today.

Inviting Annabel and Selena was, of course, Paul's idea. He thought it would be a last treat for them before they went back to school after the Christmas holiday; champagne and new people to impress. They accepted the invitation; a long letter with lots of kisses and exclamation marks, but a few days beforehand, Selena was taken ill with what seemed at first to be meningitis. She was rushed to hospital with an alarmingly high fever, Francesca and Paul remaining at her bedside while I looked after a wailing Annabel and cancelled the wedding.

It turned out that Selena's high fever was due to a wisdom tooth coming through, something that Annabel had suspected all along, but by that time I'd convinced myself that Paul, though divorced for over a year, wasn't a free man. I didn't blame him, certainly didn't condemn him for rushing to Selena's side when she'd seemed so ill, but the illness served as a warning. I no longer wanted to marry him. Perhaps he loved me more than he loved Francesca, but Francesca plus his daughters, 'the terrible trio' as I often thought of them, seemed invincible. And what had changed?

I was crying again as I reached the cottage, and the fact that Arthur turned his head towards me as I let myself in and then immediately turned away again seemed particularly cruel. I lifted him off the best chair and sat in it myself. I was hungry but too dispirited to get myself something to eat.

When I was about nine and starting to grow tall, I was always hungry, so hungry that I used to dream about food, plain food like bread and jam and digestive biscuits. Though I had a school dinner every day there seemed a permanent gnawing pain in my stomach.

Luckily, at this time of great need, I made the acquaintance of Mrs Bevan, Garth Wen. I suppose she'd always been there, working in the garden on sunny days when I passed her house on my way home from school, but perhaps it was at this time that I felt mature enough to start smiling and nodding at her. She was old with thin grey hair and glasses, the skin of her face was crinkled like knitting, but she had a very gentle smile. Hers was the last house in the village. All the other children had already reached their homes and I was alone with another long mile to walk.

After we'd reached the waving stage, she started calling me in to help her with something or other. She usually wanted me to find something she'd mislaid; a pair of scissors, her best shoes, her bottom teeth. I had no trouble finding the lost article, often it didn't take more than a minute, but she was always very grateful and repaid me with sweets or biscuits which made the uphill walk home far more tolerable. I was always disappointed when she didn't appear, a little grey ghost in the garden, to beckon me into the house.

One afternoon she took me round to the back garden and showed me the neat rows of carrots, lettuce, peas and radish her son had planted for her when he came to visit her on a Saturday afternoon. 'He told me to keep the weeds down,' she said, 'but I can't see the dratted things on account of my cataracts.'

'I'll keep the weeds down,' I said. I'd never done any gardening but that day the sun was warm on my back and I felt ready for anything. She brought me a hoe and showed me how to poke it into the soil round the little plants. 'You are a good girl,' she said. 'When you're old and have cataracts, you don't see no weeds but only great landscapes clouding your eyes.'

It was early summer and the earth was crumbly and soft, there were butterflies flittering about the gilly-flowers that grew down the path, golden gilly-flowers and bronze and chestnut; the smell of them was like being rich. I called in every day to keep down those dratted weeds.

When I'd worked for about ten minutes, Mrs Bevan would call me into the kitchen to wash my hands. She'd praise my work, though she couldn't see what I'd done, thank me and then hand me a brown paper bag with apples in it or some slices of sponge cake, once a whole swiss roll.

One day when I'd been working longer than usual, she called me into her front room to see some newborn kittens on the television. We didn't have television, I never saw it except on Christmas Day at Auntie Jane's. Mrs Bevan seemed to realise that from the way I was watching it. 'You can come in and see *Jackanory* every day if you'd like to,' she said.

'Can I bring my mother?' I asked her. 'She gets nervous if I'm not home by half-past four.'

49

'Of course you can. I used to know your mother years ago. Nice little woman.'

It became a ritual, a daily treat. My mother would walk down to meet me every day at half-past four and we'd go into Mrs Bevan's front room and there we'd stay until it was time for the early evening news.

At first my mother was very shy with Mrs Bevan but she soon got engrossed in the programmes and forgot about her.

We continued to call once or twice a week all through the summer holidays and we were always welcomed.

'I wonder if you'd like to come to work for me, mornings,' Mrs Bevan asked my mother one day as we were leaving. My mother looked startled, almost as though she was about to run away. 'You see, I'm almost ninety years old and my son wants me to go into Penparc. If I had someone here for a couple of hours every morning, I could manage nicely.'

'What would you want her to do?' I asked. 'She can do the dishes and sweep the kitchen.'

My mother came to life. 'I can do washing and ironing,' she said, her words tumbling out of her, 'and, and . . . something else as well.'

'Hoovering?' Mrs Bevan asked. 'My son bought me a first-class hoover but I can't see to use it properly.'

'We haven't got a hoover,' I said. I didn't even know what a hoover was, but I liked the sound of the word.

'I can do hoovering,' my mother said, the words pelting out of her. 'I used to do hoovering at the shop before I got married.' She turned to me. 'It's a big, noisy thing on wheels and you have to walk it about very carefully without bumping it into the furniture.' She turned back to Mrs Bevan. 'Oh, I can do hoovering. And I can make the beds and empty the slops and dust the ornaments on the dressing table. I used to do all that when I worked for Mrs Harrison when I first left school. I'll come tomorrow, Mrs Bevan, nine o'clock sharp. And thank you.'

50

'Oh, I can do hoovering,' she kept telling me all the way home. 'And Ted is always saying I should have a little job.'

I was afraid that she might have changed her mind by morning, but she was up before me, dressed in her best silk dress and ready to start. 'You must have tea and toast first,' I said. 'You must be strong to do a morning's work.'

'Yes, we'll both have our breakfast first. There's plenty of time.'

She was beginning to take charge.

By the end of the first month with Mrs Bevan, she was a different person, bossy like other mothers, sending me to bed and cleaning my shoes for the morning, though I'd always cleaned my own before, and hers as well.

By this time, Auntie Jane had resumed her Thursday visits, but Uncle Ted was still coming up in the evening to bring the groceries which she wasn't yet strong enough to carry up from the bus stop in the village. And his hour-long visits seemed always timed to coincide with my bedtime.

Now, she wanted nothing more to do with him. 'He's your Auntie Jane's husband,' she said, as though she'd only that minute worked it out. 'And I won't have him coming here and making sheep's eyes at me. When he comes tomorrow night, you'll have to wait outside and tell him we'll be getting our own groceries from the village shop from now on. He'll take it better from you.'

I was nervous about my task, though anxious to get it done. When I came home from school, I practised at the bottom of the garden. 'My mother is now working mornings for Mrs Bevan, Garth Wen, and is learning to manage on her own.' 'My mother is now quite recovered and doesn't need your help.' 'My mother and I . . . well . . . we don't want you to come here any more.'

At eight o'clock I was standing outside ready, but when I heard the car coming up the lane, I ran into the house and

51

locked the door after me. 'We'll turn the light off and keep very quiet,' I said.

We both expected him to stay for ages, banging on the door and shouting, but he accepted his fate very meekly. Within a couple of minutes we heard the car driving away and I was able to creep out to get the box of groceries from the front step. Was that going to be the end of Uncle Ted? It seemed too easy.

We stopped whispering and put the wireless on. 'Pity about the chocolates, too.' my mother said.

My mother loved Mrs Bevan and except for Thursday when Auntie Jane visited, she stayed with her until I came home from school. She talked about her in a hushed voice as Christians talk about the saints. Mrs Bevan perfectly understood what she'd suffered after my father's defection, how she'd let herself go, not able to go out or talk to anyone. Mrs Bevan quite understood about headaches and sickness and forgetfulness and being frightened of strangers. Mrs Bevan – and this is what we heard most often – thought she'd come through with flying colours and was now set to make something of her life.

'And how much a week does this paragon of understanding give you?' Auntie Jane snapped at her, clearly resentful of the way she'd been relegated to second – or third – place in my mother's life.

'She gives me my dinners, Jane, and something for Katie's tea every day.'

'And what about money?'

'And three pounds ten a week in money.'

'Three pounds ten a week! Great Heavens, she's cheating you, girl. You should be getting at least five pounds. Nobody gets three pounds ten a week nowadays. Ten shillings a day is starvation wages.'

'But she's only supposed to be there for two hours in the morning,' I said. 'The rest of the time, she's just keeping her company. It's what she chooses to do. She's happy with Mrs Bevan. She doesn't like it here on her own when I'm in school.'

'But she's got work to do in her own home. You should be cleaning this place, Miriam, and washing and ironing for yourself and Katie, instead of leaving it for me.'

'Yes, I should,' my mother said. 'And I will from now on.'

She started to cry then, but it wasn't the wild crying we were used to – wild, bitter sobbing like a child that's lost its mother – but a resigned, hopeless crying; tears, but no sound at all; much more pitiful. She sat upright on a hard kitchen chair and seemed to be dissolving into water. I was too frightened to move.

Auntie Jane got up and put her arms round her. 'Don't take no notice of me, Miri. Nobody knows better than me what you've been through.'

The silent crying went on and on. I thought it would never end.

'It was the electric they drove through my head in that place, Jane, that's what did for me. Who gave them the right to do that? Nobody should have the right to do that to anyone. It took something away from me, Jane, something I needed. I've never been to Dr Mathias since, because he sent me to that terrible place, didn't he? I only had words in my head after, instead of sentences, sometimes only pictures. Like being in the babies' class. Only words and pictures. And no sense.'

It made you shiver, the way she said, *no sense.*

We went on sitting at the table for a long time, Auntie Jane still holding my mother and crooning to her.

I could hear the clock ticking, a tractor ploughing on the 'Steddfa, seagulls calling, a crow in the distance. I wanted to go outside. I wanted to be a child, outside looking for conkers, playing with other children, but I knew I couldn't. At nine, I was already old.

*

53

Afternoon gave way to evening. I made myself an omelette but failed to eat it. I found a tin of cat food and turned it out onto an enamel plate, but Arthur wasn't hungry either. I'd already half-filled a pan with nice dry earth for him and when he cried to go out I carried him over to it, but though he sniffed at it, he wouldn't use it.

Almost eight o'clock. Paul didn't seem to be in any hurry to ring, so I left him another message on the answerphone: 'My mother died on Sunday evening. Please ring as soon as you can. I need to talk to you.' My mother was dead, had died suddenly with no sort of warning. I badly needed some sympathy and some comfort. I considered ringing the Reverend Lewis Owen. I considered ringing the Samaritans. Why didn't Paul ring? And why didn't that bloody cat stop that bloody racket and use the dirt tray?

A knock on the front door. I sniffed, ran my fingers through my hair and, ready to welcome whoever it was, hurried to open it.

'I'm your cousin, Rhydian, Kate, and this my wife, Grace. We were so sorry to hear about Auntie Miriam.' He had a soft, lazy voice and down-sloping dark eyes like Auntie Jane's.

I thanked them for coming, begged them to come in, put them to sit side by side on the sofa where I could look at them. 'It's wonderful of you to come,' I said. 'I'm so pleased to see you.' Tears were running down my cheeks, slowly, one at a time – in a way I can never manage on stage.

'We've brought a bottle of whisky,' Rhydian said. 'We didn't think Auntie'd have anything much in the house. Let me go and see if I can find some glasses.'

'I wanted to bring flowers,' Grace said.

'You needn't have brought anything. I just want company. I'm so glad you came. How long can you stay? I think I'm having a nervous breakdown.'

Grace took her coat off and smiled at me. 'No, you're not. Having a nervous breakdown isn't as easy as you think. I'm always planning to have one but I never manage it. When you have all the work of a farm and three small boys it's the perfect answer – the only way to get some attention, it seems to me – but it only happens to other people. You're just grieving after your mother and feeling lonely all by yourself up here. Your mother was a lovely woman, it's no wonder you're feeling cast down. Hurry up with that whisky, Rhydian. Are you doing the dishes out there, or what?'

Rhydian came in with three large whiskies. 'Anyone want some water?'

'Rhydian, you're so changed,' I said. 'You used to be so wild-looking, so rough. I used to think you three boys were like the Doone brothers. I was terrified of you all.'

'You've changed, too. You used to be skinny and . . . well, rather plain. Of course, we've seen you on the telly now and again, so I was ready for the change.'

'Rather plain? Iestyn wrote to me once, asking me to go to the pictures with him. He said I was very pretty.'

'Iestyn has always been a ladies' man,' Grace said. 'Different from this one.'

'I'm just a farmer,' Rhydian said, smiling ruefully in my direction. 'Turned fifty, losing my hair, the farm losing money, three children and another on the way. Well, here's to us, the three of us. And all our problems.'

For a while we drank in silence. I glanced at him again. Over fifty? Losing his hair? He looked pretty good to me.

'What about Iestyn?' I asked. 'A geography teacher. What else?'

'Deputy Head now,' Rhydian said. 'Put on a lot of weight. Important.'

'Married, divorced, married again,' Grace added. 'His second wife's very hoity-toity. Madeleine. No children, up to now.'

'Grace thinks all English people are stuck-up.'

'No, I don't. Yorkshire people can be quite homely. We do bed and breakfast now, Kate, and we get a lot of people from Yorkshire and, on the whole, they're quite decent. Quite like us.'

'And Bleddyn? He's still at Oxford?'

'No, he decided to take up teaching as well. I mean, in an ordinary school. I think he'd come to a dead end with his research. He gave it up, anyway. Head of Maths now in a Comprehensive in the East End.'

'He's never married,' Grace said, 'but he used to live with another of these dons when he was at Oxford – quite a long-term affair – and he's got a lovely daughter. She's about twenty now and going in for nursing. Siwan. Siwan *Grace* actually. She comes to stay with us quite often. The boys worship her. Anyway, what about you? Still with the same chap? Paul something? I remember your mother mentioning a Paul.'

'Yes, I'm still with him. But it's not permanent.'

What made me say that? It was the first time I had, though the thought had occurred to me from time to time. The tears welled up again, rolling slowly down my face, one after the other.

'This one could cry for Wales,' Rhydian told his wife. 'I'll never forget what she was like when my mother died.'

He turned to me. 'It was wonderful for us boys. We were desperately upset, I remember this hard lump I had in my chest so I could hardly breathe, but of course boys, young men rather, don't cry. Having you there was like having a hired mourner, our pain was eased, but our dignity remained intact. You did us a lot of good, Katie.'

'I was only about thirteen then and I loved Auntie Jane more than anyone in the world except my mother. Her death terrified me. I couldn't see how we could possibly manage without her. I remember very well how I couldn't stop crying – in the chapel, in the cemetery and back at the farm afterwards. But, you know, I've hardly cried since. Until today.'

Rhydian got up and put his arm round me. 'You used to

come to us every Christmas, didn't you, till Mam died. You seemed to us like someone from another planet, so small and serious. We couldn't help teasing you.'

Something stirred inside me. 'Was it you who made the sledge one year?'

He seemed pleased that I'd remembered it. 'Yes, that was me. We've still got it, too. The boys still get it out whenever we have enough snow.'

'How old were you? When you made it? Can you remember?'

'Thirteen, I think. Having woodwork lessons in school. Twelve or thirteen.'

'You took me out on it, once.'

'Did I? Yes, I seem to remember that. Hope I didn't frighten you,'

I smiled at him.

Yes. He took me out on his sledge. One dazzling white Christmas, the snow frosted over with stars. I remember the fear I felt. And the pride. Hold on to me, he said, and I did. He seemed so large and strong. And warm as an animal. And smelling of animals, too. How old would I have been? Only about five, I suppose. But I can still remember when he said, Hold on tight. We'll go down Parc Isa. You're not frightened, are you?

'What's the matter?' Grace asked me. 'You're looking sad again. Have some more whisky.'

'No, I'm all right. I was remembering Rhydian's sledge, that's all.'

# Chapter Six

Rhydian and Grace stayed until almost eleven and then it seemed a respectable time to go to bed. Their company, or the whisky, had managed to calm me and hoping for a good night's sleep I went out to the garden to fill my lungs with the cold mountain air. This is where I'd stand years ago reciting Shakespeare in the darkness; Desdemona, Ophelia, Juliet. 'You've got a voice like milk and honey,' my mother would say when I got back into the house. 'Like porridge and cream. Like buttermilk.' She seemed so close, I could almost touch her.

The moment passed when I saw Arthur streaking away across the garden and through the hedge at the bottom: I'd left the door open. I stood calling him for a while, but knew it was hopeless – he had no trust in me – so I went back to the house, hoping he'd turn up in the morning.

I filled my mother's hot-water bottle to take to bed with me – it would be something to hold – and went upstairs. Paul hadn't rung. He was probably still in Cambridge getting to grips with Annabel's problems.

'We had everything. Your grandmother had recently died so we were able to take over this house and we had most of her furniture as well, and pots and pans and a tea set and a half dinner set as wedding presents. I remember my Auntie Molly – she was Jane's eldest sister – asking me what she should send. "We've got everything, Auntie," I said. "We've got absolutely everything now. But an extra pair of towels would be very useful." It was true, we had a house and decent furniture and everything else we needed and a good wage coming in. And in just over a year's time, a baby girl as well, pretty as a little doll. We were happy, I swear we were, and it could have lasted for ever. Who knows what made him leave me? If only I could understand it. *No one* could understand it. Your Uncle Ted got his solicitor to make enquiries, it cost him a pretty penny too, but no one found out anything about him.'

I could hear her words all around me in the bedroom. Words don't seem to leave a place. 'If only I could understand it. We were happy, I swear we were.'

I found myself answering her as I used to, found myself remembering something I'd once dared say when I was fourteen or fifteen and she very nearly recovered. 'Perhaps he was afraid of too much responsibility. Perhaps he suspected there was another baby on the way.'

'Why did you say that?' There was a sob as well as a swell of anger in my mother's voice. 'What did you mean by that?'

I realised at once that I'd gone too far. 'Nothing. I didn't mean anything in particular. I was only trying to imagine something which might have frightened him away. Men are nervous of commitment. They're not as brave as women. That's all I meant. That's all.'

It was no use trying to comfort her. She was crying bitterly, remembering, I suppose, the abortion she'd had – or was it an accidental miscarriage? – that little coiled-up foetus I'd seen all those years ago in the chamber-pot.

Perhaps that fit of desperate crying resolved something. It was the last I remember.

She hardly cried at all when we had the news of my father's death a few years later. His body was found under the floor-boards of a cheap lodging house near the docks in Liverpool, along with the bodies of three other young men who'd gone missing in the same year.

It was a sensational case at the time, with shrieking headlines in certain newspapers about vice rings and male prostitution, but since the hostel had been closed after the owner's death almost fifteen years before, nothing was proved beyond the identity of the murdered men.

I was eighteen at the time, still at school doing my A-levels. I had no memory of my father, had never even seen a photograph of him, but I certainly mourned him deeply, realising how unhappy his life must have been and how terrifying his death. I suppose if such a thing happened today, professional counselling would be provided by the school. As it was, the Headmaster called me into his study, told me that the staff had discussed the tragedy at a meeting, decided that it would be too much of a strain for me to receive their individual condolences, so had asked him to pass on their sympathy and support. Furthermore, he continued – he was fond of that word – my subject teachers would be pleased to offer me individual tuition at any time when I felt I might be losing my concentration.

I thanked him and we shook hands.

I don't remember anyone being unkind at school. If there were any who considered the news something to snigger about, they kept out of my way. I suppose I was very lucky.

I didn't lose concentration on my work; the tragedy had the opposite effect. I worked like a demon, feeling, more than ever, that I had something to prove. I had to do well. I had to rise above my background. I realise now that the determination to succeed marked me as both judgemental and snobbish. I'm not proud of it. But that's how it was.

I mourned my father, of course I did, but at the same time, couldn't help being aware that his unexplained disappearance showed great weakness. I remember asking Uncle Ted – who had re-married by this time, but was still calling on us from time to time – whether he thought my father was homosexual. 'He was a decent chap,' was all he'd say. 'He'd worked hard and got on. Everybody spoke highly of him and he seemed to be good to your mother. Who knows what pressure he was under? Well, he may have been . . . what you said . . . but he wouldn't have wanted to harm anyone, you can be sure of that. I think you should try to get your mother to believe he was going to America intending to make his fortune before sending for her. I think she might find some comfort in that, don't you?'

'Uncle Ted thinks . . .' I started to say, when he'd left and my mother and I were on our own.

'It doesn't matter what your Uncle Ted or anybody else thinks,' she said. 'I've laid him to rest now. He left me. And then he died. It's a sad, sad story, but now it's over. I'm sorry you never knew him, but now it's over. Do you think I'm hard?'

'Hard? You've mourned him for fifteen years.'

'Fifteen years and three months. And now it's over.'

It was over, all the waiting and crying. But nothing took its place. There was never anyone else in her life.

But there was suddenly another voice in my head. The busy-body, Maggie Davies. 'And poor old George Williams will be at the funeral as well. Because he was very friendly, you know, with your mother in these latter years.'

Hers was the last voice I heard before falling asleep.

I slept deeply, but woke before it was light. I'd been dreaming again about the abortion I had had three years ago.

I'd come off the pill because of some headaches I'd been having, and in no time at all discovered I was pregnant. I was very excited for a day or so.

'What if I told you I was pregnant?' I asked Paul when he came back from some foreign trip.

'You can't be, love. We've always been tremendously careful.'

'What if I told you I wanted to be pregnant?'

'Well, that would be different, wouldn't it? If you really wanted a baby I'm sure you could persuade me to go along with it.' He sounded very tired.

'You'd have to be persuaded, though? You wouldn't be enthusiastic?'

'I wouldn't be madly enthusiastic, darling, because of my age. I'm almost fifty, you know that, and besides I thought we'd decided against it.'

'You're right. We had.'

'And you're very nearly forty, love, though God knows you don't look it. I think we should consider this quite carefully, don't you? About how old we'd be when the child was a teenager, and so on. I mean, if we did decide to go ahead.'

'We'd certainly have to consider it very carefully,' I said, all the joy seeping out of me.

'And I wonder what Annabel and Selena would think about it,' Paul continued. 'They're at an age to be rather upset, don't you think? We'd have to consider the effect it might have on them.'

That seemed the last straw. 'Say no more,' I said. 'I've decided against it. We won't speak of it again.'

I gave up without a struggle. I made an appointment at a private clinic, timed for Paul's next trip abroad, and went through with the termination, knowing quite well that I'd suffer after it. Yes, I suffered after it. Yes, I regretted it bitterly.

I never mentioned it to anyone except to my dresser at the theatre. She was a motherly fifty-year-old who knew immediately that something was troubling me.

'Come on, tell Nancy all about it. What's wrong with you?'

'What makes you think there's anything wrong with me?'

'You look different. Your face is clenched and your skin is wet as a fish. Your old man been playing you up, has he?'

'It's not that.'

'What, then?'

'Oh Nancy, I had an abortion yesterday. And I feel awful.'

She put her arms round me and hugged me. She said nothing for a long time, but I could feel her sympathy. I felt she must have had an abortion herself at some stage, to understand so much. She didn't refer to it again, but she was very tender towards me for the rest of the run.

I never told Paul about it; it was my decision and I didn't want him to feel guilty about it. All the same, it came between us.


I suddenly realise that I've never loved anyone unreservedly. I've never been able to love anyone body and soul. The words sent shivers through me. Body and soul. With my body I thee worship. And soul. Which was surely something more than mind, something deeper, almost spiritual. I'd been pleased to think that my love for Paul had been mature and comforting; cerebral, in fact. Oh, but that wasn't enough. Body and soul, I repeated mournfully. Why had I always been satisfied with one or the other?

There's nothing like death to bring you face to face with life. My life wasn't fulfilled.


Grace phoned at nine o'clock. 'I'm putting the children in the car and coming over to fetch you,' she said. 'There's no point in you being over there on your own with nothing to do but be miserable.'

'That's kind of you, Grace. But I think I need to be here at the moment. You know how people like to drop in. I don't want to be discourteous to anyone.'

'Iestyn got Rhydian's letter this morning and he's just been on the phone. He doesn't think he'll be able to get a day off for the funeral, but he said to give you his love. I bet it's that stuck-up wife of his who's against it. That Madeleine. She's probably got some cocktail party to go to on Friday.

Well, we'll be over again tonight. Yes, of course we will. What's family for? My mother will be here to baby-sit and I'm bringing over a steak and kidney pie so don't you bother to cook.'

'What about this George Williams?' I asked Lorna Davies when she called with the post – a catalogue from J.D. Williams and a phone bill.

'Did your mother tell you about George?'

'No, but your mother-in-law mentioned him.'

'Well, there you are, my mother-in-law enjoys spreading a bit of gossip. But I suppose he was courting your mother in his own way. You know, cutting her hedge at the back, bringing her beans and cabbage from his place, doing her shopping sometimes. I used to tease her about him, ask her when they were going to get married and so on, but she was never willing to talk about him. He's a nice enough man, mind, very respectable, used to work in Caffrey's the iron-monger in town. He'll be at the funeral on Friday for sure. I'll tell him to come over and have a word with you.'

'Arthur managed to escape last night and I haven't seen him this morning though I've called and called.'

'He'll be back when he's hungry. He knows now that there's someone here.'

'Won't you come in and have a cup of tea?'

'If you're sure you've got the time.'

'Of course I have. I've been waiting for you. The kettle's boiling.'

'You seem better than yesterday, anyway. You're beginning to come to terms with it, I think.'

'People are being very kind.'

'You saw the new minister, I hear. What did you think of him? Some people think he's a bit strange and abrupt.'

'I liked him. He hasn't got the outward show, but I think he's all the better for that. He put me very firmly in my place.'

65

'I like him, too, but it's a pity he doesn't look a bit more respectable.'

'He can't help his red hair.'

'No. Well, I'll tell people you liked him.'

'Is that important?'

'Oh yes. You're very important round here. On the television and so on . . . I'm sorry, I didn't mean to upset you.'

'I know you didn't. It's just that I'm feeling very vulnerable at the moment. And rather worthless.'

She decided to ignore my bid for sympathy. 'Your cousin came over from Gorsgoch, I hear.'

'Yes. Do you know him?'

'No. Only his wife is sister to Edwina Williams, Buarth, and of course, she'd heard all about you. Yes, very natural, Grace thought you were. No side. Well, I must be off. My mother-in-law asked me to tell you she's got everything organised and you're not to worry about a thing.'

I'm pleased Rhydian and Grace are coming again tonight. It's strange how close I feel to Rhydian; someone I'd half-feared, half-worshipped all my childhood revealed as mere mortal. But an interesting one with a bit of Auntie Jane in his looks and his character. And with a lazy, summer voice.

In spite of assuring me that she'd got everything under control, Maggie Davies called again at midday today. With a problem. Did I want her to use the vestry china, plain white, with several of the larger plates chipped and cracked, or should she ask for the Women's Institute china, pale green and in much better condition. Only they charged five pounds.

'I think the green,' I said firmly. 'Let me give you the five pounds now, while I think of it.'

'No, that will be a separate bill from the Institute. You think green is in order? For a funeral, I mean?'

66

'Absolutely.'

'What about the floral arrangements for the chapel? With the funeral being on a Friday, the floral arrangements would normally be left in place for Sunday worship.'

'That seems a sensible idea.'

'So who exactly is going to see to the floral arrangements? I'm sorry to say that I have too much in hand at the moment.'

'I appreciate that. I intend to see to the floral arrangements myself.'

'For the chapel and the vestry?'

'That's right.'

'Since I'm in charge of setting the tables in the vestry, can I suggest five all-white floral arrangements with trailing greenery.'

'Exactly what I had in mind. For the vestry and the chapel.'

Maggie Davies probably wouldn't have got so annoyed with me if I hadn't been using my Edith Evans voice.

'I hope you realise that all the florists in town are closed on Wednesday afternoon,' she said, 'and that they will want more than twenty-four hours' notice for half a dozen floral arrangements.'

'Ah, but I've already ordered them from London.'

She didn't believe me, I could tell that by the way her eyes narrowed. All the same, she seemed to be readjusting her opinion of me.

When she'd left I phoned Paul yet again, leaving yet another message on the answerphone. 'My mother's dead but you don't seem to care. When you finally get home will you please get in touch with me about floral arrangements.' I slammed down the receiver realising that I was still speaking in my 'grande dame' voice. *Good.*

# Chapter Seven

'I'm Edwina Williams, Grace's sister. Just calling by to express my condolences . . .' Her voice changed abruptly. 'What I mean is, I'm ever so sorry to hear about your poor mother's death. I didn't know her, myself, but everybody seemed to have a good word for her.'

'Thank you, Edwina. Nice of you to call. Grace is being very kind as well. You look alike, I could tell you were sisters . . .. But of course, you're a younger version.'

'Grace and I would have seen to the funeral for you, no problem, only we heard Maggie Davies had taken it over.'

'That's right – Lorna suggested her. Anyway, I wouldn't want to impose on family.'

'Maggie Davies was telling a neighbour of mine this morning that you were getting the flowers all the way from London. Now, there's no need for that. She was only wanting you to beg her to use her influence with one of the florists in town. I'm glad you didn't. Power goes straight to Maggie's head. I'll get the flowers for you, no problem. John Parry who owns The Flower Basket in town was a boyfriend of mine years ago and there's still a bit of interest left there, if you want to know the truth. He'll *want* to work on his afternoon off when I tell him it's for family. I'll go straightaway now before he leaves the shop. No trouble at all. One large arrangement for the chapel and five small for the vestry, Maggie was saying.

White with greenery. Was that her decision or yours? And what sort of flowers?'

'I'll leave all the decisions to your friend.'

'You won't regret it.'

Edwina hurried back to her car, chest first, waving and smiling at me as though we were the greatest friends.

I couldn't think of anyone who'd want to give up an afternoon's holiday to do me a favour. But there, Edwina is prettier and younger than I am; very rounded and dimpled and cuddlesome.

I wondered whether the interest she'd mentioned was on her side as well as his. She was wearing a wedding ring, so perhaps only a few tender smiles would pass between them and an accidental grazing of hands as she helped him choose the flowers. I could smell the sweetness of lilies and freesias and hot-house roses in the closed shop, a heavy, almost decadent smell; forbidden love, so different from the fresh, true smell of garden flowers.

Forbidden love, true love, and how should I my true love know from some other one?

My first love affair when I was nineteen. I think the boy in question was only twenty, but he seemed very worldly-wise and sophisticated. When he suggested we go away for a weekend together I didn't think of refusing though I was nervous about it. He was considered very handsome. I can't remember his face, but I remember that he was considered very handsome.

He was English, his family from the Wirral, but they often spent their holidays in a North Wales beauty spot, Betws-y-Coed, and that's where he decided we should go.

He was amazed to discover that I'd never visited the famous waterfall, though my home was only about sixty miles away. (I didn't tell him, but I hadn't been to our nearest town, six miles away, until I was eleven.) We travelled on the TransCambria from Cardiff where we were at University, my bus-fare and my share of the three days

70

and nights away making a huge hole in that term's grant. However, Handsome Boy assured me that it would be well worth it – and he didn't mean the waterfall; he was at the age when he wanted sex every half hour. And that's how we spent the first morning, missing breakfast, which I considered extremely foolish and wasteful. In the afternoon I insisted on leaving the hotel to see the famous Swallow Falls, but when I discovered how much it cost to view, I was persuaded against it. Handsome Lad knew how to get in from further up the hill; he and his brothers had done it several times. We'd wait until closing time, then see it by moonlight. For nothing.

And I must say, it seemed the right and proper thing to do. Why, after all, should I pay to see a natural phenomenon in my own country?

It was about ten o'clock before the moon rose and we went for the long walk up the hill, managing to crawl in under a fence and walk back through the larch woods to the waterfall which we could already hear crashing onto the rocks.

It was worth the effort, worth the train-fare, the cost of the hotel and the tedium of too much sex. It was my first waterfall, it was splendid as the Taj Mahal.

Naturally, I had to stand on the platform in the dazzling, moonlit spray, and as I'd borrowed my room-mate's new wool-and-cashmere dress for the weekend, promising to take the greatest care of it, I conscientiously and carefully took it off, hung it over a branch and pranced about in my bra and pants and when they got wet, pranced about without them. Being English, Handsome Lad was not entirely happy about a display of nudity and high spirits unconnected with alcohol and rugby; he waited patiently for me to finish and then offered me his handkerchief to dry myself.

By the next day I was totally bored by him and started eyeing the other guests. There weren't many, it was the beginning of October, the season almost over, but there was one grave, middle-aged man who did interest me. He had mournful eyes, I thought, and a thin, romantic face and he was alone. I imagined a dead wife or a faithless lover and from time to time over lunch and dinner, our eyes met and very briefly we gave each other careful little smiles.

We were leaving the next day after breakfast, and when Handsome One had gone upstairs to fetch our bags, I was able to speak to the stranger who was also leaving.

'Have you had a pleasant weekend?' I asked him. And was immediately aware of how tactless my question was, as he was alone, possibly abandoned.

'I've had a wonderful time,' he said in a low, sad, romantic voice. 'Would you believe that on Saturday night when I went for a walk up the hill, I looked in at the waterfall and saw a naked girl dancing in the spray.'

I wasn't at all embarrassed. I smiled at him and he smiled back at me. It seemed to last a long time, that sad, reverential smile. And I can still remember his face vividly, and his voice. Though I've completely forgotten Handsome Boy – although he'd assured me I'd never forget him.

That was my first love affair. But whom was I in love with? And how should I my true love know?

Meeting Rhydian again after so long, I find myself thinking about Auntie Jane, a truly wonderful woman, large, strong and vigorous, who found time to support my mother and me as well as battling with cancer, running a farm and looking after her own family.

Mrs Bevan's son, Leslie, used to take us over to visit her on an occasional Saturday afternoon when she'd become too ill to visit us. I can still see her, dwindled to nothing on the bed, her eyes still fighting. 'You look after your Mummy, bach,' were her last words to me. 'You're the best little girl in the world.'

No wonder Uncle Ted went to pieces after her death, drinking far too much and neglecting the farm. And soon he started staying away on Saturday nights with a young, or youngish woman called Madge, known in the village as 'a good sort', and within a few months was hardly going home at all. Madge and he got married before a year was up, but she was perfectly happy, thank you, in her neat council house and refused to contemplate taking over a great, rambling farmhouse like Gorsgoch. Rhydian came home from the agricultural institute before getting his diploma and took over the running of the farm, his father coming up from the village now and again to lend a helping hand.

Most of this we heard from Uncle Ted himself who still came up to visit us from time to time. 'I'm no good without Jane,' he used to say in a thick, drunken voice. 'Jane managed to keep me on the straight and narrow. Well, perhaps it wasn't entirely straight or entirely narrow, but at least I was usually facing the right way when Jane was alive. Now I'm anywhere.'

'You should still think about your sons,' my mother would say. 'I know what it is to lose someone, but I still try to look after Katie.'

'And she looks after you as well,' Uncle Ted would say. 'And so did Jane look after you. Don you go and forget that.'

At this point, feeling he'd had as much sympathy as he was likely to, he'd raise himself unsteadily from the chair. 'Listen, both of you,' he'd say – we knew what was coming – 'Listen, I want you to meet Madge who's a very nice woman. She's not Jane, but she's a very nice woman, a very nice—'

'No, Ted,' my mother would say each time. 'I couldn't bear to meet her, however nice she is. When I see you I can only think of Jane.'

Poor Uncle Ted. By this time I didn't dislike him as much as I had.

I walked to the village shop in the afternoon. Since Grace was bringing a steak and kidney pie, I felt called upon to make some sort of effort as well. The shop where I used to

73

buy my mother's groceries is now a small supermarket. Yes, they have wine, a fair selection, they have avocados, garlic, mushrooms, frozen raspberries, whipping cream, Stilton cheese; everything I want. When I was a girl, I can only remember sugar and tea, jam and tinned fruit. But at that time they had two huge slabs of cheese on the counter – mild and tasty – and they let you taste a sliver of each every time you went in.

There was an elderly lady standing in front of me at the check-out. 'Do you remember that tasty cheese with blue rind they used to have here?' I asked her.

'Good gracious,' she said, 'it's Kate Rivers, isn't it? Good gracious yes, I used to serve here years ago. I used to cut you little morsels of cheese so that you'd have something to put in your belly on your way home. You used to come here for old Mrs Bevan, didn't you? As well as for your mam? Yes, I heard that your poor mam had passed on. When is the funeral? I'll try to be there. Yes, I was talking to poor old George Williams earlier this week, he and I are neighbours you know, and he told me the sad news. Why don't you call in and have a cup of tea with me before you go home? For old times'sake? Ty Gwyn. It's only a step from here. Good. I won't wait for you, I'll hurry back to shake the mat and put the kettle on. See you very soon, then.'

'Do you know her name?' I asked the girl at the check-out. 'The woman I was talking to?'

'Sorry,' she sang out at me. 'I'm only here to do the till, me.'

She had a large, vacant face glistening with eye-shadow, lipstick and blusher, but she wasn't interested in anyone. She didn't care that my mother had died or that someone was hurrying home to shake a mat before I arrived for a cup of tea.

'Thank you,' I sang back at her after she'd taken my money and given me my change.

\*

74

I stared in at Mrs Bevan's house as I passed it after my tea and chat at Ty Gwyn. It had been renovated and extended. There was a too-large Victorian conservatory, all wrought iron and coloured glass, on the side nearest the village and something that looked like a stable block in the back where the garden shed had stood. Of course, Garth Wen was always a better-than-average house, it had three or four bedrooms and a bathroom, a dining room as well as a large living room and kitchen. Mr Bevan, after all, had been 'in business'. Neither my mother nor I knew what that meant, except that it meant a big house and money in the bank. 'I may decide to have an indoor toilet by the back door,' Mrs Bevan would say. 'I'll have to see if there's enough money in the bank.' Sometimes my mother and I would use the same words, but with heavy irony. Not that we resented Mrs Bevan her good fortune; indeed, we often benefited from it. After Auntie Jane's death, Mrs Bevan's bank account provided many of the extras I needed for school. 'Not a word to Leslie,' she always said when she handed over any extra sum of money. That was another phrase my mother and I often bandied about whenever we had any little treat. 'Not a word to Leslie.'

Mrs Bevan liked to think of Leslie as a very forceful character; any suggestion he made having to be acted upon as if it was God's law. 'Leslie thinks I should put all my brass ornaments away to save you work, Mrs Rivers,' she said one day. So then she and my mother wrapped them all in tissue paper and packed them carefully away in a cardboard box. In spite of the fact that she loved looking at them and telling us where every piece had come from. And the fact that my mother took great pride in polishing them.

Of course I'd long realised that Leslie was a softy; he'd spent several Saturday afternoons taking my mother and me to Gorsgoch to see Auntie Jane during her last illness, had even offered to take a day off work to drive us to the funeral, though in fact that hadn't proved necessary since Uncle Ted had found time to fetch us. 'Leslie would do anything for Kate,' Mrs Bevan used to say. 'Leslie loves children.'

So on the Saturday afternoon after the incident with the ornaments, I had no worries about calling in to explain to Leslie how his kind thought of saving my mother work had misfired. I found him in the garage, sorting out apples for storing. I can still remember the heavy smell of ripe apples. 'I'm very sorry,' he said after I'd explained the position to him. Indeed, he looked stricken with remorse.

'Don't worry,' I said. 'Just tell your mother that you miss seeing them and then she and my mother can have a lovely afternoon unpacking them again.'

He didn't say anything for a minute or so, simply stared at me as though he was about to cry. 'I took them to my wife,' he said at last. 'You see, my wife has wanted them for such a long time.'

I didn't know what to say. I was angry, of course. Mrs Bevan was ninety-four or five by this time – surely he could have waited a little longer before taking the ugly things. I was also surprised. I'd always assumed that Leslie was unmarried. Mrs Bevan had never mentioned a daughter-in-law. I think I must have just stood and gaped at him; this pathetic old man – he must have been in his mid-sixties – behaving so badly. Then, before I'd managed to say a word, he lurched towards me and started hugging me and weeping over me. I tried to pull away from him, but though I was strong – I'd be thirteen or fourteen by this time – he was stronger. He was crying in strange spasms and holding me so tightly I could hardly breathe. He was shuffling about too. And then he took my hand and put it over his penis which was big and sticky and horrible. I felt I was going to faint, but I pulled myself together and pushed him under the chin with such force that he had to let me go. 'You pig,' I was shouting. 'You pig, you pig, you pig.' He'd fallen back on to a box of apples and was standing there holding himself. I turned and rushed out of the garage. There was a key in the lock so I locked him in. There was no need for it; he was making no attempt to come after me, but I turned the key in the lock anyway. He'd have a hard time getting out of the small window in the back – plenty of time, I hoped, to think over his wretched behaviour to his mother and to me.

Especially to me, I sobbed under my breath as I ran home. It was a long time before I could get rid of that sickly smell from my hand. And even now, almost thirty years later, the smell of ripe apples still disturbs me.

Mrs Bevan died that same year, a few days before Christmas. Perhaps she'd begun to realise she couldn't trust Leslie, because the previous week she had hired a car, gone to the bank in town and taken out fifty pounds in five pound notes for my mother, a small fortune in those days. She handed it to her in a brown paper bag, just as she used to hand me the biscuits and sweets. 'For Christmas?' my mother asked her, with no idea what it was. But Mrs Bevan had lapsed into unconsciousness. She was taken to hospital later that day and died the next morning.

My mother was, of course, distraught; for several days keeping to her bed and refusing to eat, refusing even to discuss her little windfall. (What did we do, eventually, with that fifty pounds? I can't remember.)

In the local paper, Mr and Mrs Leslie Bevan were named as chief mourners. 'Great Heavens,' my mother said, when I read her the account, 'I didn't know he had a wife. Mrs Bevan told me everything, but she never told me that. I wish I'd pulled myself together and gone to the funeral so that I could have seen her. Leslie was such a lovely, kind gentleman, I'd have really liked to meet his wife.'

The house was sold soon afterwards to a local doctor who begged my mother to carry on working for him and his wife. She did. Two hours a day at a much better wage than she'd got from Mrs Bevan. But they never took over Mrs Bevan's place in her affection. It was Mrs Bevan she still talked about, Mrs Bevan she still loved.

And now my mother was also dead. I walked the rest of the way home very slowly.

There was a knock on the door while I was unpacking the shopping later. The man in the doorway was a stranger, but I immediately knew who it was.

'George Williams,' he said. We shook hands. I invited him in.

He was short and stocky; earth-coloured face and a thatch of white hair.

'Please sit down. I'll make a cup of tea.'

I was beginning to understand the social relevance of the cup of tea. It might not be needed by anyone or particularly wanted, but as well as being a gesture of good-will, making it gave you a moment to collect yourself. It suddenly seemed crucial to our civilisation.

'I'm pleased to meet you at last,' I said when I got back to the living room.

He looked me up and down. 'Likewise,' he said.

I poured out a cup of tea and passed it to him. He took a spoonful of sugar and stirred it vigorously. 'Sad time,' he said, still stirring.

'Sad time for both of us,' I said.

He acknowledged it with a slight nod of the head. He refused a digestive biscuit, but drank his tea calmly and without hurry. I wondered whether to ask him when he'd last seen my mother, but decided it might upset him.

'Did you have any inkling that she was ill?' I asked at last.

He thought about the question for what seemed a full minute, then very carefully put his cup back on the saucer and got to his feet. 'I knew she was feeling nervous,' he said at last. 'I knew she was nervous about the wedding, but her death was a terrible shock.'

'I'm so sorry,' I murmured. Tears filled my eyes again as I squeezed his hands.

She hadn't, of course, mentioned the wedding – or him – to me, but I hoped I hadn't shown any surprise. 'I'll see you at the funeral,' I said. 'And I hope you'll sit with me in the front pew.'

When he'd gone I felt quite light-headed and though it was still only five o'clock, started on the whisky.

Some time later, the phone rang. It was Paul. He was sorry he hadn't managed to ring before, but Annabel was in serious trouble. He paused, expecting me to question him, but I didn't. I didn't at all want to know about Annabel's problems, having plenty of my own. 'I think she's being charged with manslaughter,' he said. 'One of her friends died as a result of taking Ecstasy or one of these other things, and she's being accused of selling it to her. It's a lie, of course. It was some young chap from the town who'd sold the stuff, but she happened to be carrying one or two of the tablets in her bra and—'

I took a deep breath. 'Try to stay calm,' I said. 'The police have to pounce on someone so that people know they're taking it seriously, but they come to their senses after a while. I know you'll have got her the best possible lawyer. And that's all you can do at the moment.'

'Oh God, how can you be so detached? What's happened to you? We want you here. Annabel's been asking for you and so has Francesca and I'm going to pieces without you.'

'You're still in Cambridge, Paul?' I suddenly realised that he hadn't heard my news.

'Of course I am. Do you think I can leave Annabel while she's in this state?'

'My mother died on Sunday, Paul. And the funeral is on Friday. I can't seem to think of much else at the moment.'

'Oh Christ, I'm sorry. I took it, of course, that you were just visiting her while you had some time off. Oh Christ.'

79

'I'll come to Cambridge as soon as I can. Tell Annabel I'm thinking of her.'

'Listen, I'll try to make it on Friday. What time is the service?'

'Eleven at the chapel. But—'

'I'll do my best to be there. I can get there and back in a day, can't I? I'll see you, darling. Oh, I'm so sorry about your mother. I'll phone again tomorrow, darling.'

Of course, I felt wretched about Annabel. I knew I'd be going to Cambridge as soon as I possibly could after the funeral. Even as I chopped up the vegetables for the evening meal, I was rehearsing the part I'd be called upon to play. 'Look, Paul, even if you accept what the police say, even if you accept that Annabel did give, or even sell the drugs to this girl who died, she's still innocent. How could she possibly have known what effect they were going to have on her? Paul, a wasp sting can prove fatal to certain people. You can be quite certain that Annabel takes these drugs and that they make her happy. How could she be expected to know that this particular supplier was selling contaminated goods? I took drugs when I was young, didn't you, Paul? Pot, of course, and LSD from time to time. Well, there wasn't any Ecstasy then, but I'd certainly have taken it if there was. How could anyone resist Ecstasy?'

Of course, I was truly sorry for the young girl who'd died, and for her parents and friends, but that didn't make me any less sorry for Annabel. Yes, she was a stupid, stupid child, but she must be going through hell at the moment.

# Chapter Eight

Rhydian and Grace were late because Aled, their youngest lad, aged four, had objected to being left with his grandmother. I think they'd also had something of a row coming over, so that the first half hour was rather fraught. Grace's pie had to be put in the oven for twenty minutes and by that time my dish of jacket potatoes with mushroom and garlic sauce had dried up and the avocados had, in any case, proved too hard to eat. However, the pie was good and so was the wine and by the time we were on to the pudding, we were all fairly relaxed.

'I hope you're going to stay here for a while now that we've got to know you,' Grace said. 'You won't be going back as soon as you've come, will you?'

'Damn, she's got her work to think of, girl,' Rhydian said. 'She's not going to give up her work, is she, because you and Edwina want to show her off.'

Grace glanced at him, with pity, I thought, rather than malice. 'Are you working on anything at the moment?' she asked me.

'Not at the moment.'

I must have looked worried; in fact, I was thinking again about Annabel and her problems. 'But I've got to leave here very soon. On Saturday, I think.'

Not wanting to worry them with that problem, I switched to a lesser one. 'A chap called George Williams called on me today.'

'What did he want?' Grace asked crossly.

'You know about him, then?'

'Edwina has mentioned something about him, yes. But he's got no right to trouble you at this sort of time. Some people have no feelings.'

'He didn't trouble me. I just felt very surprised about the whole thing and very sorry for him.'

'Could one of you please tell me what you're talking about?' Rhydian asked, his voice an aggrieved drawl.

'Pity you don't listen to me a bit more. I've told you loads of times about Edwina mentioning something about Auntie Miriam and this fellow George Williams. You never listen to a word I say. You turn round and go to sleep as soon as your head touches the pillow and then accuse me of not telling you things.'

'My God, if I listened to every bit of gossip that passes between you and Edwina I'd be well on the downward road by this time.'

I was enjoying their bickering. Paul and I were much too civilised – or too distant – to quarrel.

'Oh, be quiet,' Grace said. 'Can't you see how you're upsetting Kate.'

'You're not upsetting me. I feel envious of you. You're so obviously happy together.'

They both looked at me with some surprise. 'Come on,' I said, 'you *are* happy together, aren't you?'

'I suppose I'm as happy as I can be with an ugly, bad-tempered chap who thinks I'm having another baby just to spite him.'

'I'm happy enough about another baby and I suppose I'm fairly happy with her,' Rhydian muttered. 'Even though she's only got bubble-wrap between the ears.'

'I'll come down to see your new baby. I hope it's a girl this time.'

'If it's a girl, we're going to call her Jane,' Grace said.

And I realised by the way she said it, that she was making Rhydian a definite and important concession.

'I don't mind what you call it,' he said, with so little gallantry that I was immediately annoyed with him.

'Oh yes, you do,' I said. 'You want her to be called Jane because that was your mother's name and she was a very wonderful woman. So you should tell Grace how pleased and thankful you are that she's agreeing to it.'

'Well, it'll be in private if I do,' he said. His voice held out a warning to me as well as a tiny shiver of tenderness. 'Anyway, what about this George Williams? Was he courting your mother, or what?'

'It was more than that. He said they were going to get married. It took me completely by surprise because she'd never mentioned him to me.'

'He's making it up,' Grace said. 'He wants something from you.'

'No, I believed him. He seemed totally trustworthy. Anyway, what could he want from me?'

'I don't know,' Grace said. 'But don't be too ready to trust him. Would a woman of Auntie Miriam's age be likely to want to get married? How old was she? She had a nice little cottage and a pension and a holiday in London twice every year. She had everything she could possibly want.'

By this time, we'd finished our meal and were sitting by the fire. 'My father was courting your mother at one time,' Rhydian said, stretching out his long legs. 'Did you know that?'

'Honestly, Rhydian, you're really witless, aren't you? Poor Kate has had one shock about George Williams and now you give her another. And I don't believe this latest thing either. After all, Auntie Miriam was his sister-in-law.'

'Just like me and Edwina,' Rhydian said, 'so please bear that in mind and don't throw us together so often . . . Only she wasn't his sister-in-law. Auntie Miriam was my mother's niece. So, strictly speaking, he was her uncle-in-law. Isn't that right, Kate? Anyway, I hope I haven't shocked you. Have I?'

'Not really. Though she never mentioned your father either. Only it doesn't entirely surprise me. He used to call here even when he was married to Madge.'

'He never married Madge. He used to say he had, but that was only out of respect for your mother. And when Madge left him a few years later, he did his best to get your mother to marry him. Yes, he actually told me that. But she refused him. I can't say I blame her either. He was drinking like a fish by that time. And it killed him, of course. When he was only a couple of years older than I am now.'

'Poor Uncle Ted. What year did he die? It must have been after I'd left home in 1974.'

'1977 I think it was, the year of the drought. Or was that '76?'

'When I was at university, do you know, my mother was younger than I am now. And I thought she was really old. I wonder if they were happy together now and then. What exactly do you mean by "courting", Rhydian?'

'Now, how should I know? He didn't confide that in me, did he? I only know that I'd call at his place now and again – Madge had swanned off somewhere by this time, leaving him the council house and all the arrears of rent – I'd call, wondering why I hadn't seen him for some days, and when he eventually got to the door, he'd mumble that he'd been up staying with your mother. Perhaps she was only giving him a bed and looking after him during one of his bad spells. But I used to think it was a bit more. I used to hope so, anyway.'

'I hope so, too. I'd like to think she had something in her life.'

'Even if it was only Rhydian's broken-down father,' Grace said.

'Did you know him?' I asked, hurt by this dismissive reference to Uncle Ted.

'No. He'd already passed away by the time Rhydian and I

84

first met. Rhydian was nearly forty, you know, when we got married. No one would have him when he was young and wild.'

'I was too busy to think of girls when I was young. I had a farm to run single-handed – or single-handed except for the occasional day when my father turned up. I worked like a slave every day including Sunday and saw to the books at night. Everything had been neglected ever since my mother's illness. I was years getting it to rights. Did I have any time to run after girls?'

He looked at me and smiled, as though I wasn't to take him absolutely seriously. His smile was slightly one-sided and his eyes were dark; sometimes brown, sometimes ash-black.

'You know, I admire you, Rhydian. You stayed on and made a success of life here. While all the rest of us felt the need to escape to a different life and a different culture where we don't really fit in. At least, I don't feel I fit in anywhere. I seem an outsider now, wherever I am.'

'I'm not sure that I fit in too well, either. I can't get worked-up about politics, for instance. I usually vote Welsh Nationalist in elections, but it's only to avoid having to vote for one of the other parties. I voted for the Welsh Assembly, of course I did. But I don't feel really positive about anything.'

'But you don't need to be particularly positive. You and Grace are part of the Welsh community, you live the Welsh life, attend Welsh functions, talk Welsh as a matter of course, so you don't have to get worked up about it. It's people who don't quite fit in who feel the need to go on and on about what we once had and what we're losing. You don't feel so much nostalgia for that past if you actually lived through it.'

'You may be right. Bleddyn, for instance, is far more fervently Welsh than I am because he's lived in Oxford most of his life. And what is this great Welsh Culture that everyone gets worked up about? Yes, we've got some good singers and some good poets, but they're not world class. Well, perhaps R.S. Thomas is world class, but luckily he writes in English, otherwise we'd be boasting that he's the greatest poet of all time. I can't bear it when people say that Saunders Lewis is as great as Pinter and David Hare, because he's definitely not, and Kate Roberts is not a patch on Elizabeth Bowen and Katherine Mansfield and it doesn't help us to pretend she is. Why should we be so defensive? I think Nationalism has had its day. It's time for us just to be people and good neighbours, it seems to me. Do you feel particularly Welsh?'

'I do when I'm in England. At least, I never feel English. One certainly has a deep, almost unaccountable love for one's place of birth. But on the other hand, I like what London has to offer and I'm grateful for it.'

'You've had a great career,' Grace said.

'No, I haven't, Grace. I've been moderately successful some of the time, but it certainly hasn't been a great career. You wouldn't have heard of me except that I'm family. Well, perhaps I'm fairly well-known in Wales because of this endearing Welsh preoccupation with anyone Welsh. But that's all.'

'I've only seen you in a few things on the telly,' Rhydian said, 'so I can't really judge. Bleddyn went to see you as Lady Macduff at Stratford and he thought you were very good. I should have gone with him. He wanted me to, but the weather was bad and we were lambing.'

He's a farmer, this cousin of mine. Why should that suddenly surprise me? Why shouldn't farmers be interested in politics and literature and music? On stage and on television, farmers are usually rough, tough men with side-burns and gaiters who grumble about droughts and bad harvests. And come to that, actors are always flamboyant and vainglorious. People are more than stereotypes, I know

86

that. All the same, Uncle Ted was the farmer, in my eyes. 'You don't seem a typical farmer,' I said.

'He isn't,' Grace muttered. 'He doesn't care enough about his property. He lets people get away with things, and it's his children will suffer.'

Rhydian looked at me and sighed. 'I won't fight over trifles. I won't take someone to court for a few feet of ground, especially when it's old Abraham Williams who was my Sunday School teacher years ago. If the poor old boy gets any pleasure from pilfering a few feet of upland grazing he's welcome to it.'

'All the same,' I said, 'you'd think a former Sunday School teacher would have some notion of moral principles.'

'He's eighty-three, though, and having a lot of trouble with his teeth.'

Rhydian has lovely teeth, a lovely smile. Rather abruptly, I turned to Grace. 'Are any of your boys interested in farming?'

'They'll all have to have other jobs, as far as I can see. Farmers are all doing badly these days. *We* certainly are. Gwyn says he wants to be a vet, but I suppose it's only because of the telly. All the best programmes are about vets.'

'You're lucky to have children,' I said. 'Step-children are the most I can boast.'

Rhydian looked over at me. 'Everyone wants what they don't have,' he said. 'That's a fact of life, it seems to me.'

I was getting more and more attracted to Rhydian. The previous day I'd been able to tell myself that I was interested in him because he reminded me of Auntie Jane, by this time I knew I was drawn to him because he was the most sexually disturbing man I'd come across in years. I hadn't had this ache for anyone for years and years, and it was for someone I could do nothing about. If only we'd met in London, with Grace a wife mentioned only in passing! Just one night, I'd

87

say. Life is short, and we're bound together by family ties and our common inheritance Oh my dear heart. Cariad annwyl.

'No, I won't have any more wine, Rhydian, thank you.' My mouth was swollen with desire; I was finding it difficult to talk normally.

'And I don't think you should have any more, either,' Grace said. 'You've got three children, don't forget, and another on the way.'

It was as if she'd been tuned in to my thoughts. 'I'll make us some coffee,' I said.

They went soon afterwards. Grace kissed me but Rhydian only looked at me – oh, that lingering look – and smiled his crooked smile. He didn't seem the sort who'd kiss unless it meant something. Unless it meant everything.

But I could do nothing about it, shouldn't even be thinking about it at such a sad time.


I'm too old for this sort of nonsense, I told myself when I was in bed, too old to be having this stupid adolescent fancy for another woman's husband. It isn't love, it isn't that great shining thing, it's merely desire, an agitating physical attraction, flawed and tarnished and rather shameful. I'm in lust with my beautiful cousin, I told myself, plagued again by what Jonson called the loathsome itch.

Come off it, I said later, sitting bolt upright in bed and turning on the light again. I know lust pretty well. I succumbed willingly enough to several bouts of it at university and drama school and during my early career. A typical young woman of the seventies, I had many affairs, in fact with practically everyone who suggested it: Jack Yarborough who kept me awake for nights on end, Chris Matthews who taught me some sweet perversions which still make me giggle and blush to think of them, Alain something, a very hairy Frenchman who shouted out Baudelaire as he rode me. Perhaps those encounters could have developed into deeper relationships but they didn't because there was something missing. They all had built-in obsolescence.

I could never understand how some of my friends, starting off with the same excitement, the same 'falling in love', managed to salvage something good and lasting from it. Was it a matter of luck or were they more easily satisfied than I was? If one starts with physical attraction, and surely one has to, what else does one need? If physical attraction is only lust, is it lust plus knowledge, plus experience, plus instinct?

Whatever love was, I was suddenly sure I'd found it. It wasn't only Rhydian's physical presence, but also a mysterious and quite overwhelming affinity I'd never known before. The fact that I loved him with all my instinct and all my experience fitted into my mind like a key into a lock and lodged there. I'd never felt so sure of anything.

For a time the absolute certainty comforted me. Soon though it seemed huge and inescapable. I became far too restless to sleep.

At about three o'clock, I went downstairs, put on the electric fire and made myself a cup of tea. There were a few magazines on a stool near the fire and to escape my thoughts, I picked up the top one. And as I opened it, I came across a letter my mother had been writing to me. *My dear Katie . . .* At one time, she used to write to me every Sunday morning, but for the last ten or fifteen years I'd been phoning her once or twice every week, so that her letters had become less frequent.

> *. . . This is to tell you something I didn't manage to say on the phone though I planned to. As you probably know, I've got a friend called George Williams and I think it's time for us to get married as he's been asking me for years now and I'm not getting any younger. To tell you the truth I often wish I'd married him when he first asked me and I was about seventeen,*

*and then I would have been happier in the long run*
*and how different your life would have been, but you*
*wouldn't have been you, would you? But saying that, I*
*can't forget how I felt about your father and how that*
*was my life's great moment and I couldn't miss that,*
*could I, in spite of all that happened after. And your*
*poor Auntie Jane too suffered and I think it killed her*
*in the end. But I'm trying not to think about that*
*terrible time when you and I were like little rabbits in*
*the headlights of a car. And now I want to tell you*
*that . . .*

That was the letter. That was the letter she was writing to me on the morning of the day she died. Why had she stopped when she did? What else had she wanted to tell me? *And now I want to tell you that . . .* Had the stress of writing the letter brought on the massive stroke that killed her? Or was it some doubts she'd had about what she intended to do. *And now I want to tell you that . . .* that I love you. Oh, why hadn't she written that?

I re-read the letter. I read it so many times that I had it by heart in no time. And I knew it would remain with me, though not to my comfort, not to my comfort. I was more than ever aware of the distance I'd allowed to grow between us. And I her only child who'd slept with her through all her tormented years.

# Chapter Nine

It was already light before I went back to bed, but I did manage to sleep for an hour or so. When I woke, though, I was immediately aware of all the pressures on me; the sadness of my mother's death at a time when her life should be starting a new and happier phase, the guilt I felt at being so distanced from her, the knowledge of Paul's anguish about his daughter. This isn't a time for falling in love, I told myself, there's no space in my brain for any other emotion. I have to forget Rhydian. It simply didn't happen, that shock of recognition, that lurch of the heart, that terrifying moment; it didn't happen. I'm going to get up, have breakfast and think sanely and positively about getting through the next few days. Only of that.

The phone rang as soon as I got downstairs; another pang of guilt as I recognised Grace's voice asking how I'd slept. I swallowed hard, unable to tell her what a frightful night I'd had, how I was even now finding it difficult to keep my eyes open.

'A silly question,' she said. 'You couldn't have had a good night and I'm sure Rhydian and I didn't help, inflicting our worries on you. Anyway, we want you to come over to us tonight. Yes, we've got it all arranged. Bleddyn is arriving from London in time for supper so Rhydian will come over to fetch you at seven o'clock. No, I won't take no for an answer. You'll have a hard enough day tomorrow and having a bit of company tonight will be some help and you'll be able to see our boys as well, before they go to bed, and Gwyn, he's the eldest you know, almost nine now, he's really excited because he's seen you on the telly in that Shakespeare thing, what was it now? He'll remember. And I've asked Edwina and David over as well. By the way, Edwina says that the flowers will all be in place by ten tomorrow morning, so no worries on that score.'

'Grace, you're very kind, but I really can't come this evening. Please forgive me, but I feel I must have a quiet time on my own this evening. I've really appreciated your company for the last two nights, but . . .'

I tried to go on, but felt my words being pushed back at me. Grace was at Gorsgoch, I told myself, eleven miles away at Gorsgoch, but I could still feel the force of her determination.

'Rhydian said you wouldn't come. He said we'd upset you by our quarrelling.'

But I was stubborn, too. I had to be. 'It's not that, Grace. I enjoyed last night, you were both so open and friendly. I really enjoyed feeling a part of the family and I shall remember it. But tonight I have to be by myself and that's that.'

I recognised her kindness as well as the steely determination to have her own way, but knew I had to ignore both. 'So I'll see you tomorrow,' I said. And put the phone down feeling dazed and foolish.

For almost an hour I sat at my mother's table with a cup of weak tea in front of me, too listless even to re-read her last sad letter. I looked forward to Lorna calling, to her loud, harsh voice and her gossip about her bossy mother-in-law and the chapel and the red-haired minister. But she didn't come. There was obviously no post, not even a brochure from a Friendly Society offering a five percent bonus on a once-in-a-lifetime saving scheme or from The Reader's Digest announcing you'd already come halfway to winning a million pounds.

At least my headache and extreme lethargy gave me an

excuse not to go to the hairdresser in town. I might wash my hair and curl it a bit tomorrow morning before the funeral, but no more. I had a gorgeous black velvet hat at home, but hadn't had time to plan what to bring. All I'd done was throw a few essentials into a bag and take a taxi to Paddington.

After sitting still for about an hour, I managed to muster enough energy to go upstairs to see if my mother had any sort of half-decent hat I could wear, even in my present low state, I still had that craven desire to create something of an impression. The grey suit I'd bundled into my suitcase wasn't new but had cost a fortune and so had my grey suede shoes. But they had three-inch heels and I'd done nothing about getting a car to fetch me; I certainly couldn't walk a mile and a half in them – couldn't even walk a hundred yards in them if I was honest. If Paul intended to get to the chapel by eleven, he could surely call for me by half ten. Oh, why hadn't he left me a phone number so that I could contact him.

I opened my mother's wardrobe. No hats – I hadn't really expected any – the dresses and suits I remembered, most of which we'd bought together during her visits to London, but also a sky-blue suit I hadn't seen before, swathed in plastic and carefully hung up on a satin hanger. Her wedding suit, of course. She'd already bought her wedding suit, a young style, a young colour, a row of mother-of-pearl buttons. If I'd needed another jolt to the heart, I'd certainly got it. She'd always pretended to admire my taste in clothes, but when something was important to her, she'd gone to town on her own without even consulting me. I hadn't been necessary to her.

I closed the wardrobe door and lay back on the bed and cried. Not only because she'd been so late telling me her plans, even buying her wedding outfit before I'd been told, but for the sheer sadness of it all; the pale blue suit she must have bought with such pleasurable anticipation, and would never wear.

What I felt was more than sadness, it seemed almost an

amputation. Something was gone from me, something which was a part of me, something I still needed.

The wind seemed to be weeping in the stunted trees outside the window. I remembered the sound from my childhood. It seemed the same wind, draining out my life, dragging it out of the window, leaving nothing behind but an empty husk.

The next thing I remember was waking up. It seems insensitive to have fallen asleep at that bleakest moment, but that's what had happened. Now it was almost midday; the wind had dropped and I felt calmer. And as I sat up in bed I realised that someone was tapping at the front door, that it was probably that sound which had woken me.

It was Lewis Owen, the minister. 'I'm sure I'm the last person you want to see,' he said.

It was all I could do not to laugh out loud. His words were so delightfully uncharacteristic of his profession. When the Reverend William Pierce, former minister of Horeb, used to call on my mother, he'd stand, large and stern, on the doorstep saying, 'Mrs Rivers, I've come to bring you words of comfort from Our Lord.'

'Do come in,' I said. 'You've cheered me up. Religion has always seemed rather pretentious and turgid, but you seem . . . so ordinary. That sounds rather unflattering, I know. What I mean is, well . . . you're not at all the last person I want to see. Not at all. Will you have a cup of tea?'

'No, thank you. I have to drink too much religious tea.'

'What about a small whisky? Or a large whisky?'

'Perhaps a small one would help.'

'Help? That sounds ominous. Do you intend to talk to me about religion? The afterlife? Something like that?'

'No, but you see, I don't even know how to talk to you about anything. I'm not sure whether you're making fun of me or trying to flirt with me. I don't know how to take you. You seem determined to undermine whatever confidence I have.'

'I'll get us both a whisky.' On my way to the kitchen, I turned to look at him 'You're wonderfully different,' I said, 'but please don't spoil it by being . . . hard.'

'Do you mean rude? I'm often accused of being rude.'

'It's not rudeness exactly, it's just a lack of courtesy. Of course, that's much better than having too much, which leads to obsequiousness. You know, like the Reverend Collins. Hard is like the craggy old pastors in Ibsen. Don't get like them.'

I brought in whisky and glasses and a jug of water. He took a very small whisky and a large amount of water. I did the same.

'Are there any decent priests or ministers in literature?' he asked me. 'Or are they all fools?'

'Of course not. On the whole they're extremely interesting and intelligent.' My mind was a complete blank. 'Trollope,' I said after a moment or two. 'The Warden is a wonderful man and I must say I have a sneaking admiration for the Dean as well. In Welsh literature, they're a bit too saintly perhaps, but certainly not fools. I think books are always more interesting as soon as the priest is introduced.'

'I never find that. Anyway, I shouldn't have said you were flirting with me. It was presumptuous. I say something and think afterwards.'

'No need to apologise. If I were twenty years younger I probably would be. Are you married?'

'No, not married.'

His eyes warned me that I was stepping out of line again. Blue-green eyes, pale as water.

'So what did you want to talk to me about?'

'George Williams came up to see you, I believe.'

'Yes. And he told me that he and my mother intended to get married. It was a complete surprise to me, but I hope I didn't let him see it.'

'Your mother had been to see me about the wedding. It was to be soon, but she didn't set a date for it. I think she wanted to find out when you were free.'

'Why didn't you tell me that when I came to see you on Tuesday? It would have saved me the shock of finding out from poor old George.'

'You seemed very upset on Tuesday. I didn't think you could take it.'

'What makes you think I'm any better today?'

'Don't make it more difficult for me, Miss Rivers. I've come to ask if I may mention their wedding plans in the funeral service. I think it would please George Williams. According to another of my older members, he and your mother were childhood sweethearts. And though your mother looked elsewhere, he remained devoted to her, and unmarried.'

'Mention it, of course. It's very moving. There won't be a dry eye in the house.'

'Don't be . . . hard, Miss Rivers. I shan't be giving a theatrical performance. I shall refer to it only as an instance of a faithful love which reflects in a small way, the infinite love of God.'

'I shall look forward to the service. I'm sorry if I sound cynical. The thing is, I've never managed to discover much about the nature of love. But perhaps there's still time.'

'I do hope so, Miss Rivers. Thank you for the whisky.'

Although Annabel and Selena despised me, they'd always got on well with my mother. They didn't have a grandmother, so she became something in between a substitute grandmother and a retired nanny. They patronised her but seemed fond of her at the same time. I'm not quite sure what she thought of them. 'They're very pretty,' she used to say, 'but, you know, I'm afraid they may be consumptive. There was a girl in my class at school, June Roberts her name was, the same build exactly, and she died in a sanatorium. Do they drink enough milk, say?'

'Am I getting deaf?' she'd ask at other times. 'I'm afraid I never understand much of anything they say. Their English is very strange surely. Is it a Crete accent they've got? Or is it just posh?'

She'd sometimes let them style her hair and put make-up on her face. They'd sit her in a chair, put a towel round her shoulders and give her the full treatment; moisturiser, foundation, blusher, eye-shadow, liner and lipstick. I'm not sure whether she was submitting gracefully to their ministrations or enjoying it; when they brought the hand mirror to show her what they'd accomplished, she'd look at herself in a bemused way and then look at me. 'You're very beautiful,' I'd say. 'I used to tell the girls at school that you were a famous model.' She liked that and so did Selena and Annabel. Occasionally they dropped their guard and seemed not to dislike me too much.

She used to knit for them. She'd done a great deal of knitting when she was young, but during her breakdown years it seemed to have gone completely out of her mind. But when she was working for Mrs Bevan and found herself helping her with some unrecognisable purple garment she was trying to finish, all her forgotten skill came flooding back and after that she was seldom without some piece of knitting. She used to make endless cardigans and jumpers and scarves and shawls for herself and Mrs Bevan, but I would never accept anything, knitted things being completely out of fashion when I was young.

But they were very much in vogue and very expensive eight or nine years ago, so that Annabel and Selena were always hanging over the back of her chair waiting for her to finish the little tight, sleeveless tops with plunging necklines they got her to knit for them. She thought they were vests and was very pleased to make them a couple each. 'They're sensible little girls, Katie, but you really should teach them to talk properly. You had el-o-cution in school, didn't you? I remember how you used to shout out poetry in the garden. You could talk like a preacher, you could.'

One Boxing Day she and the girls went to see *Swan Lake*. The previous year Paul and I had taken them to *Giselle* and had been amazed at how moved and thrilled they were. Yes, eleven-year-olds love ballet, but as they were always determined to be different, far more sophisticated and worldly-wise than other children, we'd been delighted by their reaction. The following year I was in a play in the West End, so Paul had arranged to take them. At the last minute, though, he persuaded my mother to go instead.

He took them to the theatre, bought them a programme each, ordered ices for the interval and went home to put his feet up and watch *Morecambe and Wise* on the telly.

When I got back, they were already home.

'I don't think that was any great success,' Paul told me in the hall. 'The girls were in tears all the way home and your mother wasn't much better. What's the matter with them? The bloody thing finishes happily, doesn't it?'

The girls looked pale and exhausted. Yes, they'd enjoyed it, it was even better than *Giselle*, brilliant really, but they didn't want to talk about it, just wanted to go to bed. And no, they didn't want a sandwich or even drinking chocolate, thank you. 'And what about you?' I asked my mother when they'd gone upstairs.

'It was too beautiful,' she said. 'I never want to see anything like that again. Too beautiful and too sad.' She looked very young that night, but there was a deep yearning in her eyes. She was only twenty-four or five when my father left her.

What a lovely person she was; kind and simple and guile-less. To his credit, Paul was always very fond of her.

I should try to think about Paul. My partner in life. He is kind, generous, civilised, urbane. And totally unexciting.

Whereas Rhydian has opened me up again to the huge tides. After tomorrow I'll never see him again. Oh God, what am I to do? He has a wife and three children and a baby on the way, he couldn't be more committed. He belongs to them, I know that. But his eyes say he's free, that he's mine. For one moment last night I'd looked at him and his face had been laid bare, had been naked with desire.

98

No, I'm simply confused. I'm in a state of shock. I'm in mourning. I'm not myself.

I'm sick of being myself, docile and wifely. I've been faithful to Paul for ten years and I'm tired of it.

It's three-thirty and Lorna Davies knocks at the door. 'I thought I'd look in on you since I didn't see you this morning. How are you feeling now? Any better?'

'Not much, to tell you the truth. But I'm sure I'll be better when tomorrow's over.'

'Of course you will. How soon will you be going back to London?'

'Straight after the funeral, I'm afraid.'

'In that case I'd better tell you now. There's a rumour in the village that your mother was going to marry George Williams. Someone said that Hilda Griffiths had it from Lewis Owen himself. She said that he said that she said—'

'It's quite true, Lorna. I found a letter she was writing to me on Sunday just before she was taken ill.'

'Oh, so you already know about it. That's all right, then. Only I didn't want you to have another shock tomorrow. Hilda – she's a cleaner at the hospital, you know – was telling my mother-in-law that George Williams was up here last Sunday afternoon when she had the stroke and it was him phoned for the ambulance and went with her to the hospital. Did you know that?'

'No. I'm afraid I took it for granted that she was the one who'd phoned. The hospital only told me she'd arrived by ambulance just before three and that she'd died almost exactly twelve hours later. They phoned me at eight on Monday morning. They didn't contact me on Sunday because they hadn't realised how ill she was till she had the second stroke in the early hours.'

'Only my mother-in-law was wondering whether George Williams could have upset her in any way.'

'I'm sure he didn't. He seems a very gentle, kind man

and devoted to her. He came up here to see me yesterday.'

'That's all right then. Only my mother-in-law doesn't get on with George's sister, Mali, they haven't spoken for years, so she thought you ought to know about this rumour so you could have it out with George. But if you're happy about the whole thing, that's fine. My mother-in-law will be disappointed, though. To be honest, there's nothing she likes more than a really hearty row.'

'I'm sorry I can't oblige her.'

'Don't worry. She'll get busy now on Edwina Williams's affair with John Parry, the chap who owns The Flower Basket in Vaynor Street in town. I'm not sure how she got wind of that, but she certainly won't let it rest. She's been on about it all day today. "Oh, these modern women!" '

'I think Edwina'll be a match for her, though, don't you? Cup of tea?'

'Yes, please.'

There's still a tidal wave of misery about my heart, but Lorna's gossip and her loud cheery voice help pass the time. I manage to keep her talking until five.

What am I going to do for the rest of the day? Tomorrow will be easier. Paul will be with me. He'll say kind, thoughtful, comforting things about my mother. He'll squeeze my arm through the Reverend Lewis Owen's doleful service. He'll protect me from being too heartbroken about poor George Williams. He'll stand by me as I drink tea and eat a ham sandwich, and, oh God, a slice of cold quiche. He'll hand over cheques to Maggie Davies and Edwina's heart-throb florist, knowing to the penny how much to tip. He'll also know, as if by magic, the exact moment when we can decently, unhurriedly leave. All that.

But will he be able to protect me from the spell of the eldest of the savage Gorsgoch boys; he of the midnight-dark eyes, lazy voice and rough farmer's hands.

100

# Chapter Ten

I suddenly started thinking about my father, a thing I hadn't done for years. Some people, I know, will go to endless trouble to find out exactly who they are and where they've come from. Possibly because I'm an actor, I've always been more interested in the person I can become. I'd never had a passionate urge to discover every detail of my father's life and death; he'd always been a shadowy figure and I was satisfied with that. In old Welsh myths, it was the mother's brother who was responsible for the young hero's upbringing, not his father: he could be sure of his mother, not so certain, perhaps, of his father. That has nothing to do, I'm sure, with what I felt, but all the same, it's an interesting fact.

I'd been told that my father was slight, fair-haired and very quiet. I imagined that fairly soon after marriage he'd discovered his homosexuality and had been determined to escape before it engulfed him. I liked to think that he'd once intended to make contact again, at least to the extent of making some financial commitment, but hadn't had time to get it done. The date of his death hadn't been accurately assessed, but was definitely in the same year that he'd left us.

He must have been a bright lad. I shouldn't think many boys from Barnardo's got to a grammar school at that time, or did well enough to get a decent job in a bank afterwards. He must have been serious and hardworking at school. As I was. I found it strange to think of traits I'd inherited from him.

It seemed the right time to sort through some of my mother's papers. I'd surely find a snapshot or two, if nothing else. Perhaps an account of their wedding from the local paper. If I took my time, it might well get me through most of the evening.

There were three cardboard boxes in the glass-fronted cupboard next to the fireplace, large chocolate boxes with garish chocolate-box country cottages – very different from ours – on the covers. I knew they contained my mother's souvenirs, though I'd never been invited to look through them.

My hands were shaking as I undid the ribbon on the top box. I found that it was full of newspaper cuttings; my entire career from the earliest appearances in school plays to the latest television series, every one carefully dated. I'd had no idea that she collected them. I was moved, of course, and even more so when I discovered that she'd bought copies of *The Times* as well as her usual tabloid when any review was due. And she'd kept every single notice of every single play I'd been in, whether I was mentioned or not, had saved even the unkind ones. 'Kate Rivers gives her usual breathy performance.' 'Kate Rivers expresses distress, anger and fear with the same glassy-eyed stare.' I read through them all; more good than bad, but none ecstatic. Ah well, it was as I thought. I was a competent actor, but no more.

The thought came to me unbidden: I could give it up and not be missed.

I made myself a meal, egg-bread and baked beans, one of our favourite suppers years ago, though not as good as egg-bread with mushrooms – field mushrooms, which had the added advantage of being free. 'Fry the mushrooms till they're black,' my mother would say. 'It takes away the taste of horses.' I didn't care what the taste was. I loved it. Cultivated mushrooms are probably safer to eat but have next to no flavour.

I finished the meal with three cups of strong tea. It was half-past seven. In three and a half hours I'd have a stiff whisky and go to bed.

The second box. This one had family photographs and accounts of weddings and christenings. I looked out for a photograph of Rhydian and Grace's wedding and found it. Two good-looking, happy, loving people. I made myself study it. A wedding. A religious sacrament. Whom God hath joined together.

Empty, empty words. Rhydian and Grace got married because they were neighbours, because the time was right. Rhydian wanted help and comfort, Grace wanted children. They got married because it was suitable. Not because they were oceans deep in love. As I am now.

If I had stayed home and become a teacher, as I was meant to, perhaps I would have re-met my cousin-once-removed and married him. Perhaps I could have become a farmer's wife, perhaps I could have endured all the back-breaking work, the bitter cold and the mud and even the draughty old farmhouse if I was brimming over with love. As I am now.

I make myself look at other photographs. A haughty young girl in cap and gown. Was that me? I'm afraid so. I was insufferably conceited at twenty-one. Life has taught me something if not everything. By this time, I don't think I'm better – or worse – than anyone else.

I catch my breath again: a photograph of the three brothers together. Bleddyn is the one who hasn't changed, he's scowling as he used to, taller than the others, hair still unruly. Iestyn has a fuller face and a gentle smile. And Rhydian, lean and dark, deified by my love.

Iestyn's first wedding, another pretty, round-faced bride, now superseded by the self-regarding Madeleine. Bleddyn with his one-time partner, a rather stern-faced woman, and a four-year-old child, Siwan Grace. An old sepia photograph, slightly creased and curling at the edges: Auntie Jane's wedding. She and Uncle Ted and a tribe of relatives,

103

a great deal of lace and hats, my mother a buxom brides-maid, about fourteen years old, shy and very pretty.

I didn't want to carry on, but I had time to kill. And I still hadn't come across a photograph or even a snapshot of my father. I went through the entire collection, at least fifty old-fashioned studio photographs of members of my extended family, dressed in their best, hair combed and tidied, smiling at the camera. It was a sad experience, but it suited my mood. The only missing photograph seemed the one I'd been searching for; my mother and father's wedding.

At last I had a phone-call from Paul, who seemed much more cheerful. His solicitor had been optimistic from the beginning, but on visiting Annabel and seeing her and Selena together, was certain that he could release her from the charge. For how could any of their acquaintances be at all certain that it was Annabel and not Selena who had supplied the dead girl with the fatal tablets? There was what amounted to a complete lack of evidence. As a matter of fact, Selena hadn't been at the rave, but no one else need know that. He had been able to assure them that their nightmare was over.

I didn't feel quite as optimistic about the outcome as Paul. I felt certain that Annabel would finally be acquitted of the charge, but it seemed too much to hope that the police would drop it at this stage. After all, they needed to charge someone. Of course I kept my doubts to myself.

Paul repeated that he'd be at the funeral and would be happy to pick me up first. He said the girls and Francesca were sending a wreath and that he'd also sent one from me. 'I knew you wouldn't have time to think of it,' he said, 'so I ordered white chrysanthemums from the girls and me, and a large heart-shaped wreath of white roses and freesias from you. "To my dearest mother. With love from Kate" .'

'Thank you,' I said. No, I hadn't remembered a wreath – I don't set any store on flowers for the dead – but felt hurt and annoyed that he'd taken it upon himself to act for me. And if I were sending flowers, I'd want to write my own message. In Welsh. How was it that he knew so little about me?

Of course I felt glad of the better news about Annabel, but on the whole I felt worse after his phone-call than before. And I wasn't looking forward to seeing him again. I was certainly in a bad way.

Almost nine o'clock. Another phone call. This time from Rhydian. 'How are you feeling now? We've finished supper and Bleddyn and I are coming over to see you. Just a short visit. No, Grace doesn't mind. She's got Edwina here and her husband. And Bleddyn's daughter is here as well. Grace will be fine. Fifteen minutes then.'

It was what I'd been hoping for all along. That he wouldn't be able to keep away. Fifteen minutes. Fourteen minutes. Thirteen.

'This is Bleddyn. I suppose you'd recognise him.'

'Yes, I've been looking through old photographs.'

We talked about the old days, Rhydian and I, but our eyes spoke a different language.

Bleddyn didn't help much. Perhaps he understood too much and didn't approve, perhaps he was always the strong, silent one.

'Whisky?' I asked. 'There's still half a bottle left. Or would you prefer white wine?'

'We mustn't stay long,' Bleddyn said.

'Why not? This girl's on her own with her mother being buried tomorrow. I think we should stay. And I think we could all do with a whisky, too.'

I got up and went out to the kitchen and Rhydian followed me. As I'd expected. 'When can I see you?' he asked. His voice an urgent whisper.

'I don't know. I've got to go back tomorrow.' My heart beating wildly.

'No, you haven't. Stay for a few days. I've got to talk to you. Promise me you'll stay.'

'I'll come back as soon as I can.'

He took my hands in his, crushing them so that I almost cried out. Then he picked up the tray with the whisky and glasses and followed me to the living room.

We drank to family ties. We all relaxed a little. I tried not to look at Rhydian.

'My earliest memory is of your mother's wedding,' Bleddyn said. 'I had a white shirt and long black trousers and I was supposed to give her a silver horseshoe as she came out of chapel, and I cried because I wanted to keep it.'

No one had ever been willing to tell me anything about my mother and father's wedding. I was fascinated. 'How old were you?' I asked him.

'About five. Rhydian was a pageboy, but they only gave me a minor role.'

'And you didn't do that very well,' Rhydian said. 'I remember Dad slapping you about that horseshoe.'

'You were a pageboy? I've never even seen a photograph of my parents' wedding.'

'I'll get Grace to look through ours. We may have some. Give me your address, in case she doesn't find them for tomorrow.'

He passed me his diary and I wrote in it. My address and telephone number. And Love Kate.

'Are you married?' Bleddyn asked, his voice chilly again.

'I've got a partner, Paul, who'll be here tomorrow.'

'Actor?'

'No. Photographer.'

'Rhydian, I really think we'd better go now. We told Grace we wouldn't be long. Thanks for the drink, Kate. I saw you, by the way, in the Arthur Miller play at the Hampstead Theatre last year. Good performance, I thought.'

'Thank you.' Briefly, I met his eyes.

He knew how it was between his brother and me and couldn't wait to separate us.

When we got outside, the stars were white and the moon was rising. Rhydian put his arm round me and held me for a moment before getting into the car so that I could feel the warmth of his body and his heart beating. 'I'll see you tomorrow,' he said, giving me one swift, voluptuous kiss. As he broke away from me, a white owl flew from the rowan tree by the gate, slicing the darkness. And I found I'd clung to him again.

There didn't seem much chance of keeping our secret from Bleddyn. 'Good night,' he said from the car, his voice cold and worried.

But Rhydian wound down his window and touched my face again. 'I love you,' he whispered.

It seemed a small miracle. He felt as I did. I went back to the house, but couldn't stop thinking of his kiss. And the owl flying like a medieval omen above us.

The myths are very close, in moonlight, in the countryside, in the heart of Wales.

He felt as I did. A truth only guessed at for the last two days had now been spoken. 'When can I see you? I have to talk to you. Please don't leave tomorrow.' And finally, 'I love you.' In all my misery and worry, I'm suddenly so happy, so triumphant. There's no future in it. This man can't be mine. But I'm shaken with love again so that I know my future can't lie with Paul, who may be decent and safe as an old tweed jacket, but is ultimately arid, all his passion already spent on Francesca, Annabel and Selena. How could I have stayed ten years with a man who never once made me feel young and reckless and dangerously, indecently aroused? As I feel now.

Ten-fifteen. Still too early for bed. A walk in the dark? Another whisky? A cup of tea? How should I get calm? But did I want to lose this raw sexual excitement?

Anyway, it was obvious that I was far too excited to sleep. And tomorrow was going to be long and difficult. Perhaps I should wash my hair and iron my grey suit and white blouse . . . Or should I make some excuse to phone Gorsgoch, hoping Rhydian would answer?

I shouldn't be feeling like this on the eve of my mother's funeral. I should be thinking of her, of her sweet nature and her blighted life . . . I *am* thinking of her blighted life, determined that mine is going to be different. I'm not going to be sweet and longsuffering.

Leaving the back door open to give me some light, I walk out into the garden, a sloping patch of rough grass, with the valley falling away beyond it. The air is balmy and smells of flowering currant, the only shrub that flourishes here. The flowers come early in April, brave little pale pink clusters shaking in the wind from the sea, but to my surprise the leaves have the same pungent smell. The smell of home.

Paul was always offended that I referred to this place as home. 'I think I'll go home for a few days.' 'I thought this was your home.' 'No, this is my London home.'

This is my home. I should have come here more often. I love this patch of ground.

I always had the vague feeling that there was something artificial and pretentious about our Mediterranean garden in Camberwell; blue walls and white pots and strange, spiky plants. I prefer grass. Why do I discover so many self-evident truths when it's too late? *Is* it too late, or can I decide to make a new start? Of course I can.

Perhaps all this self-assessment, self-doubt, is due to my being in love, but it must still be of value. I'm mature enough to realise that my life can't lie with Rhydian, but to arrive, in spite of that, at the conclusion that my life can no longer lie with Paul must surely be liberating and good.

I don't want to go back to London. I know I shall have to return to Cambridge with Paul until Annabel's trouble is sorted out, then I shall come back here, soldiering on

108

through winter and hard weather like a middle-aged Rosalind.

The night closed round me, not many stars visible, the half-grown moon swathed in a long transparent cloud. 'Slowly, silently now the moon, Walks the night in her silver shoon.' I remember how disappointed I was, as a small child, to discover that 'shoon' was simply an old word for shoes. I'd imagined something far more romantic – a glow, a shimmering, a dazzle. And the child is mother of the woman. I was still wanting the dazzle, still wanting to be Rosalind, even a middle-aged one. Couldn't I settle for spending a season or two in this small, not-much-renovated cottage without any dazzle or any role-playing?

I was beginning to feel cold. There was a smell of mist. I could see the mist, rising white from the valley. I could hear an owl in the distance.

As I was about to turn back into the house, I almost screamed as I felt something wet and cold rub itself against me. 'Arthur! Oh Arthur, I'm so glad you've come back. Oh Arthur, shall we go in now?'

He followed me in and purred as I shut the door. He circled round my ankles as I opened a tin of food and put some in his dish. He ate, not ravenously, but politely, looking up at me from time to time, and when he had quite finished, followed me into the living room, stretching out on the rug in front of the fire to give himself a thorough all-over wash.

Life was short and he seemed through with grieving. He was, after all, an indoor cat.

Half-past eleven. I'd got undressed for bed, but came hurriedly back downstairs, realising that I hadn't opened the third cardboard box. There could still be a photograph of my parents' wedding in that, perhaps one of Rhydian as a six-year-old pageboy.

I got the box down from the cupboard and sat on the armchair before opening it, having a sudden intimation that I could be in for a shock. I raised the lid as though something might explode in my face.

The box was crammed full of tiny scraps of paper which I first took to be packing material. It took me some seconds to realise that every minute shred was part of some precious momento which had been thoroughly and systematically destroyed. The greyish scraps were perhaps torn newspaper cuttings; the cream, writing paper, possibly love letters, the shiny bits, old, torn photographs, but nothing remained large enough to be further examined or deciphered in any way.

My mother's life torn to shreds.

But why, if she'd been set on obliterating all memory of her marriage, had she preserved this confetti-like detritus? That night, when it was almost midnight, it seemed like a message from her. What was she trying to tell me? It was like the last unfinished sentence of her letter. *And now I want to tell you that . . .*

I shut the box and put it back in the cupboard with the others.

*And now I want to tell you that . . . you must live life to the full. Not give up on it as I did.*

Perhaps that had been her last message to me. That certainly seemed the message of the third cardboard box.

# Chapter Eleven

I was awake for hours, almost pleased to be awake grieving for my mother. I'd always been a dutiful daughter, I knew that, but hadn't been as loving as she'd deserved. From the time I was sixteen or seventeen, there'd been a distance between us; perhaps I'd never quite been able to forgive her for the wretched years of my childhood.

Yet, I'd always known that she'd suffered far more than I had, so why had I been so hard? How, for instance, had I been able to justify going away to university, leaving her alone in this isolated cottage? I could have gone to the nearer college at Aberystwyth so that I'd have been able to come home more often. No, I'd wanted to break away, to be completely free. I'd been utterly selfish. Not that she was as helpless as she'd once been. She had a job as dinner-lady in the village school by this time, which meant she had a certain amount of contact with others. I know she loved the children, especially the naughty ones, used to tell me stories about them in her Sunday letters. Perhaps my absence had forced her to find other interests.

In this way I spent most of the night, blaming myself, defending myself, remembering the past.

At last, though, I fell asleep and had a dream about her. She was dressed in the cap and gown I'd had to hire for my graduation, she was standing in front of a full-length mirror admiring herself and smiling. At last she turned round to me and said, 'I'm glad I'm not fat and ugly like the other mothers. Look at my feet. Aren't they slim and beautiful? I've always wanted red court shoes.'

It was a consoling dream, though very short. She had come to Cardiff for my graduation, and though she hadn't, as far as I can remember, tried on my cap and gown, she had been happy. And many years afterwards I had bought her red court shoes.

It was too late to make amends for my shortcomings, so I had to take what comfort I could from that vivid snatch of dream. She had certainly loved those shoes.

I suppose the dream came because I needed it; needed the reminder that there had been good times.

During my first years at grammar school, as soon as I'd got to know the town, we used to go shopping every Saturday afternoon. She had a little money by this time as she was working for Mrs Bevan, and a great desire for what she called 'finery', though this might turn out to be only a quarter of a yard of veiling for a hat, or some violet eyeshadow.

It was the late sixties, early seventies – Biba time – and if you couldn't get to London, dressy clothes from antique shops were all the rage. There was no antique shop in Abernon and my mother wouldn't have been able to afford the prices even if there had been, but Mrs Bevan had several old coats and dresses which she was delighted for my mother to have. After all, Mr Bevan, as his wife never failed to remind us, had been 'in business', so that her clothes had always been expensive, acquired from catalogues from the very best London stores – Barkers, Derry and Toms, Pontings. Mrs Bevan would repeat the names like a rosary. The clothes were of beautiful soft material and were also rather elegant, I think, and though my mother wasn't a great needlewoman, she had a flair for adapting these twenties and thirties garments; a wide, shiny, patent leather belt and some large safety-pins would sometimes be enough for their

112

transformation into what she – and I – considered the height of chic.

When we went out on a Saturday, she wore a lot of white face-powder and hat and gloves, and I used to be very gratified by the admiring, or perhaps startled looks that people gave her. I always wore my navy-blue school coat, bought for me, with ample room for growth, by my Auntie Jane – 'the very best quality, Katie' – though my mother assured me that I should inherit some of her smartest clothes as soon as I got 'a figure'.

Not that she had much of a figure, but she was small and slim and looked very young. 'People will think we're sisters,' she used to say when she caught sight of us in a shop window.

There were two smart dress-shops in town and we would go to them in turn, I being expected to do all the talking. 'We're looking for a wedding-outfit,' is what I'd usually say. 'Something rather special.' Some of the haughty-faced assistants had heard this many times so that they weren't over-eager to help us, but in fact we preferred searching through the racks for ourselves. 'We'll try these on, please,' I'd say, after a happy half-hour.

'Very well, madam.' They were always icily polite.

My mother would try on the most expensive dresses and suits in the shop, without, of course, the slightest intention of buying. The smallest sizes fitted her perfectly. Sometimes she was so pleased with the way she looked that she'd walk out of the dressing-room to admire herself in a larger mirror in the showroom.

'You'll never find anything to suit you better,' an assistant might say, but without hope of a sale. They treated us quite well. They knew we weren't going to buy, but they also realised we were fairly decorative and entirely harmless; that I would hang every garment back in its rightful place, thank them and assure them of our return.

I've often been asked by various interviewers whether

113

there's any tradition of acting in my family. 'No. Members of my family are mostly farmers and shopkeepers,' I tell them.

It's only now I realise what a consummate actor my mother was, how much she could convey without speaking a word. Perhaps the non-speaking was part of the role. I think she aimed at being a woman of mystery and romance and on those Saturday afternoons she achieved that. Her clothes were eccentric, but expensive; she wore French perfume – sprayed on from the make-up department of the store, yes, but not until she'd tested several sorts. The purchases she did eventually make might only cost pence, a slip of a scarf or an artificial rose, but they were as carefully chosen as any theatre props.

It's only now I realise that the pleasure she got from my career was at least partly from knowing that what talent I had, had been inherited from her. So that when our shopping sprees came to an end when I was fifteen or sixteen, she was able to accept it readily, knowing that, from then on, I was attending a Saturday drama class which she considered much more important.

We'd still go to the September hiring fair together, a night when there was a special late bus back to the village. No one else took their mother with them to the fair, but no one else had such a fun-loving, young-looking mother. I often felt she was far younger than I was; more excited, more exuberant, more frightened of height and speed and noise. My friends thought she was 'brilliant' – that was the in word, then. She didn't say much, but laughed and shrieked a great deal – giving, I realise now, a thoroughly different performance.

She was always an attractive woman, but I'd almost forgotten how very pretty she was when she was young. At certain times, when things were going well, I think she was beautiful.

On the morning of her funeral, I got up determined to

remember the happy times, the special meals she'd make for birthdays and holidays, the surprise neither of us could hide when cakes rose and puddings set as they were supposed to. Culinary success for my mother was always a surprise, failure was normal, but tasted surprisingly good. She didn't believe that anyone could manage to get two courses right for any meal. We only attempted one; egg and chips for lunch and apple crumble for supper was the sort of menu we aimed at, with bread and butter if we were still hungry.

When I was about thirteen, my class at school was taught to make meringues, and one Sunday morning I decided to demonstrate this new skill, but with disastrous results. Instead of the crisp little confections I'd whisked and beaten so hard for, there were only sticky yellow splodges like chicken messes at the bottom of the baking tin, which we scraped out with teaspoons and tried, but failed, to eat. For years the word meringue was our synonym for failure, 'the marriage turned out a total meringue,' reducing us both to fits of schoolgirl laughter . . . We had been close, of course we had.

At ten-fifteen I was still sitting at the table in my night-dress, having done nothing but feed Arthur. I felt completely separated from reality. There was a great deal happening inside my head, but it didn't seem to have any connection with the funeral.

It was a phone call from Grace which brought me back to the present. 'Is there anything I can do? Would it help if Rhydian dropped me at your place so that I'd be with you when the car comes for you? I honestly don't like to think of you being on your own.'

'I think Paul is going to be here, Grace. But what car is coming for me?'

'The undertaker's car will be fetching you.'

'I don't think I arranged that, did I?'

'I phoned them just to make doubly sure of everything, I hope you don't mind. And they said you'd been very vague.

Goodness, that's only natural. They were going to phone you again, but I thought I'd save you that.'

'Thank you, Grace. I must go and get dressed now. And have a cup of tea.'

A nervous silence. 'You're still not ready? I think I'd better come over. I'll be with you in fifteen minutes.'

She must think I'm buckling under the strain, that I'm some sort of weakling.

I spend ten minutes over tea and toast. I'm not a weakling, Grace. Three minutes for make-up, three minutes for costume, and even without a hat, I'm in the part, my lines rock-solid. Is this reality? I'm not sure.

There's no sign of Paul.

By the time Rhydian and Grace drive up, I'm ready for them; Gucci suit, Prada shoes and handbag, a double layer of Elizabeth Arden's matte foundation, miel doré, Rubenstein lip-line, sable rose, black eyeliner, pewter eyeshadow, both Steiner, with a black georgette scarf – property of Miriam Rivers – round my head.

The funeral car draws up behind Rhydian's.

'Do we need to be at the chapel so early?' I ask Grace. 'I think I'll give Paul another ten minutes. Would you like to come in and have a cup of tea?'

'No time for that, love. We'll go, now we know you're all right.'

'I knew you'd be all right,' Rhydian muttered from the car, 'but it's easier not to argue. We dropped Bleddyn and Siwan at the chapel so we'd better go along and join them.' I could read nothing in his funeral-dark eyes.

I stood watching the two large cars, one shiny, one mud-spattered, manoeuvring to change positions in the narrow lane; it looked like a strange courtship, advance and withdrawal, advance, withdrawal. Grace wound down her window to say something to the driver of the funeral car, probably that he was on no account to let me wait for more than five minutes.

116

As soon as Rhydian's car leaves, Lorna arrives pushing her bike. 'I'll be finished before long,' she says cheerfully. 'I'll see you in the vestry.' She hands me a letter from Annabel – oh God – which I put in my handbag.

'I think you ought to go now,' she says, 'or people will think you're making an entrance.'

'I'm waiting for Paul,' I tell her.

'Don't hang about any more,' she says. 'You should be there before the coffin arrives. Off you go.'

She notices how I flinch and gives me a hearty hug. 'Your poor Mam died last Sunday. Today isn't important. It's just something you've got to go through, that's all.'

'Just something to go through,' I tell myself. 'Just another part to play.'

I'm in the chapel at a quarter to eleven and it's already full. I sit next to George Williams in the front pew. I don't bow my head, pretending or even attempting to pray, because I don't believe in prayer and neither did my mother. I'm soothed by the atmosphere of the little chapel though; the white-washed walls and the plain glass windows. I seem quite pleased, somehow, that some people have Kept the Faith. Perhaps attempts to worship a man, kinder and more forgiving than any other before or since, is to be admired, however much false sanctity and hypocrisy goes with it.

I wish there was some marvellous music, St Matthew's Passion, from some famous organ. No, I don't. This anthem played inexpertly on this small organ is more than enough to be going on with. I'm aware that listening to the beautiful, craggy language of Bishop Morgan's Bible will be comforting and enriching; it will be Lewis Owen's halting words that will be unbearably moving. Services in Welsh Congregational chapels are altogether too personal, too demanding. Roman Catholics and Anglicans with their ritualised responses have it easy.

'Just something to go through.' I hang on to Lorna's words as I listen to the red-haired boy in the pulpit trying to say something relevant and true about my mother. Who is dead. He seems certain that she has lived the good life and fought the good fight and begs the congregation to learn from her example. So far, so predictable. Now he's faltering, needing a prompt. No, this is an ad lib, he's out of his text. 'I hardly knew her. But every time I met her I was aware of two things: The pain in her eyes. And the love.'

Truth is always an unexpected punch in the stomach.

And then the wheezing notes of the organ and the hymn I asked for which is the saddest in the world, 'Their sleep is so gentle', and I can hear Grace sniffing quietly in the pew behind me.

And I fall over in a dead faint, knocking my head on the front of the pew, upstaging everyone.

Water – is this holy water? – is brought up to my lips, but I can't drink it and someone with bright red hair says, 'Don't crowd round her,' and carries me outside, lays me down on the cold September earth and then disappears, presumably to oversee my mother being laid into a hole in the same September earth, a ceremony I have to forgo since I'm noisily vomiting up my tea and toast over my Gucci suit and my Prada handbag.

Is this reality? I can't, surely, be acting now. Anyway, I'm certainly pleased that there's no audience, that everyone but Grace has gone to the cemetery.

'Isn't Paul here?' I ask her after what seems a very long time.

But she's too busy cleaning me up to answer.

I perform pretty well after that, thanking people for coming and saying, 'Yes, feeling much better now, thank you,' and drinking cups of tea. The vestry is warm and muggy, sun streaming in through the tightly closed windows, with everyone chatting and enjoying the food. It's not exactly a wake, but as near as we get to it in this part of Wales, not exactly a celebration, but a recognition that life, while not in

118

the same league as death in chapel terms, is still occasionally worth living.

I'm introduced to Siwan, Bleddyn's daughter, and we work out our relationship: second cousins.

Lorna is one of the helpers. The moment I see her, I kiss her on both cheeks, realising as I do that it will be seen as wildly histrionic. 'You warned me not to make an entrance, but I'm afraid I made quite an exit,' I tell her.

'So I heard,' she says, putting a large stick of celery – a punishment? – onto my plate.

I seek out George Williams. 'My mother thought the world of you,' I tell him in a sudden rush of warmth. (Did she? She must, surely, have thought pretty highly of him or she wouldn't have considered marrying him.)

'No, no,' he says, gently putting me right, 'but I thought the world of her. That's how it was.' He doesn't seem prepared to say much more.

'I may be coming back here for a while. If I do, I hope you'll come up to see me from time to time.'

He gives the suggestion his deepest consideration, nodding his head, but not committing himself.

'What do you think of the flowers?' Edwina asks me.

'They're beautiful. Please thank your friend. Do you have a bill for me?'

'Yes. Ten percent discount for family, and no hurry to pay.'

It's several hours later before Grace thinks it's time for us to go home. 'I'm going to collect all the flowers from the tables' she says, 'otherwise Maggie Davies will have them all. You just sit there till I've finished.'

But I have to thank Maggie Davies and pay her. She flushes with anger as Grace gathers up the flowers, but my effusive words and large tip seem to soothe her. 'I may be coming home for a while,' I tell her, 'so I hope to see you again soon.'

I thank Lewis Owen very sincerely for his loving words, but only succeed in embarrassing him. He blinks his pale sea-green eyes very rapidly at me and turns away. He thinks I'm playing a part, even when I'm not.

I haven't spoken a word to Rhydian. He and Bleddyn are already in the car when Grace – with flowers – and Siwan and I get into the back. I'm worried that they'll feel obliged to keep me company for another evening. 'I don't know where Paul got to,' I tell them. 'One of his daughters is in trouble with the police, so I suppose he decided he had to stay with her. I'll have to go back to the house, though, in case he phones.'

There's a long silence, but at last Grace says, 'Well, we certainly can't leave you on your own, tonight of all nights.'

'But people sometimes like being on their own,' Siwan says. 'Kate, what would you like us to do?'

'You must all go back to the farm, obviously. The children will be home from school, won't they? I'll phone you later to tell you when I'm going back.'

'I'm not at all happy about leaving you,' Grace says again.

'Right,' Rhydian says. 'We'll drop you off here, give you time for your phone-call, and when I've finished the milking I'll come back to fetch you and we'll have supper at our place. All right?'

I can hardly get my breath. 'All right. About seven?'

'About seven. And don't do any more fainting.' He gives me a long tormented look as I get out of the car.

They drive off and I go back to the empty house.

# Chapter Twelve

I pressed caller-return, but no one had phoned. What had happened to Paul? He'd been fairly cheerful last night, assuring me that he'd be able to pick me up for the funeral at ten-thirty, but six hours later, there'd been no word from him; no explanation, no apology.

Arthur was already at the back door waiting for me. As I let him in, he looked me straight in the eye for a moment. 'We both know she's dead, but life goes on, for me as well as you.' I opened a tin of tuna and forked it onto his plate. What should I do with him tomorrow when I went to Cambridge? 'You're a heavy responsibility, Arthur,' I told him and he purred his agreement. I'd have to ask Gwenda Rees from the farm if her sons would feed him until I got back.

Until I got back. Getting back was assuming a tangible reality. I intended coming back, at least for a time. The relationship between Paul and me seemed to have been floundering for months, even years, and now, while he was preoccupied with his family, seemed as good a time as any to make a break.

I wasn't too worried about Annabel. She'd weather the storm as she'd weathered so many others at boarding school. There'd always been incidents of various kinds; orgies of drinking or drugs, or boyfriends secreted in her room.

I suddenly remembered the letter she'd sent me and took it

out of my handbag. But it wasn't from Annabel but from Selena – even their handwriting was almost identical. *Dear Kate, I was most awfully sorry to hear about your mother's death. She was a lovely person and I shall miss her. Love from Selena*. I was surprised and pleased to get it; sometimes, when they dropped their guard, Paul's daughters didn't seem as bad as I painted them. Perhaps we'd be better friends when Paul and I were no longer together.

I went into the garden and stood looking down at the valley; complete stillness, an apricot sky, the trees beginning to show traces of autumn, the river glimpsed here and there in the distance, and beyond it a blue haze of round-backed mountains.

My mother would often stand out here in the evening, listening to the last thrush – 'He'll go on singing while he knows I'm listening to him,' – or waiting for the first stars, the first glimpse of a new moon.

I turned back to the house, my mother's and now mine. It was built about two hundred years ago, by my grandmother's great-grandfather, according to Auntie Jane. He'd built well; there'd been very little done to it over the years. My mother had had a grant for having the walk-in pantry extended and converted into a bathroom when I was about fourteen; apart from that, it was much as it had always been – a sturdy stone-built house like a child's drawing; a door and four windows, a roof with a chimney at either end.

Arthur comes in with me and winds himself round my legs.

Yes, this is where I'm going to stay. For the autumn and winter, if not longer. Is it because I've fallen in love with my cousin? Probably. But at least I'm aware of the problems I'm facing, aware of his kind, infuriating wife and his family, aware that they must always come first. Shall I *ever* come first with anyone? Probably not. But perhaps I can snatch a few moments of pleasure. And manage to survive.

My heart is thumping against my ribs, but my head feels cold and clear as ice. I'm at the middle point of my life and I'm taking stock. The most critical day during my relationship with Paul was that terrible day when I had the abortion. That day, because of his reluctance and caution, I threw away any hopes of a future with him, and though I stayed with him for three more years, it was only because no crucial event happened to effect the inevitable break. My mother's death and my journey into the past has given me the chance to see my relationship with Paul for what it is; safe and dull. And I want intensity. I'm no longer young but I need to feel that I'm alive. Yes, I'm frightened of what will happen. But even that fear proves I'm alive. Rhydian has made me feel alive. I don't intend to steal him from Grace – even supposing I could – but there's no way I can pretend this momentous thing hasn't happened to me. It has.

I go upstairs to change. Fear is making me shiver and sweat.

'I know this isn't the right time,' Rhydian says, leaning back against the door and looking at me as though catching sight of me for the first time. 'Bleddyn came out with me to do some fencing this morning before we went to chapel and gave me a proper earful. How you were in a vulnerable state because of your mother's death, how there was nothing between you and me but a crude sexual attraction, nothing but biology, nothing but middle-aged lust. Well, he may be right, Katie, but oh Christ, it feels like a whole lot more to me.'

He comes towards me and I'm in his arms. 'And what about you?' he breathes into my ear. 'Do you feel as I do?'

I don't say anything. All my love words have left me. All I do is fit my body more closely into his, clutching him so that we're like one body, turn my face up to his, taste his tongue. Our deep kisses leave us shuddering.

No time to undress each other, no time for mouth-play,

only time for a shocking, wonderfully brutal giving and taking and gasping for breath and wanting even more, even more, even more, clinging together as though we're both drowning. Our eyes, open wide in wonder, are like drowning eyes.

'We've got to go, Katie, or they'll know something's up. Katie, love, come on. You can comb your hair in the car.'

Adrift and dreamy with love, I stumble after him to the car. 'Do I look all right? Do I look fairly normal?'

'No. You look like a sinner. God, I won't be able to take my eyes off you all evening. Bleddyn will know, even if Grace doesn't. I won't be able to carve the joint.'

'I won't be able to say anything. I'll only be able to think of what's happened. I can't bear to let it go.'

'We mustn't let it go. You mustn't go back to London.'

'I have to. But I'll come back.'

He stopped the car and we kissed; a long, long kiss of longing and promise; lips and mouth and tongue. 'We're lovers,' Rhydian said. 'Isn't that wonderful? Isn't that terrifying?'

He drove on again until we came to the farmhouse. Two black and white sheepdogs rushed out to meet us, sniffing us all over. 'Even the dogs know,' Rhydian moaned.

Grace was in the kitchen when we arrived, which gave us a moment or two to pull ourselves together. I was so happy I felt I could die of it.

'Oh Kate, you look so much better,' Siwan said. 'You've got a bit of colour in your cheeks now. The boys want to see you. Do you feel up to it? We've got five or ten minutes before supper. My fault. My cheese and potato pie isn't ready.'

The farmhouse was very different. In Auntie Jane's time, it was all flagstones and flaking whitewashed walls, now there were Laura Ashley floral wallpapers, pink and turquoise curtains, brass wall-lights and wall-to-wall carpets, even a carpet on the twisty old staircase. I wondered what Rhydian thought of the changes.

The boys were in their pyjamas, but playing computer games. Seeing them was not the ordeal I'd imagined. And I was pleased to find that they weren't at all interested in me. 'Are you our Granny?' the little one asked, when at last he did look up. 'Something like that.' 'Of course she's not your Granny,' Siwan said briskly. 'She's your Auntie Kate. Say goodnight, Auntie Kate.' 'Goodnight, Granny Kate. Goodnight, Siwan.'

'Your youngest son thinks I'm his Granny,' I tell Grace. She laughs. And the moment I'd dreaded is over.

We sit at the table, a new mahogany table with lace table mats, instead of the old scrubbed pine. Siwan serves the cheese and potato pie – the pototoes are not quite cooked but we all pretend they are – and Rhydian carves the baked ham. Grace pours out some red wine and asks me to pass round the broad beans. And Bleddyn frowns and says nothing.

We begin the meal. Siwan tells us about an exciting new nursing technique which is saving the lives of some of the tiniest premature babies. Grace supposes her new baby will be late as usual, but would love Siwan to be with her if at all possible. Siwan assures her that she's already got the date starred in her diary.

The conversation washes over me; a family argument about whether Gwyn, the eldest son, who has an outstanding soprano voice according to Grace, should apply to Wells Cathedral for a choral scholarship. Rhydian concedes that the boy's voice is passably good, but doesn't want him to leave home. Bleddyn, whose soprano voice was quite as good if not better than Gwyn's according to Rhydian, is not in favour of specialised education, but offers, for what it's worth, the theory that music and mathematics are often closely akin. Grace, while not prepared to deny that Bleddyn may have had a truly magnificent voice as a boy, is adamant that a particular timbre in Gwyn's voice has come from her

125

side of the family, and would like to remind all present that her cousin's son has turned professional and has sung in the Albert Hall with The Welsh Choir of a Thousand Voices and is set to become another Bryn Terfel. Siwan wishes that Grace had told her about the Albert Hall concert with The Welsh Choir of a Thousand Voices, since the nurses at St Thomas's, where she's doing her training, are sometimes given free tickets. Grace promises to get in touch with her when her cousin's son is giving another concert in London, though she rather thinks his next engagements are in Leeds and Cardiff.

Cardiff's Millennium stadium is a sore point with both Bleddyn and Rhydian, a shocking waste of money and what was wrong with the old Arms Park? Bleddyn asks me whether I'd ever gone to international matches when I was at Cardiff University and I said I had, which was a lie, adding that I still watched rugby matches on television when Wales was playing, another lie. Siwan, braver than I and with not so much to lose, admits that she'd never been to a rugby match in her life, but she had visited the International Eisteddfod at Llangollen last June and wonders whether Grace's cousin's son had ever sung there, but Grace replies, rather abruptly, that that was only for foreigners.

We have blackberry-and-apple tart for pudding, which Grace has made specially for Bleddyn, who says she makes the best blackberry-and-apple tart in the world. Rhydian then praises the damson cheesecake Siwan made for last night's supper and Grace says she must, please, give her the recipe before she leaves.

And all the time, whatever was being said, I sat thinking about the moment when Rhydian had blindly crossed the room towards me, and wondering whether he would be taking me home and what would happen if he did.

Coffee and mints in the lounge – dove-grey dralon with touches of maroon – and more desultory conversation, then

126

a tape of Mozart's *Requiem*, with everyone sighing and looking a little embarrassed, and the evening seemed to be over.

Rhydian got to his feet to take me home, but Bleddyn,
knowing a thing or two, and possibly three, insisted that
Siwan go with us. He would be more than pleased to help
Grace with the washing-up, but felt his daughter would like
a quick look over her great-grandmother's cottage.

'Won't Kate be too tired?' Rhydian and Siwan asked
together.

'Of course not,' I said, with more enthusiasm than I felt.
'I'll be delighted to show you the house. It will only take two
minutes, Siwan. It's very small.'

We went out to the car. The night was dark and cold, the
sky silvered with stars. I clung to Rhydian's arm. Bleddyn
might be suspicious of us, but I felt sure that Siwan
considered us old and quaint. Rhydian's calloused farmer's
hand held mine as he drove one-handed along the
murderously twisted lanes. And quivering with sinful
thoughts, I looked out for lay-bys where we might meet
when I returned.

The drive was soon over and we were back. (How distance
has shrunk. It used to take two buses and half a morning for
Auntie Jane to get to our house.) As we got out of the car, we
could hear the phone ringing, but I couldn't find the key,
couldn't find the lock, couldn't find the light switch, and by
that time it had stopped.

'That was probably Paul,' I said, 'but he'll ring again. This
is my mother's cat, Siwan. Arthur. He didn't like me at first,
but now he's getting quite friendly.'

He seemed intent on tripping me up. Did cats have yet
another meal at half-past ten at night?

'Will you be taking him back to London with you?'

'I think I may be staying here for a while. At least until I
get my next job.'

The phone rings again. It's Paul. 'Hello. Where have you
been? I've been ringing you all evening.'

127

'Where have *you* been? You promised to be here in time for the funeral.'

A long silence. 'Kate, I've got some terrible news. Kate, it's Selena. Selena has committed suicide.'

'Selena? Good God. Oh God, how frightful. Oh Paul, I'm so sorry. Paul, give me a minute and I'll ring you back. At the moment I simply can't think. I've just got to sit down and take this in. Oh my dear, I'm so very sorry.' The room swirls round me.

'What the hell's wrong?' Rhydian asks.

'I know it's very bad news. Let me make you a cup of tea,' Siwan says.

'One of Paul's daughters. Killed herself. God knows why. Twenty-one. Oh God, how frightful. Oh God, what a frightful day.'

Rhydian is chafing my hands which have turned white with shock.

Siwan has made me a cup of tea and is holding it to my lips. 'Have one sip. It's got a lot of sugar in it. Just one sip. Good girl. Good girl.'

'There, I feel better. I'll have to ring him back now. Rhydian, I think you and Siwan had better go and let me deal with this in my own way. I'll get in touch again when I can.'

'I think Grace will be very angry if we leave you in this state,' Siwan said. 'Rhydian, you need to go back, but I can stay here for the night. And I'd really like to.'

'We'd both better go. I think Kate needs to be on her own. Kate, will you phone later? At eleven-thirty? We'll want to know that you're coping.'

They leave. Siwan kisses me and Rhydian touches my face with the back of his hand and when Siwan turns towards the door, traces the line of my mouth with his fingers.

But I'm back with Paul again; Paul and Selena. I pace about the living room trying to get to grips with this new trauma, trying to find a way to bear this new pain.

\*

128

'What happened, Paul? What did she do?'

'Took all Francesca's sleeping pills. We don't know why. She wasn't at all implicated in the drugs affair. She wasn't even at the rave. That's all we can get out of Annabel. She screams if we ask her any more.'

'Had they had a quarrel?'

'We daren't ask her, Kate. She gets hysterical and has to be sedated if anyone asks her anything.'

'Poor girl. No wonder she's hysterical.'

'And Francesca's almost as bad. Can you possibly come tomorrow? I know you've had a tough time, but I really need you. I've had to cancel the Spain thing – not that that matters. Nothing matters now, that's how I feel. I'm at rock bottom, Kate.'

'Of course you are. Nothing in the whole world can be worse than this. And I know that nothing I can say or do will help, I know that too. But I'll come, of course I will. I'll ring you tomorrow morning as soon as I find out about trains.'

'Thank you, love.'


At exactly eleven-thirty, I phone Gorsgoch and Rhydian answers. I fail to say anything except that I have to leave the next day.

He doesn't try to dissuade me, doesn't say anything at all except those three words that mean everything and nothing.

Will he forget me? Will I forget him? I don't know. I don't know.

# Chapter Thirteen

How can you comfort a man – your partner – whose twenty-one-year-old daughter has committed suicide? You can only hold his hand and be very loving, I suppose. Which would be easier if you hadn't made violent love to another man, whose image was still in your mind, less than twenty-four hours before.

It was the first time I'd been unfaithful to Paul since the beginning of our relationship. We'd discussed the ground rules: we were to consider ourselves married, it was to be everything except the scrap of paper. I remember the hours we spent talking it over, even making wills so that everything was settled, signed and sealed.

I can't be totally wicked, I kept telling myself as my train drew nearer and nearer Cambridge, or I wouldn't be feeling so guilty. I honestly believed I'd be able to break it off with Paul. Now that has to be postponed, perhaps indefinitely, but that's due to circumstances beyond my control. And behind that legal terminology is a young girl; Selena, my step-daughter, lying white and cold and dead in a mortuary. Such a horrid, icy image that I shivered in the warmth of the compartment.

I'd bought a newspaper and a paperback at Shrewsbury, but couldn't read either. Throughout the journey I sat back against my seat, eyes tightly closed, hands clenched together. Even travelling to Wales immediately on hearing of my mother's death hadn't been as traumatic and shocking as this.

'Would it help to talk?' the woman sitting opposite me asked. I looked at her for the first time, a woman of about my own age with a strong, intelligent face; concerned, but definitely not a busybody.

'Thank you. But I don't think so. A young girl, my step-daughter, is dead. She's dead. There's nothing to talk over, is there?'

'No, I suppose not. When did you get this news?'

'Last night. She committed suicide the previous night.'

'Suicide? Oh, God! Was she a student? Was it because of her studies?' She leaned across the small table between us and laid her hands on mine. 'I never usually talk to strangers,' she said.

I looked up at her and nodded to assure her that I believed her, trusted her. 'I never usually reply.'

'Have we met before? I know it sounds a cliché, but I feel I know you.'

'You may have seen me on the box. I'm an actor. I'm usually reluctant to tell people, because they either want to know everything I've done, or ask whether I've ever met John Thaw . . . What do you do?'

'I teach at the University. German Literature . . . And *have* you ever met John Thaw?'

'Not yet.'

'There, you smiled. I won't pretend this is going to be easy for you, in fact I know it will be devastating, but go on working and let people help you negotiate it. It's the only way. We're arriving now and I suppose you'll have someone meeting you, but here's my card. Please get in touch with me. Let's meet and have a drink. I'm in London most weekends.' I took the card and glanced at it. Dr Joanna Morton.

'I'd like that. Thank you. You're speaking from experience, aren't you? About suffering?'

132

'Yes. My daughter died of leukaemia when she was just seven. Thirteen years ago now, but I still need people's help.'

When we were out on the platform, I took her arm and squeezed it. 'My partner's over there, so I'll leave you. But I will get in touch. I'd really like to.'

She smiled and walked away and I hurried to join Paul who, without a word of greeting, led me out of the station. He looked old, the lines on his face deeper than I remembered. We walked to the car park, still without either of us managing to say a word. He unlocked the car. 'Will you drive to Newnham?' he said then.

'I'd rather you did, Paul. I don't know Cambridge.'

I willed him to pull himself together. I wasn't prepared to let him go to pieces, not even for a day. I got into the passenger seat and smiled at him and after what seemed a whole long minute he got into the driver's seat and started up the car.

'I keep on wanting to drive into something,' he said, when we were out on the busy road in heavy traffic.

'That wouldn't help anyone and could prove quite painful. I remember playing a woman whose lover had deserted her. That Christmas she bought a bottle of gin which she intended to drink before throwing herself out of the window. But a friend happened to call who told her that a second-floor flat wasn't high enough to kill, but only to maim, so she gave up the idea and they drank the gin instead.'

'That was the Jean Rhys autobiography,' Paul said in an almost normal voice. 'You played it on BBC 2 about seven years ago. *Smile Please*. You were pretty good in it, I thought. I'm very sorry about your mother, by the way. Sorry I couldn't come to the funeral. Did everything go well?'

'As well as could be expected, I suppose. I mean, it wasn't much fun but we got through it.'

'God, I didn't mean to say that. Did everything go well! I'm not myself, Kate.'

133

'Of course you're not. I don't mind what you say as long as you keep talking. Tell me about practical things. Where are we staying tonight? Where are Annabel and Francesca? Where are we eating? How long are we staying in Cambridge? Have the police dropped their charges against Annabel?'

The last question seemed to galvanise him. 'Yes. They seem to have accepted that it must have been . . . Selena who passed on the drugs.' He turned to look at me. 'I find it almost impossible to say her name.'

'She wrote to me about my mother's death.'

The car swerved, almost hitting the kerb. 'Really?'

'I was very moved by it. Let's find somewhere to eat and I'll show you the letter. Have you eaten today?'

'No idea.'

We drove into the car park of the Garden House Hotel. When we were shown to a table, he leaned across and kissed me. 'I couldn't face this without you,' he said. 'We've been drifting apart lately, I know. But please see this through with me.'

At first I thought Annabel looked remarkably normal. Paul had been telling me about her bouts of screaming and head banging. Now, dressed in Paul's dark green sweater, she was very pale but seemed composed.

I think I was too tense to say much, which may have been a good thing. Perhaps too many people had been giving her too much fairly useless advice, so that she was pleased that I was prepared to squeeze her hand, smile at her and say very little.

After a few minutes she made some coffee, so dark and horrible that I wondered whether she intended poisoning the three of us. 'I don't think I can drink this,' I said. 'Is it something Turkish and expensive? Or something cheap and nasty? It tastes like creosote.'

'It is rather terrible,' Paul said. 'I've complained about it before. What is it?'

134

'Some supermarket stuff. I put three spoonfuls in each cup, but it's no better, is it?'

'I'll make some tea,' I said. And, waiting for the kettle to boil, I started telling them about all the people I'd been making tea for; Lorna, the postwoman, Gwenda Rees from the farm, bossy Maggie Davies, George Williams, my mother's secret lover, and the red-haired boy, the Reverend Lewis Owen.

'Tell me about the funeral,' Annabel said.

For some reason, certainly not to humour me, she wanted to hear about my mother's funeral. So I told her about the isolated cottage, the funeral car, the little chapel full to the door, the flowers, tastefully arranged by the fancy-man of my cousin's wife's younger sister, the wheezing organ and the funeral meal in the vestry with the WI green china, five pounds extra.

I worried that she'd think I was making light of it; I suppose I was, but you can make fun of something while delighting in it at the same time.

'I wish I could have been there to support you,' Paul said. 'It must have been unbearably sad. Your mother was a lovely person.'

We drank our tea in silence.

And then Annabel spoke. 'I want Selena to be buried there,' she said.

Paul and I stared at her in disbelief. 'Darling, Mummy's arranging to have the funeral at St Botulph's,' Paul said.

Annabel's voice became shrill. 'For God's sake don't call her 'Mummy'. We've been calling her Francesca since we were children. I've never had a 'Mummy.' And I'm the one who was important to Selena so *I'm* the one who's going to decide everything. Francesca wasn't important to her and neither were you.'

'Annabel, listen to me. Selena is dead and everyone is devastated, you most of all, but the funeral is only something we've all got to get through. That's what Lorna, the village postwoman told me and it's absolutely true. It's not important, Annabel.'

'It is important, it is. I don't want Father Anthony and all Francesca's silly friends gawping at me. It might be just a bit more bearable if it's only Francesca and Paul and you and me and the sad hymns. Please Kate, I've never asked you for anything, but please do this for me. Please.'

'Can we talk about it tomorrow?' Paul asked, his voice parched, almost a whisper.

Annabel stood up and started trembling like someone with a fever. 'No. You must tell Francesca tonight before she and Matthew go back to Holland Park and start arranging everything.'

'Perhaps she needs to have something to arrange, love,' Paul said. 'People have their own way of dealing with unbearable tragedy. Many people have a great need to keep busy. Couldn't you please try to let her deal with it in her own way?'

'Why are you always on her side? She led you a terrible life, remember, and finally she dumped you. And yet you always, *always* stick up for her. Why?'

Her angry words hung over us. She was asking a question I'd wanted to ask many times, but never had, perhaps because I knew the answer. And now it no longer mattered.

We all seemed suddenly too tired for any more talk or argument.

'I've been sleeping in Selena's room to keep Annabel company, but she says she'll be all right on her own tonight.'

'Nonsense. We'll both sleep there.'

'Tiny room, single bed.'

'All right, you go to a hotel and I'll stay here. Is that OK, Annabel?'

'Are you sure? I may start screaming.'

'Me too, love. You go, Paul. Come round in the morning.'

He kissed us both and left. He looked like one of the

soldiers in First World War photographs; a man stumbling out of the trenches.

Annabel and I listened to his heavy footsteps on the stairs. For a time we were both silent, both of us, I suspect, desperately wondering how to get through the rest of the evening.

Annabel turned on the television. *Match of the Day*, *Stand-Up-Comedy*, *Horror Movie (1977)*, *Prison Drama*, *Sex in the Nineties*. After a while she began switching channels feverishly as though deriving some grim satisfaction from the noisy, surrealist kaleidoscope she was able to produce.

I put up with it as long as I could. 'What about some music?' I said at last. She seemed amenable to the suggestion, moving over to the pile of CDs on the book shelf.

But suddenly she spun round to face me, her eyes round and childlike and sparkling with tears. 'You never even tried to help Selena, did you?' she shouted at me. 'You were as hopeless as everyone else.' She was shaking with anger and distress.

'Annabel, neither of you took kindly to anything I said or did. So I usually thought it wiser to say as little as possible.'

'You couldn't be bloody bothered. You couldn't even see what was in front of your eyes, could you?'

'Say what you've got to say, Annabel, then we can both go to bed.'

She came over and stood only a few inches away from me. 'OK, this is what I've got to say. You never even bothered to notice that Selena and I were two separate people. That she was sensitive and clever and I was a stupid show-off. You could never be bothered to work that much out, could you?'

'I think you're exaggerating. I'm not trying to defend myself – I did cut myself off from you as much as I could, I admit that. But I know it's difficult not to idealise someone who's died. I think you were both a mixture of good and bad, like the rest of us.'

137

'Don't give me that garbage. She wanted to be completely independent from me. She was sick of being my double, the weaker and less-noticed half of identical twins. She hated me because she couldn't get away from me. That's why she killed herself. Because she despised me and was frightened of me.'

'Darling, you're being melodramatic. Please come and sit down and let's talk quietly and rationally. Please. Please Annabel.'

'We hated each other. Everyone thought we were so close. We were, of course, but it was a suffocating closeness. It was hell. She hated me because she thought I'd managed to get away from her. And I hated her because she'd never try to break away. And I feel sure she killed herself because she thought someone else – a boyfriend – was more important to me than she was. He wasn't, of course, he was never in the least important. But somehow I couldn't tell her that. I somehow wanted her to suffer.'

She threw herself at me and started to cry and fling herself about. I knew exactly what to do because I'd gone through the same excesses of grief years ago with my mother. I made her comfortable, stroked her hair and rocked her, saying absolutely nothing, until at last the storm of weeping was over.

Then it was my turn to say something. And I was out of my depth, I knew it. I remembered Paul suggesting that identical twins often retained an element of the rivalry they'd experienced in the womb. Perhaps it was true. Perhaps Annabel and Selena had hated one another to some extent. But I had to set aside that idea.

'Annabel, she didn't hate you, didn't despise you. You may have developed in different ways and I'm really sorry I didn't notice it. Yes, I accept that you had problems, but I know you truly loved one another as well and you must hold on to that. She loved you and you loved her. There may have been difficulties, you may both have begun to feel stifled by your closeness, I can believe that. The same thing happened to my mother and me when I was a teenager, but I was able to break away from her and go to university. With you two, the relationship was much closer, and more suffocating, but the love was always there. That's something I'm absolutely certain of. Won't you believe me? Don't make things harder for yourself than they are.'

She sniffed and looked up at me. 'Did you really hate your mother?'

'Often. She needed me too much, depended on me too much, wouldn't try to make a life without me.' It was true to some extent, I suppose, though it was the first time I'd faced up to it.

Annabel eventually grew calmer and said she would go to bed. She took two sleeping pills which the doctor had prescribed for her – I noticed that there were only two in the bottle, probably a sensible precaution – and then, while still in the sitting room, she got into a pair of pyjamas as though she was a little child. 'Don't forget your teeth,' I said, enjoying her excursion into childhood. I expected her to glower at me, but she just murmured, 'I won't,' and went off meekly to the bathroom.

A few minutes later I went to Selena's bedroom, a tiny cell of a room; white walls, white bedcover, books and files organised with the utmost care and neatness on the shelving units, the only incongruous items being the three large posters of Chagall's most surreal pictures on the walls, lovers flying hand in hand over gardens full of butterflies and flowers; a farmyard; a milkmaid, a blue cow, two cockerels, watched over by a huge green eye; a flying grandfather clock with a blue wing. I got into bed, wondering what this revealed about her character . . . and immediately fell asleep. And was still in that first, deep sleep when Annabel was suddenly by my side, shaking me. (And Paul had endured three nights of this? No wonder he was looking so old and defeated.) 'I never wanted to come to this damn place,' she

139

said, her voice shrill again and on the verge of hysteria. 'I only applied because Selena wouldn't come here without me. For her, of course, it was easy, but God knows how I got in. We both read English up here and she wrote most of my essays and if she didn't, I'd threaten to leave. All I did was have a good time and she did my work as well as her own. And no one noticed that she was brilliant and I was a cheat and a slob. And it killed her in the end. *I* killed her.'

I couldn't decide whether to shout back at her or remain calm. I took a deep breath, reckoning that cool reason required less energy. 'You didn't kill her, Annabel. She took her own life. And I'm pretty sure it wasn't because of overwork.' I was so tired I hardly knew what I was saying, but words came out.

'Do you think it was because I might have been charged with manslaughter? She couldn't, surely, have thought that would stick? Even the solicitor chap said there wasn't a chance of it coming to court. And she was here at the time, she heard him say it. I wasn't even the one who got the Es that night. I'd done it plenty of times before, I admit it, but that night I was making out with Laurie Bridgewater and we didn't get to the rave till about three.'

'And Selena wasn't there at all?'

'Of course not. Selena was working. She never went anywhere.'

I was about to say that that might have been the trouble, but luckily stopped myself in time. 'You're getting cold,' I said instead. 'You must go back to bed now and we'll talk again in the morning. I'll come with you and tuck you in. Up you get.'

She was a tired little waif again, all eyes and straggling blonde hair. I tucked her in and kissed her.

What would tomorrow bring? I had no idea, but felt pretty sure it would be nothing worthwhile or comforting.

# Chapter Fourteen

When the phone rang, I was amazed to find that it was ten o'clock and that I'd slept for four or five hours. Soon, I could hear Annabel talking in the sitting room; quite animatedly at first, then getting more and more excitable, and finally slamming the phone down and starting to sob.

I waited as long as I could before barging in on her. 'I'm sorry if I'm intruding, Annabel, but I've got to have a pee.' I looked back at her before going to the bathroom. 'Try to stop crying by the time I get back, love.'

Not a chance. 'Tell me about it,' I said, rather reluctantly. She glared at me. 'Piss off.'

'And then have you say I don't care about you? I do care about you and want to help you. Tell me what this latest thing is all about. Otherwise, there's no point in my being here. If I'm no help, I may as well go back home.'

I put the kettle on and made a pot of tea. There didn't seem to be any bread, but I found some cream crackers and some soft cheese. Annabel was still sobbing, but I put some tea and cream crackers in front of her. 'Horrible breakfast,' she said, swallowing air and gulping. 'Horrible. I'd get better than this in prison.'

'What's happened now, Annabel? Is there bad news?'

'Bad news? Yes, haven't you heard? My sister's dead.'

I drank some tea and tried again. 'Who was on the phone? Was it Paul?'

'No, it was Laurie, this friend of mine.' She took the tissue I passed her and dried her eyes. For a moment or two she stared in front of her, almost in a trance. I was really frightened, then. For those few moments, she seemed somewhere in between life and death, contemplating both. Then she seemed to pull herself together. She drank some tea and looked up at me as though ready to talk.

'So what did Laurie tell you?'

'There was an item about us, he said, on local radio. About me and Selena. It said that Selena had killed herself because she was ashamed of causing Miranda Lottaby's death.'

'Oh God. Listen to me, Annabel. If I've learnt one thing in life, it's to ignore the media; particularly local radio. No one is aware of anything that's been said after about five minutes.' I blew into the air. '*Phooh!* Gone! No one remembers it.'

'I'll remember it for the rest of my life. It's a terrible, terrible lie. Selena never got drugs for anyone in her life, and she'd never even met Miranda Lottaby.' Suddenly she jumped up from her chair.

'Where are you going?'

'To the police station. I'm going to tell them it was me.'

I reached the door before her and wouldn't let her out. 'I'm sorry, but I'm not going to let you.'

'You can't stop me.' She was shouting again.

'Yes, I can. I'm bigger than you and much stronger. If you go to the police station, it'll be when you've calmed down, and when Paul is here to go with you. And anyway, why should you tell them it was you? It wasn't. You told me that and I believed you.'

'But it wasn't Selena, either. Don't you understand that? It wasn't Selena. Just because she's dead, it doesn't mean that she can be blamed for something she didn't do. We can't just dump it all on Selena and forget about it. Truth is important.'

'Of course it is. But so is compassion. Paul and Francesca won't be able to bear it if you get involved again. Paul is

142

really brokenhearted and he says Francesca's no better. They've lost a daughter, Annabel. I accept that it's even worse for you, but you must admit that it's pretty agonising for them too. And Paul is fifty-four, a dangerously common age for heart-attacks in men. How will he bear up if the police start questioning you again – all that hassle?'

Annabel was sitting on the floor looking at her hands, turning them this way and that. I couldn't help thinking what a superb Ophelia she'd make; she looked about fifteen and more than half mad.

'Don't make them go through all that,' I said quietly. '*We* know that Selena was innocent, all your friends, all the people who matter know she's innocent. Is what they write in the police files so important? Think about it, love.'

Silence settled into every corner of the room. I didn't have anything more to say. What was Annabel thinking? Had she been listening to me? I wanted to suggest another cup of tea, but didn't dare break the silence.

'You never used to bully me,' she said.

'I intend to from now on. Someone has to.'

She seemed pleased with that answer, looked up at me with what was almost a smile. 'I'll make a bargain with you, Kate. I won't go to the police if you let me have my way about the funeral, and secondly, let me leave this place.'

'I think you should leave this place, if you only came for Selena's sake. And you're old enough to make your own decision about it. About the funeral, I'm not the one to decide that. If your parents agree to it, I'll certainly try to arrange it, but I can't say more, can I?'

'Oh yes you could, if you had the guts. If you made a definite arrangement, they'd go along with it. Why won't you? Why? Why can't you phone someone now? Why? Why can't you?'

'Because I'm forty-three years old and I've learnt to behave in a fairly civilised way most of the time. As Paul said last night, having to make the arrangements for the funeral may be of enormous help to Francesca. And though I care more about you, I also care about her. Let's at least discuss it with her. Is she back in London now?'

'I don't know.'

'Why don't we go out and get some breakfast somewhere? Croissants and some decent coffee? When we come back we'll try to contact Francesca. All right?'

It wasn't. She started to sob again and rock herself from side to side. All the same, I felt less nervous about her by this time, now that some sort of truce had been agreed between us.

When Paul – and Francesca – arrived at the flat at about eleven o'clock, Annabel and I were still sitting on the floor by the door, sizing each other up.

'Are you meditating?' Francesca asked.

'I've brought some freshly-ground coffee and some hot walnut bread,' Paul said.

I hadn't seen Francesca for some years. She was as beautiful as ever, but had grown smaller and older – she was a year or two older than Paul – and didn't seem quite as brittle and cold.

'Where's Matthew?' Annabel asked. Matthew was her mother's current boyfriend, a partner in the art gallery.

'He has the children every Sunday. You should know that.'

I left the sitting room to make coffee in the kitchen and Paul followed me. 'Has Annabel been difficult?' he asked me. 'Did she keep waking you?'

'Yes. Did you have a good night's sleep? You look better. You'd better go back in there, Paul. Annabel's about to tackle Francesca about the funeral.'

'I've already done that. And she's agreed. She says it'll be restful and uplifting, just the four of us.'

'Thank you for arranging the funeral for us,' Francesca said, in a grand but gracious voice, as soon as I returned with the coffee. 'Whatever you and Annabel want will be fine with me. What's the name of your church, by the way, and what religion is it? I need to know so that I can get the cards printed. I'm sure no one will turn up, the place sounds so remote, but I'll simply have to have announcements printed. People will expect that much.'

'Horeb, Congregational Chapel, Glanrhyd,' I said.

'No announcements,' Annabel said at exactly the same moment.

Francesca turned to me, ignoring her daughter. 'Horeb? Is that the name of a Celtic saint?'

'I don't quite know how these things are arranged,' Paul said. 'I mean, what if it's members only? Something like that?'

'Then we pay,' Francesca said briskly. 'And if that doesn't work, we pay more. And afterwards I'll commission Agnes Miller-Thorpe to design a stained-glass memorial window there. Nothing too modern, of course.' She turned to Annabel. 'Lilies and doves, darling, and perhaps a very young Saint Catherine.'

Annabel's eyes narrowed as though she was about to say something fairly rancorous, but I cut in. 'No, Francesca, Horeb isn't the name of a saint, it's a Hebrew place-name. Many of our chapels are named after Hebrew places. There's Seion – Zion, Saron – Sharon, Salem – Salem, and Ebenezer, the stone of God, then there's Bethlehem, Bethany, Bethel, Calfaria – Calvary, and of course Moriah and many more which . . .'

They were looking at me as though they weren't sure whether I'd had a slight brainstorm or was acting mad. I wasn't sure myself. Perhaps people all become actors under extreme stress. Perhaps Francesca was just playing a Francesca part, 'Lilies and doves, darling, and a very young Saint Catherine,' and Paul the decent husband and father part, 'I've brought some coffee and some hot walnut bread,' and I was playing grumpy step-mother.

145

Anyway, I felt I had every excuse. I hadn't had a decent night's sleep since hearing of my mother's death. When was that? Only a week ago? Too much had happened in one week; two deaths, one of them extremely sad, one hugely tragic, and one small miracle that lit up a corner of my mind but couldn't be thought of at the moment in case my face broke into an unseemly smile.

'But we do have Celtic saints,' I said. 'Dewi, our patron saint, Beuno, Padarn, Garmon and Rhydian.' There, I'd pronounced his name and felt better for it. 'And in fact I have a cousin called Rhydian. He was at my mother's funeral. Rhydian. Rhydian Jones.'

'Jesus, Kate,' Annabel said. 'What's got into you? We're not interested in your bloody Celtic saints. Just shut up about them.'

Meanwhile, Francesca had withdrawn herself from the funeral talk. 'You were born first,' she told Annabel, sounding like an old woman, 'and Selena wasn't born for another hour and forty minutes. She was so small, not quite two pounds, and I was hoping she'd die. She looked so frightening – bloody, like something the dogs used to bring in when they'd been hunting and torn the skin away. Even when the nurse had washed her, I couldn't look at her or hold her. I just hoped she'd die.'

'They were both tiny,' Paul said, 'but I thought they were beautiful.'

'Why didn't she die, then? When I wanted her to?'

Paul went to Francesca's side and held her against him. Even Annabel was moved to pity for her mother. Her eyes shone with tears and her mouth trembled. 'We'll never forget her,' she said quietly.

We sat in silence. I wanted to be somewhere else, almost anywhere else.

I thought about the little bay a few miles from my home. Not many people know it because there isn't a road leading down to the sea at that point, only a track through very tall,

146

ancient-looking trees, with the river, the same river that we see from the back of the cottage, a stone's throw away. And there are no noisy holidaymakers with surf-boards and ghetto-blasters, only a few local families with rugs and baskets of food and beach-balls. When I was a child, I only went there on rare occasions; a Sunday School outing or a geography field day, but when I got to the Sixth and had acquired a second-hand bicycle, I went fairly often. Being in the sea never meant much to me. I could swim, but not well; I always liked it better at a distance. I wasn't over-fond of sunbathing, either. What I liked was walking on the sands, collecting stones and pieces of driftwood, and along the cliffs with the heavy smell of gorse drugging the senses and making a fire on the beach afterwards, not to cook anything, but because it lit up the sea and the sky and smelled of tar and salt. Sexual experiences were lovely, too, on the beach, with the tumult of the sea like a swelling film score in the background. In the Sixth, a boy called Brynmor Richards and I were too nervous to go 'all the way', but the way we did go was sea-sweet and dangerously exciting.

I think of the sea at Cwmllys whenever I'm nervous at First Nights or at difficult social events or medical examinations; cervical smears, for instance.

'When will you phone the vicar?' Annabel asked, dragging me back to the place I didn't want to be in, to the situation I wanted to escape from.

'He isn't a vicar, he's a minister. He doesn't wear a cassock, for instance, no sort of robe. In fact, he's not at all a romantic figure. I hope I haven't given you the wrong impression of him or the chapel. I mean, it was obviously the right setting for my mother's funeral, but the minister, for instance, he's very young and he's got bright red hair. And I'm not sure that he's all that religious either. And the organ wheezes like an old man.'

They were still looking at me strangely.

'None of us can be expected to be normal or sane at the

147

moment,' Paul said briskly. 'We simply must go out to have a proper breakfast.'

Paul drove us back to the Garden House, and Francesca had a word, or several words with the manager – words I've never managed to acquire – so that we were brought exactly what we asked for even though they had long finished serving breakfast.

We talked about Annabel's future. Francesca said she would give her a job in the Gallery and Paul said she could go to Japan with him, if he got a particular assignment, which he felt he would. 'What about you?' Annabel asked me. 'Don't you have anything to offer me?' I felt she was suddenly trying to pull me into the family circle, just at the time I wanted to be out of it.

'My profession is nothing but sweat, toil and tears,' I said, making an effort to be flippant.

'Does your work seem to be drying up?' Francesca asked, looking fairly cheerful for the first time.

'It does rather, I'm too old, now, for the parts I used to get.'

'Nonsense,' Paul said. 'The phone doesn't stop ringing.'

'I was sorry to hear about your mother,' Francesca said. 'I never met her, but Paul used to say she was quite a character.'

Life, real life, seemed to be resuming. 'I must go back home tomorrow,' I said. 'I have so much to do.'

Annabel gave me a look which I tried but failed to interpret.

After a long and satisfying breakfast we went for a walk along the river. The day was completely still, no sun, no wind, the sky a uniform grey, the Cam dark, like antique moss-green silk.

The Cam. I started to think of all the places where I'd never taken my mother. She'd have liked to go to Grantchester, she'd learnt a great chunk of that poem at

148

school, and also to Ireland, 'where the mountains of Mourne go down to the sea'. She always favoured places associated with school and her childhood. In London, she wanted, above all, to see the Tower where the little princes had been imprisoned and Lady Jane Grey beheaded, and when I once took her to Paris for a weekend, all she'd wanted to see was Napoleon's tomb. 'I liked him better than Nelson,' she'd confided, as though they were two old schoolfriends. I'd always intended to take her to Ypres where her mother's uncle had been killed, she'd expressed a great desire to see those rows and rows of graves and crosses. She'd had a romantic attachment to death.

'Why are you smiling?' Paul asked me.

'I'm trying to stop crying, that's all.'

'I'm trying to stop crying, too, but I can't smile,' Annabel said.

She and I fell behind the other two. 'I've got something to tell you,' she said.

She must have sensed my apprehension because she didn't say anything for a moment or two. But whatever she wanted to say was hanging in the air between us so that finally I said, 'Is it to do with Selena?'

'No. To do with Paul and Francesca.'

'They're getting back together?' I asked. I'd only that moment thought of it, but it immediately struck me as possible, even probable. 'A tragedy of this sort can often bring people together,' I said in a small voice.

'I haven't been told anything. It's only that I'm getting certain vibes, that's all. I just thought I ought to warn you.'

'Thank you. I appreciate it.'

'No you don't. You think I'm an interfering bitch, I know you do. I suppose you think I'd welcome my parents getting back together, but I wouldn't. Well, I would in a way, but I'd be afraid my mother would dump Paul again as soon as she got over Selena's death. I know he's safer with you. You wouldn't let him down. And though I try not to care about people, I do care about him.'

'I care about him, too, but . . .'

'But?'

'But strange things happen to everyone, mysterious things like falling in love. Even to unremarkable people like me.'

'Kate, what are you saying?'

'I'm not saying anything at this point. But I don't want you to think of me as some wonderfully stable and dependable person. I'm weak and vacillating like everyone else. That's all I'm saying.'

Why should I be feeling as though I'd been punched in the stomach? If Paul wanted to get back with Francesca, wouldn't that solve my problems, or at least some of them?

# Chapter Fifteen

Laurie Bridgewater, Annabel's beau, was in the flat when we got back.

I deliberately use that old-fashioned, almost archaic word, because no other does him justice; he was tall, dark, elegant, elegantly dressed, beautiful, charming – the sort of young man you usually see only in old French films. When he put his arm round Annabel, she burst into tears, looking fragile as a snowdrop. Still holding her, he shook hands with Paul, Francesca and me, offering us his most sincere sympathy. He was so handsome, so gallant, that for a time we all found it difficult to do anything but look at him with wonder. And within a couple of minutes he seemed to have taken charge of all the arrangements we still had to make: he'd call on all Selena's tutors to make sure they'd heard of her death; he'd pack everything left in the flat when Annabel returned with her parents and take them to London during the following week; he'd see about letting the flat, he'd drive us to the funeral, we could leave absolutely everything to him.

We all seemed to relax in the power of his presence. We'd all, even Francesca, been fumbling our way uneasily through the pitfalls of the day, nervous of putting a foot wrong, afraid to speak our minds about anything. Now Laurie was in control and we breathed more easily.

He'd contacted the police and they'd confirmed that it

wasn't necessary for Annabel to spend another night in Cambridge, he'd help her pack some things, while Paul and Francesca could fetch their belongings from the hotel and be ready to drive to London in half an hour, Paul taking me, Francesca taking Annabel.

'But I need to borrow Paul's car,' I said. 'I have to go back to Wales, and it's too late now to get a train.'

'I'll come with you,' Annabel said. 'And tomorrow we can arrange the funeral.'

We were all, even Laurie, loath to argue with her. Her eyes were glittering and there were spots of high colour on her cheeks: she seemed feverish. 'I'll come with you,' she repeated, her voice even more determined and steely.

'Fine,' Laurie said.

Paul and Francesca went off obediently to fetch their bags from their hotels and I made a pot of tea, wondering whether Annabel was intent on coming with me to give her mother and father more time on their own. Didn't children always want their parents to get back together, however unsuited they were? Annabel and Selena had hated me when they were children because they'd thought, quite wrongly, that I was the cause of the break-up.

I switched my thoughts to another direction. 'How well did you know Selena?' I asked Laurie when Annabel was still sorting out her things in the bedroom. 'I don't think I knew her at all. Annabel says I'd never taken the trouble to distinguish between them.'

He conferred on me his full attention, his intent gaze. 'It was Selena I knew first. She was in my tutorial group. Very clever, a very original mind. I got to know her, liked her a great deal, we were often together, but there was never anything between us. We never went out together, or anything like that. What I mean is, please don't think that I'm in any way responsible for her suicide.'

'Of course not,' I said. 'Has Annabel suggested that you were?'

'Oh no, she'd rather blame herself. She keeps saying that Selena hated her and was frightened of her. But, you see, no one really knows the reason. Did you know that ninety per cent of people who commit suicide leave a note, an explanation or a vindication, but the police didn't find anything here, though they went through the place with a toothcomb. I'd really like to understand what she was going through. Whenever I was around, she always gave the impression of being distant and rather impassive.'

'She was perhaps terribly disturbed that she and Annabel had become so different, that Annabel seemed to be having all the fun and she all the work.'

'But I was always begging her to come out with me and Anni. Don't you believe me?' he asked, when I made no response.

'Yes, I believe you. But if, by any chance, she was in love with you, that might not have been too easy for her.'

'But she wasn't in love with me. Why suggest that?'

'You're the type women fall for. That can't have escaped your notice.'

'But Selena didn't even seem to like me. Good God, she was totally against the life I was leading. And she thought I was a bad influence on Annabel.'

'You can be in love with someone though you disapprove of him.'

Annabel came back to the sitting room. 'What are you two arguing about?'

'Your step-mother thinks Selena was in love with me,' Laurie said.

Annabel looked from him to me, then back at him. 'No, it was nothing like that. Selena considered Laurie beneath her notice. She ignored him as she ignored everyone else.'

Laurie looked hurt. 'I'm not too sure about that,' he said crossly.

During the course of the day, Annabel's anger had

153

changed to a profound sadness. I couldn't decide whether or not it was a sign of improvement.

Why was she so determined to come home with me? What was I going to do with her? How would she spend her time? I certainly wouldn't be able to see Rhydian while she was with me, though perhaps I'd be able to talk to him on the phone, hear his low, sensual voice. I felt weak at the thought of him, then ashamed to be wanting him so much at a time when I should be thinking only of others. All the same, I gave myself up, for a moment or two, to a trembling contemplation of our sudden, ferocious passion.

'What are you thinking about?' Annabel asked me.

'Why do you ask?'

'You looked so intense. As though you were solving all our problems.'

'Afraid not. I'm worried about the journey home, that's all. It's a long way from here. Two hundred miles, at least.'

'I'll do the driving. I enjoy it.'

'Why do you suddenly want to come with me? You've never wanted anything to do with me before.'

She didn't answer. Perhaps it was as much of a mystery to her as it was to me.

'I'll be following on tomorrow,' Laurie said. 'When will the funeral be?'

It was five before we left the flat. The evening was mild and sunny, the sky a coppery green. Annabel drove through Cambridge and as far as Northampton where we stopped for a pub meal, Annabel looking so pale and wan that everyone stared at her.

I felt wonderfully revived after some pasta and a glass of red wine and insisted on taking over the driving. I knew my way across the Midlands. I'd worked for two seasons in Stratford and for two months in Worcester years ago; even in the dark, the roads seemed familiar and I had a moment's exhilaration at the thought that I was driving home.

154

'Are you going to drive all the way at forty-five miles an hour?' Annabel asked.

'Of course not. Thirty is my top speed in Wales. Very dangerous roads.'

'Why are you so old?'

'It's all those years piling up on top of me and all the griefs.'

'If you'd let me drive, I'd at least have something to concentrate on.'

'Go to sleep.'

We seemed to be getting on well. I stopped dreading the days ahead. I opened the window and felt the clean mountain air on my face. I looked over at Annabel and smiled at her.

'I'm pregnant,' she said.

I breathed steadily in and out, determined not to say the wrong thing. And everything I thought of seemed the wrong thing.

'Don't look so frightened,' she said. 'Girls get pregnant all the time. Even the Virgin Mary. For God's sake say something, even if it's only a bloody platitude.'

'OK, you're pregnant. How pregnant? How certain are you? Have you had a test?'

She didn't answer. There seemed scorn, even contempt, in her silence.

'Anyway, none of it matters. I refuse to worry about you. Your parents are rich and supportive and your boyfriend is exceedingly handsome. Whether you have an abortion or an extremely beautiful baby is up to you. All I intend to do is make you nourishing meals, cabbage and so on, and buy you multi-vitamin tablets and folic acid while you make your decision.'

We drove several miles in silence.

I remembered how terrified I was of getting pregnant while I was a student. For me, it would have meant the end of all my dreams, all my ambitions. When at last I worked up enough courage to confront a doctor and ask him to put me on the Pill, it was the beginning of a new life. A new heaven and a new earth.

'I *had* decided on an abortion,' Annabel said. 'And my exceedingly handsome boyfriend was even more enthusiastic than I was. He came with me to a private clinic, The Langland, where all the rich bitches go, to make an appointment. Which was for Tuesday of this week. The day after tomorrow.'

'But you've changed your mind?'

'Of course I've bloody changed my mind. Selena's death altered everything. Don't you understand that?'

I drew into the side of the road and stopped the car. She threw herself at me and I hugged her. And we both cried for a long time.

'Laurie isn't upset that you changed your mind?' I asked at last.

'No, he understands. And I understand that he doesn't want any part of it. He's very ambitious, doesn't want to be held back. Anyway, I shall prefer being on my own.'

'You've told Paul and Francesca?'

'No. You can do that. I can't seem to talk to those two.'

'I think you'll have to. After all, they'll have to support you. Babies cost a lot of money.'

'Think what they'll save in university fees. Anyway, they're generally all right about money. Francesca had all Grandfather's when he died last year and she can't have gone through it yet, though she's trying hard. I'm not going to start worrying about money. It's so . . . so demeaning.'

Is that what it was? Worrying about money? So . . . demeaning. What a pity my mother and I hadn't understood that. It could have changed our lives.

'Did Selena know you were pregnant?'

There was another long silence, so long that I thought she intended to ignore the question. I started up the car and drove away.

'I didn't tell her. I didn't want to worry her, especially as

156

I'd already decided on an abortion. But I'm sure she knew. She always knew what I was up to. It might even have been the thing that tipped her over the edge.'

'I don't think so,' I said, simply to comfort her. And before she could question this, added inconsequentially, 'I had an abortion once and regretted it bitterly.'

I found myself telling her how surprised and excited I'd been at finding myself pregnant a few years ago, and how Paul's complete lack of enthusiasm had made me change my mind.

'That's terrible,' she said. 'I hope he regretted it too.'

'I never told him about it. Not in so many words. Anyway, I was almost forty and my nerve failed me. I suppose the blame was all mine.'

Another long silence, the miles speeding, or at least trundling by.

'What do you get out of living with Paul? I've often wondered. I mean, he's quite a boring person, isn't he? I like him because he's very dependable, but I'd have thought you'd want more than that.'

I wasn't prepared to answer her question, so countered with one of my own. 'You like your father. Do you like your mother, too?'

'No, but she's more interesting and more challenging. When we were children we always liked him, but admired her. Wanted to be like her. We were very spoilt, I know that. And desperate for more and more attention. We were rich and spoilt.'

'I wouldn't argue with that.'

'And we despised anything we considered ordinary. We liked ignoring people, but we couldn't ignore Francesca.'

'You admired Francesca and tried to out-do her.'

'Something like that, I suppose. And Selena has, in a way. She not only despised ordinary middle-class life, as Francesca did, but despised life as a whole. Life with a capital L. To the extent of finishing it.'

157

'Oh, I think that's going too far. You're trying to elevate her suicide into something grand and meaningful. I think it was much more likely to be a momentary mood of despair – too much work, too little attention, no one to love, you being in trouble with the police – at a time when Francesca's sleeping tablets happened to be on hand.'

Even as I spoke I realised that Annabel might find my words hurtful or even offensive. 'Of course, I may be totally wrong,' I added hurriedly. 'After all, you knew her much better than I did.'

'I hope it wasn't as haphazard as that,' she said, in a small, child-like voice, which I hardly recognised. 'But life is pretty haphazard isn't it, so perhaps death is, too.'

By this time the moon had risen and I drew into a lay-by again, turned off the engine and got out of the car. At first, the silence seemed total and overwhelming. Soon, though, I could hear the river in the distance and the bleating of an occasional sheep. 'Have we arrived?' Annabel asked.

'Look at the mountains,' I said, pointing at some vague charcoal-coloured shapes in the distance. 'That's Cader Idris on the right, and Pumlymon on this side. What do you think? Are you glad you came?' I felt light-headed and expected a scathing reply. It would mean nothing to her. To me it was beautiful because I knew it so well, knew the colours; the blues, violets and greys, in sun and rain. Especially in rain.

When I turned towards her, I realised that she was crying again. 'You can moan and howl here as much as you like,' I said. 'No one will hear you but the sheep and the foxes.'

She went on crying, but still silently. After a few moments I put an arm round her and she leaned on my shoulder. 'Say some poetry,' she said. 'Shout out some sad poetry.'

> 'Fear no more the heat o' the sun,
> Nor the furious winter's rages;
> Thou thy worldly task hast done,

158

Home art gone and ta'en thy wages:
Golden lads and girls all must,
As chimney-sweepers, come to dust.'

I was crying too, by this time; for my mother as well as for Selena. My voice cracked and shivered in the amphitheatre of the mountains. I tackled a few lines of *Lear*, some of Wordsworth's 'Prelude', Keats's 'Bright Star' and finished with a Welsh englyn on the death of a young girl.

It was a cathartic experience for me and, I think, for Annabel, too. Before we turned back to the car she took a deep breath and shouted out, 'Selena! Selena!' It was very moving. It was like the Last Post.

When we arrived home, we were too tired to do anything but go straight to bed.

I put Annabel in the tiny spare bedroom – with the curtain across the corner for a wardrobe – leaving her a tin of biscuits and a glass of milk in case she got hungry in the night. But before I'd got myself undressed, she was calling for me: Arthur had got in through the window and was drinking the milk. I'd forgotten him, but he hadn't forgotten me. He circled round my ankles, purring and sneezing with excitement until I went downstairs again to feed him.

The phone rang as I got to the living room. I guessed it would be Rhydian and it was. 'How did you know I was back?' I asked him.

'I ring every night at eleven-thirty. When can I see you?'

'It won't be easy, love. I've got my step-daughter with me, the twin sister of the girl who died. The funeral's going to be in Horeb – I don't know when. I've got to see the minister tomorrow.'

'I can call by, though, can't I? I am your cousin.'

'And my lover.' Oh God, I shouldn't have said that. I intended to be aloof, but hearing his voice confused me.

'Can I come over now?'

'Of course not.'

'Oh, please don't sound so tortured. I'm not trying to make things worse for you. I know our position isn't easy, but we mustn't give up. You don't want to give me up, do you?'

'No, but I may have to. But I'll never forget you, Rhydian.'

'I don't want any of that bloody stuff. That's just bullshit. I'm not into the marriage of true minds, all that rubbish.'

'Just sex?' I asked. Lovingly.

'That first and foremost, yes, and mixed up with everything else. Like our background, our inheritance, our beliefs.'

'I haven't got any beliefs.'

'Yes, you have, and they're the same as mine.'

He sounded so sure of himself, so determined. 'What are we going to do, Rhydian?'

'As much as we can, for as long as we can.'

'That doesn't sound very safe. But it does sound exciting.'

'And there's one other thing too. I love you, Katie. I love you.'

# Chapter Sixteen

I slept well that night, with no visitations from Annabel. I got up early, but decided to let her sleep on. I phoned Paul but he wasn't in; he had either gone out or had stayed the night with Francesca. If he had stayed with her, I should be feeling pleased because it simplified my course of action. But of course feelings aren't logical; if I was going to be thrown over for Francesca, I wanted to be consulted about it, wanted to be apologised to, grovelled to, made much of. At times it was convenient to forget that I'd already done what I thought Paul might be doing, and without as much excuse as he had.

There was an unopened business letter lying on the dresser. I must have picked it up last night and been too tired to bother with it. I had a moment's unease as I slit open the envelope.

It was from Mr Gomer Richards, a solicitor in town, sending me his condolences on my mother's death and a copy of her Last Will and Testament, which he had drawn up for her a little over a week before her recent untimely death.

My unease grew, formed a small tight lump in my chest. Had she had some bad news about her health? I couldn't imagine why else she'd felt the need to make a will. I could hardly bring myself to open it.

Being of sound mind, etc, etc, she, Miriam Rivers, bequeathed to her only daughter, Katherine Jane Rivers, her gold wedding ring, her opal and pearl brooch, her silver pendant and whatever she should desire of the contents of her house, Maendy, Glanrhyd, Ceredigion. The said house and the remainder of the furniture and contents she bequeathed to George Rhys Williams of Two Brook Cottages, Glanrhyd, Ceredigion, to use and enjoy during his lifetime, after which it would revert to her afore-mentioned daughter, Katherine Jane Rivers.

I had to read it three times before the truth sunk in. This house wasn't mine. This house where I'd been born, which I'd always considered home, now belonged to someone else. I probably had no right to be sitting at this table, looking out at this tree and this sky. This view, this silence, this damp smell which we'd never succeeded in eradicating, the garden, the smooth white stones from Cwmllys outside the back door, the stunted bushes, the grass, the rabbits, the air even, these things were no longer mine. And I'd planned to live here for at least a part of every year. Arthur jumped up onto my knee and I cried into the soft fur at the back of his neck, cried for things I'd only recently realised I needed, things I'd always taken for granted, as much mine as my own flesh.

'What's wrong with you?'

I looked up at a stern-faced Annabel. 'What the hell's wrong with you?' she repeated. Anxious for sympathy and discussion, I was suddenly pleased she was with me.

However she didn't wait for my explanation, but rushed to the bathroom where I could hear her being sick. I dislodged Arthur and got up to make her a cup of tea. In George Williams's kitchen. When would he be expecting to move in? I reminded myself that he was a kind, respectable man who'd been faithfully in love with my mother for almost half a century. And he lived, I'd been told, with his sister and her husband and their fifty-year-old unmarried son in the small council house they'd taken over from their parents. Wasn't it fitting and proper that she should bequeath this cottage to him rather than to me, part-owner of a semi-detached Edwardian villa, four bedrooms, two bathrooms, in a fairly desirable and increasingly trendy part of Camberwell?

Lorna came to the door. 'I don't want any more letters,' I told her.

'What's the matter now?'

'How long can you stay?'

I settled down with the teapot and the tin of digestive biscuits and gave her the full details of my mother's will. She flung her chest out, about, I think, to make an indignant protest, when Annabel joined us. 'I'll just have water and lemon,' she said.

'This is my step-daughter, Annabel. We're here to arrange her twin sister's funeral.'

'Her twin sister's funeral?' Lorna put down the tea I'd poured her and blew her nose. 'You poor little thing,' she said then, looking at Annabel. 'God love her,' she said, looking at me. And then she blew her nose again, wiped her eyes very thoroughly and said nothing more.

And of course, I said nothing more. Under the circumstances, how could I possibly carry on bemoaning the loss of a house?

'Do you feel well enough to come with me to see the minister?' I asked Annabel when Lorna had left.

'Give me half an hour, my stomach's still churning. Hey, what's this on the table? What's all this about?'

'You can read it if you like,' I said, since she was already studying it and looking very perplexed.

'Who is this George Rhys Williams?'

'The man my mother was going to marry. I didn't know of his existence until last week.'

'And she's left him this house? That's a bloody shame. I was planning on staying here . . . What's so amusing?'

'What would you find to do here, Annabel? You'd have no sort of a life here.'

'What sort of a life would I have anywhere? Would I be

163

better off with Francesca? With you and Paul? Or with Laurie, who doesn't want me? I'm twenty-one, I've been a child all my life so far and now I've got to grow up and be a mother all at once. What should I do? And please don't try to advise me because I've got to try and work it out for myself.'

We sat in silence for a few minutes, Annabel sipping her cup of hot water while I re-read the solicitor's letter and my mother's will.

'Do you fancy a day at the sea?' I asked. 'A walk on the cliffs and a picnic? We could call on the minister on the way back.'

'Selena and I were brought up by the sea,' Annabel said as we walked along the sand and pebbles at Cwmllys. 'The waves crashing on the rocks was probably one of the first sounds we heard.'

'Was that in Crete?'

'Crete,' she said in a child's voice. 'In Crete our entire life was a poem.'

I looked up at her, hoping she was being at least slightly ironic, but she was deeply serious; tears in her eyes, her lips quivering. My impulse was to hug her, but I knew it wasn't the response she wanted. For a moment or two I simply stared out to sea, saying nothing. Then an old excitement took over. 'Look, look, there's a dolphin! Over there.' Can you see it? Or it may just be a seal. No, it's a dolphin! Definitely!'

She ignored me, wasn't even prepared to locate the creature, let alone enthuse about it. 'Francesca and Paul had this cabin right at the edge of the sea. Did you ever go there? Did Paul ever take you there?'

'No, he didn't.'

'He probably didn't think of it. Or perhaps it would have made him think of past times. Why did you two never get married?'

'Perhaps he was still in love with Francesca.'

164

'Do you think it was that? Do you really? Oh, I'm sorry. I shouldn't have brought it up.'

'It's all right. It's all water under the bridge now.'

'What does that mean? All water under the bridge?'

'It's all in the past.'

'It's not, it's not. It's here all around us. We're all bound together for ever. With Selena. Please don't say it's all in the past. Please don't leave us. I couldn't bear it.'

'Annabel, you're so emotional at the moment that you're talking nonsense. I'm not a part of your life. Please don't get worked up about me. Look, we'll walk up the cliff path to the top and from there, we'll see all the coastline of West Wales and the mountains of three counties and all the lovely sky.'

'That's not going to do anything for me.'

'It might.'

After about fifteen minutes, she looked at me pitifully. 'How far do we have to walk? It's so cold up here.'

The weather was unusually mild, a Michaelmas summer, not a cloud in the sky.

'We'll turn back.'

'And now the wind is facing us.'

'Have my jacket.'

She let me zip her into my shabby old anorak. Her face was white and clenched. Why hadn't I realised how unfit she was? We still had almost a mile to walk along the cliff path before getting back to the beach and the car.

I almost stumbled into the man sitting reading in a grassy hollow at the edge of the path. I'd started to apologise before realising that it was the minister, Lewis Owen, who was scrambling to his feet. 'This is my step-daughter, Mr Owen. She's not feeling too well so I'm rushing her back to the car.'

'This is a lovely sheltered spot, Miss Rivers. I think you should both sit here for a moment or two.' He must have noticed how pale she was.

Annabel sank down onto the patch of flattened grass he was offering us, while he and I stood looking down at her. 'Annabel, this is the minister of Horeb, the Reverend Lewis Owen.'

'Why don't I go and get you both some tea from the kiosk?'

'The kiosk has been closed since the end of August,' I said. 'But I've got some tea and sandwiches in the back of my car, if you'd be kind enough to fetch them.'

I handed him my keys and he went hurrying off, Annabel and I watching the flaming red head until it disappeared from sight.

'Do you feel any better?' I asked her.

'He looks like a pre-Raphaelite angel, doesn't he,' was all she said. 'Who did you say he was?'

'Very good sandwiches, Miss Rivers. Won't you try one, Annabel?'

'No thank you, Lewis.' They were already on Christian-name terms.

'I'm so pleased I came here today. I haven't had a picnic for years.'

It wasn't much of a picnic. I'd only had time to pack a flask of tea and some raspberry jam sandwiches which had become rather limp.

'We were going to call on you on our way back through the village, weren't we, Kate?'

'That's right,' I said, aware again of what we had to discuss.

But it was difficult to contemplate the funeral; Annabel and the minister were two youngsters, newly acquainted, and eyeing each other rather more than was strictly necessary. I wanted them to savour these few moments, which might, in the future, leave a little blurred stirring of pleasure in both their minds. Annabel had stopped shivering and seemed to be looking around her, for the first time taking in the sea, certainly not a Mediterranean aquamarine, but a creditable Cardigan Bay slate-blue for all that, with pure white frillings where it broke onto the pebbly beach with the splash and suck you hear in your dreams, the seagulls, of course, wheeling round with their desolate cries, the gorse fringing the cliff path, the flowers like bits of torn paper stuck on haphazardly, and the strong sea-shore smell which the first settlers must have inhaled when they decided to stay. 'It's nice here,' she said. 'Couldn't we buy a house down here?'

'There's no houses till you get to the village, half a mile up the hill,' Lewis Owen said. 'People weren't daft enough to build down here in the teeth of the wind. In the old days views weren't as important as shelter. In any case, the fishermen who lived in those houses, saw more than enough of the sea. My father was a fisherman. Down the coast in New Quay. Ever been there?'

'No, we always went to Crete. My grandfather had a house in Crete. My sister and I loved it there.'

'I've only been abroad once and that was a school trip to Brittany. Quite pretty countryside. Big ugly churches, though, and the little towns not a patch on New Quay.'

I tried to join in the conversation, but could only think of the moment when I'd have to break in and mention the funeral. We couldn't delay it any longer, Paul would be phoning later in the evening wanting all the details; there were many arrangements to be made.

Annabel seemed to sense my unease. 'Have you heard about my sister?' she asked Lewis Owen in a very gentle voice, leaning over towards him and putting her hand on his arm. I could hardly believe this was the girl who loved to shock and bewilder everyone.

'Annabel's twin sister, Selena . . .' I said. And failed to go on.

Lewis stiffened, realising that the pleasure of the afternoon was over. 'No,' he said, as though he, too, couldn't bear more.

167

'She killed herself. And we . . . and I . . .'

'Annabel and her parents would like her to be buried at Glanrhyd if you think that would be possible.'

'I don't know,' he said. 'I don't know.'

There was silence for a moment or two, then Annabel gave a little half-choked sob.

Lewis Owen got to his feet and looked out towards the sea. 'I'm not sure I could do it. You see, I've only had to perform three burial services so far. And they've all been for old people. But I know the Reverend Henry Parry would take over for me. He's a retired minister who lives just outside the village, a thorn in my flesh, actually, with his kindly advice about this and that and everything else. But very experienced and highly respected.'

'I want you to do it,' Annabel said. 'There won't be anyone there except me and Kate and my parents. I don't want anyone experienced and respected. And I don't want anyone old. I hate old people. I just want you to say those words about ashes to ashes and be very sad.'

Lewis Owen turned to face her again. 'I think it's only right to tell you that I'm not even convinced about "the certain resurrection".'

'Not Faith, but at least Hope,' I said, quoting Betjeman.

'That's all a lot of balls,' Annabel said. 'Just say she was lovely and that we'll never forget her and that we'll love her for ever. And I want you and no one else. Certainly not that horrid old man with his advice.'

Another long silence. 'All right,' Lewis said at last. 'Anytime this next week except Tuesday. Give me a bell when you decide and I'll see to everything. I have to go now. A hospital visit this evening.'

'Can we give you a lift?' I asked him.

'No thanks, I've got my bike.' He had become extremely downcast as though he was personally implicated in our tragedy.

'I love this place,' Annabel said after we'd watched him walking down the path and across the beach.

'You mentioned your parents and you and me, but you didn't say a word about Laurie.'

'Oh, Selena never cared for Laurie. Anyway, he'll be far too busy to come. He's got such a lot of such very important work. No, I shan't be seeing Laurie any more.'

'Annabel, try to remember that you're a pregnant lady and that you're not to go lusting after respectable ministers of religion.'

'Can we go back now? Can we have sausage and chips later on?'

Poor Lewis Owen, I said to myself as we walked back to the car. He doesn't stand a chance against this one.

When we arrived home, we found Rhydian leaning against the wall waiting for us. For a moment before he turned, I saw his profile; high forehead and thin, fine nose, and it was like seeing someone who was a stranger and yet very close and familiar – a new lover whom I'd known for ever. I'm sure he felt the same; his smile was both very shy and very intimate.

I introduced him to Annabel and he squeezed her hands. 'I've got a little niece, just twenty-one,' he said, 'so I know how your family must be feeling.'

'We're all numb with shock,' I said, since Annabel didn't seem able to say anything. 'But of course it's Annabel who's suffering most.'

'What's all this about your mother's will?' he asked me, after a few moments' silence. 'Lorna had a word with Edwina about it, asking her to contact us. She felt you needed someone in your corner, I think. So here I am.'

'Lovely to see you, anyway. Come in.'

'Grace and I feel that your mother made that will thinking she'd be married to this George Williams long before she passed away.'

169

'I suppose so. It was only made in the week before she died.'

'So it could be contested.'

'But I don't think I'd want to contest it.'

'No, I didn't think you would.'

Rhydian and I sat one on each side of the table looking at each other. 'I shall miss being down here, though,' I said. 'I intended to stay for a month or two.'

'Yes, I was hoping you might.'


'You two are in love, aren't you?' Annabel asked me, as soon as he'd left.

'I tried to tell you about it,' I said.

'Are you going to live with him?'

'No. He's married with children.'

'Are you going to tell Paul about him?'

'Do you think I should?'

'How should I know? How should I know anything?'

She suddenly hurled herself onto the sofa and was sobbing again, sobbing so uncontrollably that I could hardly make out what she was saying. 'I don't want you to leave us. I don't want you to leave us.'

Annabel's world had turned upside down. For ten years, I'd had to get used to being the despised intruder in her life; now she didn't seem prepared to live without me. Laurie Bridgewater was shortly to be dispensed with and the baby she'd planned to get rid of was to take Selena's place. I tried to think of something comforting and wise to say, but failed to come up with anything. My world was pretty unsteady too.

170

# Chapter Seventeen

When Paul phoned that evening I was able to tell him that we'd spoken to the minister and that Annabel and I had arranged the funeral for two o'clock on Friday afternoon, which would give him and Francesca plenty of time to drive down from London.

'You're so good to me,' he said in such a humble voice that I knew there was more to come. 'I don't deserve you, Kate. You're having to cope with Annabel immediately after losing your mother, and Annabel's not your responsibility, but mine. And I know how difficult she can be. How is she, darling? Did she like the minister?'

'She loved him.'

'Is Laurie with you?'

'No, he phoned earlier, but Annabel put him off.'

'Why was that? I thought they seemed very close?'

'That was yesterday.'

'Francesca will be so disappointed. She really took to Laurie. I wonder what happened?'

'I'll let you talk to her. I think she has some other news for you, too.'

'Don't go yet, I need to talk to you . . . I don't know how to tell you this, Kate, but I have to . . . You know how badly shocked Francesca was – well, last night when we got to her home, she had a terrible fit of near-hysteria and I

171

simply couldn't leave her. I stayed with her . . . Do you understand what I'm trying to say?'

'Not really. Do you mean you had to stay with her until the doctor came to sedate her?'

'Kate, you know what I mean. And I'm terribly sorry. I didn't mean it to happen and I feel wretched about letting you down. Please say something. Please say you understand. You know how tragic the circumstances are. We've lost a child, Kate. It's not altogether surprising that we need to cling together, is it?'

My anger, or fit of pique, left me. 'No, it's not surprising. In fact, Annabel and I talked about the possibility of you and Francesca getting back together. And I've always known how much she's meant to you.'

'But you've always meant a great deal to me, too, Kate. I've always loved you, you know that. I still do love you. And admire you. And respect you. It's just that . . .'

'Yes, I know. I know all that . . . But I don't think there's much point in prolonging this talk now, do you? We'll still be friends, I'm confident of that. But let's get the funeral over before we start on any other emotional matters. Would you like a word with Annabel?'

'Not now. Tell her I'll ring again tomorrow. Oh, you don't know how upset I am, Kate.'


What was the matter with me? As soon as I put the phone down I was full of pity for Paul. Though I knew I should have been feeling hurt and aggrieved at the way he'd treated me – it was obvious I'd been nothing but a stop-gap for years – I knew how guilty he was feeling, and more than that, realised he was going to be hurt again. He was letting himself believe that Francesca had turned to him at last out of some hidden but abiding love for him, but I felt sure it was only from a very temporary need. I was ready to blame Francesca, but couldn't find it in me to feel much anger towards Paul. He was behaving foolishly, but at least he had the best possible excuse for it: he'd always loved Francesca. I'd been as foolish as he had, trying to believe it was over.

'You were right about your parents,' I told Annabel when she came in from the garden. 'They are getting back together. It was Paul on the phone.'

'Oh Kate, I hope you don't mind too much. Of course it was what Selena and I planned for and dreamed about for years, but now I feel sorry for both of them. Francesca's at a desperately low ebb, but she'll bounce back before too long, and then Paul's going to suffer all over again.'

Was Annabel unnaturally mature, or was I unnaturally naïve? 'They may live happily ever after,' I said. 'Or at least, learn to tolerate each other.'

'We both know that's not at all likely. Listen, I'm frightfully hungry. Can we go out for a curry?'

'A curry?' I tried to hide my amazement. Where did she think we were? 'Well, I suppose there could be an Indian restaurant in Abernon, six or seven miles away. There are a couple of fish and chip shops there anyway and two or three hotels. Yes, let's go out. By all means. There could be a nightclub and a sex shop there now, for all I know.'

'Do you think Lewis would like to come with us?'

I tried to appear equally nonchalant about this suggestion. After all, he wasn't a Roman Catholic priest who'd taken a vow of chastity. I tried to dismiss visions of the Reverend William Pierce, large and stern, from my mind. 'He said he had a hospital visit. But he might be back home now. We could ring him, I suppose.'

I fetched the telephone book from the cupboard by the fireplace and passed it to her.

My mother's handbag was in the same cupboard. I held it close for a second or two but found I couldn't open it. I still wasn't ready for the well-remembered smell of spilt powder, eau de cologne and peppermints, or to come across her worn black purse stuffed full of special-offer coupons, old receipts and out-of-date guarantees, and her precious reading glasses in the tooled leather case Paul had once brought her from Florence. He'd always been fond of my mother. And she of him. Though I don't think she'd be ready to forgive him for dumping me. I sighed, put the handbag back in its place and closed the cupboard. Annabel was already on the phone. Life went hurtling on.

'I said we'd pick him up in five minutes. I think Selena would be quite interested in Lewis, don't you? He'd probably remind her of that picture of the young Rossetti. Shall I leave my hair as it is, or put it up?'

I looked over at her, giving her my fullest attention. 'Put it up,' I said. I felt we were playing some complicated game of which neither of us knew the rules.

I found myself seeing Lewis Owen in a different way, not as a gauche youth trying to be wise beyond his years, but simply as one of Annabel's contemporaries whom she'd fallen for. I failed to see him as pre-Raphaelite angel, but could see that the pale, almost translucent skin, sea-green eyes and bright red hair made a startling statement. And Annabel approved of startling statements, I was aware of that.

How experienced was this boy? When I was at university, theological students were regarded as dangerously fast, 'getting it in while they could,' being the widely-held explanation. Experienced or not, I hoped he wouldn't be alarmed by Annabel's apparent sophistication which was only, I realised by this time, a cover for a pathetic lack of self-confidence. I wished I could tell him how hurt and vulnerable she was.

Perhaps he understood, because he listened to every outrageous thing she said, showing neither surprise nor shock.

'I was hoping to live in Kate's cottage for the next year or so,' she told him while we were still munching poppadums, waiting for our meal to be cooked. 'You see, I'm two months' pregnant and I don't want to marry the father, and he certainly doesn't want to marry me – in fact, he and I are no longer together, so I thought living up there would give me a chance to settle down and grow up.'

'It would have been far too isolated,' I said.

'And settling down and growing up sounds much too extreme,' Lewis added. 'It would be punishing yourself.'

'Anyway, Kate's mum left it to a certain George Rhys Williams, so it's not an option. And Kate doesn't feel like contesting the will, though I think she should. What do you think, Lewis?'

'No, I don't think she should. Mrs Rivers and George Williams were childhood sweethearts. They intended to get married.'

'And in any case, it reverts to me after George's death.'

'I think you're a very old-fashioned, romantic boy, Lewis,' Annabel said. 'Do you have a childhood sweet-heart?'

'No. I'm fancy-free and open to offers.'

Luckily, our food arrived before Annabel had a chance to follow that up and for a while they both seemed content to concentrate on eating to the exclusion of everything else. 'Try this.' 'Oh, try this.' 'This is really good and hot, this is.' 'Fantastic.'

I felt middle-aged in their company, eating moderately, being less than moderately impressed by the food, and soon thinking again of my personal problems: my life after Paul, how different it would be, the initial loneliness, the challenge of building a new life, the part Rhydian might be able to play in it. Rhydian. Would he ring me later tonight?

It suddenly came to me that Annabel might end up living with me: Annabel and her baby. And strangely enough, the thought didn't appal me, but slipped smoothly and pain-lessly into my consciousness. It would make some sort of sense of the years I'd spent with her father; the baby might compensate, in some measure, for the baby I hadn't had the courage to have. Tomorrow I'd phone my agent to see if there was anything going for me. I needed work. I had some money saved, but not enough for three people.

'I had decided to have an abortion,' Annabel was telling Lewis. 'As a matter of fact it was arranged for tomorrow morning. But when Selena died, it changed everything. Can you understand that?'

'Absolutely. You were perfectly right. Don't you think so, Miss Rivers?'

'Oh, don't call her Miss Rivers. It sounds so affected.'

'Annabel bullies everyone,' I said. 'You'll have to get used to it.' I stopped short as I realised that I was implying some sort of relationship developing between them. 'I mean, *people* have to get used to it. But they're usually fairly happy about it.'

'What are you talking about, Kate? I'm not bullying anyone. I'm simply letting Lewis know that he doesn't have to be so formal with us. We're not his parishioners, after all, and this isn't a Jane Austen novel.'

'I've never had time to read much Jane Austen,' Lewis said. And was then treated to a diatribe from Annabel on what an overrated and rotten writer she was, how *Emma* was the most boring book she'd ever read, apart, possibly, from *Sense and Sensibility* and *Pride and Prejudice*.

I looked up, expecting to see Lewis smiling wryly, but no, he was clearly ready to be impressed with everything she said.

We ordered ice creams, two large and one small, and three coffees.

The young Asian waiter who brought them, pushed a piece of paper at me. 'Sign please,' he said and I took a pen from my bag and wrote my name, adding the date and my best wishes.

'Whatever are you doing, Kate? Haven't you got your cheque-book? Good Lord, was he asking for your autograph? Whatever next.' She grimaced at Lewis, afterwards looking rather pleased.

176

'Do people often recognise you?' Lewis Owen asked. 'You've got a very exciting job, haven't you?'

'Completely inessential, though. Essentially inessential.'

'Nonsense. You contribute to people's well-being. Which is what I try to do, too. To a lesser degree, of course.'

Did I contribute to people's well-being? Was that what I did? I smiled into my coffee, sat back and let the rest of their conversation wash over me.

They were still talking in the car as I drove home, Annabel now telling him how intelligent and wise and hard-working Selena had been, while she'd been an attention-grabbing delinquent, as different from her as possible. Having heard all this before, I could only sigh with some impatience, but Lewis Owen took both her hands and said, 'From now on, you have to be Annabel *and* Selena. That way, you'll keep her alive for everyone.'

'There's no way I could manage that,' Annabel said, her voice anguished.

We'd reached the Manse by this time. I stopped the car to let him out. 'You'll manage it,' he said, leaning over to kiss her. He got out of the car and waved to us as we pulled away.

I was again aware of some impressive streak in his character. Perhaps it was grace.

Early next morning while I was still in my dressing-gown – and would have been still in bed if it hadn't been for Arthur's loud and persistent demands for food – someone came to the front door, ringing the bell several times.

It was Mrs Tudor Davies, Lorna's mother-in-law. 'Can't stop,' she said, pushing past me into the house, 'I'm on my way to work. Only I've just heard about your mother's will and I'm tamping mad. I'm going to have a word with George Williams, I can tell you.' Her large chest, encased in tight pink overall, rose and fell.

I took a deep breath. She was terrifying even when she was on your side. 'It's good of you to be so concerned, but

177

I'm glad you contacted me before doing anything. The thing is, I like George Williams and I'm pleased to think he'll have this house in his old age. Lorna was telling me that he's always lived with his sister and her family and it can't have been easy for him.'

'Easy? Not easy at all. His sister is a terrible woman, everybody dislikes her. She's got a tongue like a whiplash.'

'And it does revert to me after his death. And, you know, I couldn't live here full-time and that doesn't do a house any good, does it? I think George Williams will take good care of it and of Arthur, too.'

I thought she'd consider me weak and foolish, but she looked at me with something close to approval. 'If that's what you want,' she said, 'I'll say no more about it.' She nodded her head several times, then looked over at me again. 'The other thing I wanted to mention was the organ fund. I suppose you know that Horeb is celebrating its bicentenary next year and we're aiming to replace the organ. Now I know Lewis Owen is too much of a milksop to mention it to you as you're not a member, but I thought you might like to make a contribution in memory of your dear mother.'

'I would. I certainly would. Thank you for bringing it to my attention.'

'And I hear you've had another tragedy in the family and that there's to be another funeral at Horeb.'

'That's right. My young step-daughter, Selena. Twenty-one years old.'

'Terrible. Terrible. Is there anything I can do in the way of a small private repast, family only? No charge. Cost of food only.'

'That's very kind of you, but I feel her parents and her sister might be more at ease back here. There'll only be the four of us, you see, so it might be less of a strain. But I'll certainly mention the organ fund. Yes, I think I can safely say that the new organ is home and dry.'

A small relaxation of the mouth, not quite a smile. 'I'll go

178

then. I wanted to know what you felt about the will, because if you were contesting, I'd be fighting for you, you can be sure of that.'

'Thank you, Mrs Davies.'

She nodded at me, but with her hand on the doorknob, turned and said, 'Oh no, Maggie I am, to friends.'

I felt as though I'd done well in some important audition.

Rhydian hadn't phoned the previous night as he'd promised. I'd had to fight hard against the desire to phone him as I waited and waited for his call. Even when I gave up and went to bed, I still couldn't sleep, realising how much hearing his voice meant to me. Did this foreshadow my life from now on? Over the years, I'd had many friends and colleagues with married lovers; they all had a certain fragility, a wavering look whenever a telephone rang, at times almost a caged expression. Was this to be my future?

In the middle of my self-examination, I heard his car drawing up, saw him passing the window, heard his tap on the door. 'I couldn't ring last night,' he said.

'It doesn't matter. You're here now.' I was in his arms and nothing else counted. Until the next time.

'Annabel's upstairs and the postwoman will be here soon and she mustn't see your car. We must be careful. You know that.'

'I know.' Oh yes, he knew how careful we had to be. 'Only I need to touch you. Here.' His eyes were wide and pleading as he put his hand inside my dressing gown, stroked my breast very lightly, ran the flat of his hand down my belly. But one touch led to another and the hands which were so gentle became urgent and probing and my longing for him was so intense there was nothing else in the world, nothing else mattered, nothing else existed. He knelt before me, his tongue like a flame inside me; I wanted to be consumed by him, broken in two, destroyed. I'd never known such long-drawn-out climbing or such a heavenly,

heavenly fall. I knelt on the floor with him, my arms around him, whispering love words in his ear, adoring him.

'Go and put a dress on. I'll drive you to a place I know where I can lie on top of you. Hurry.' His eyes were no longer gentle, but dark and demanding.

When I went upstairs I could hear Annabel getting up. 'I'm going out for half an hour. I'll be back to make breakfast.'

'Can I come with you?'

I clattered downstairs, pretending not to hear.

# Chapter Eighteen

The next day, I phoned Gomer Richards, my mother's solicitor. He sounded very worried and contrite when I gave my name, as though he thought I might be holding him responsible for the terms of her will. To put him at his ease, I had to assure him that it was exactly what I'd expected.

'Then that's very satisfactory,' he said and I could almost see him rubbing his hands together. I've never had much to do with solicitors. I was imagining a Dickens character, elderly, with black suit and wing collar, when he suddenly said that he remembered me from school: I'd been a prefect when he was in the first form, he still felt a bit nervous of me.

And then I remembered him. Of course. Gomer, a little plump boy with an engaging smile who was always late getting into lines.

'I'm ringing to ask about the time-scale,' I said. 'How long am I allowed to stay here before I hand it over to Mr Williams?'

'You've got any amount of time. As much as you want. No hurry at all. You see, probate has still to be granted. Your mother's executor has to apply for probate. And I'm her executor, as a matter of fact, so I could very well delay things for a week or two. And after that it could be a further six to eight weeks before it comes through. Can I take you out to lunch today? Take you through it? There's a new restaurant opened last week in Castell Dyffryn. Very good reports.'

'I'd really like that, Gomer, but I've got too much on this week.'

'Well, don't hesitate to get in touch. That's what I'm here for.'

How strange life was. Little Gomer Richards inviting me out to lunch. I could remember his little fat knees in his P.E. kit.

Annabel had had another bad night, had woken me two or three times. In her dreams, Selena had been calling her. What if she *had* called her after taking the sleeping tablets and she'd been out with Laurie? What if she'd regretted taking them? What if she, Annabel, had been around and able to contact 999? Would they have been in time to pump out her stomach? Would they have been able to save her? What if she'd only meant to make a bid for attention? What if she hadn't meant to die? The questions went on and on. And then started again. 'Please help me,' she kept saying, her eyes red and swollen.

I was desperately sorry for her, but couldn't help. She was far too intelligent to be fobbed off with comforting lies. All I could do was stay awake with her, trying to share her suffering. She'd slept at last and I hoped she'd wake in a different frame of mind.

When the phone went I thought it would be Rhydian, but it was Laurie Bridgewater. I explained that I couldn't call Annabel because of the troubled night she'd had, but all he wanted was directions to the cottage. He was on his way down, but couldn't find Glanrhyd on the map.

I warned him that Annabel, at the moment, didn't want to see him, but he said he was aware of that. So I told him how to find the house and asked him to pick up some coffee in the village shop as he came past.

On the whole I was glad he was coming. If Annabel was

182

mad at him, and I felt she would be, it would at least rouse her from the hopeless despair of the previous night. I took her a cup of tea and told her he was on his way.

She sprang out of bed shouting at me. 'But I *told* you I didn't want to see him. Why can't you protect me from people who're harassing me?' Her whole body had stiffened. 'I'm not going to stay here. You must let me have the car and I'll drive to the sea. I'm not going to stay here to be bullied by Laurie Bridgewater.'

'What is it, Annabel? Why are you frightened of him? If you don't want anything more to do with him, you should surely tell him that. Have it out with him.'

'Stop trying to understand me. How can you understand me when I don't understand myself? I don't want to see him. That's all I've got to say. And I don't want anything else to do with him ever. It's over. That phase of my life is over.'

I was still standing in the little bedroom, patiently waiting for her to calm down, while she was throwing on her clothes and rushing downstairs. By the time I'd got down she'd finished in the bathroom and was demanding the car keys. 'I have to go, Kate. Just believe me. I need to be on my own. Laurie and I are finished. *Finished*. But I'm not going to get involved in any fuckin' arguments till after the funeral. Can't you understand that? Please get rid of him. That's all I ask.'

'He phoned from Crossgates, Annabel – that place where the sheep were on the road. He won't be here for at least an hour. Have some toast and coffee before you go. Take a flask of tea with you.'

She glowered at me, snatching up the keys from the table.

'At least take my anorak. You know how cold you were yesterday. OK, take my new jacket. It's cashmere.'

With the air of a martyr, she took my new reefer jacket, and strode out to the car. She looked very small and frail. I stood at the window waving to her as she drove away.

\*

'She's gone out, I'm afraid. I couldn't stop her. No, I've no idea where she was going. And I honestly don't think you should try to look for her. She's in a very disturbed state. I don't think you quite understand what she's going through at the moment.'

'Of course I do. And she's being over-dramatic as usual.'

Laurie Bridgewater stood – uninvited – in my mother's little living room, six foot tall and glowing with health and vitality.

'You do? Who have you lost? What do you know about it? What do you know about losing someone who developed with you from the same egg? Who swam about with you in the womb? Who suffered the trauma of birth with you? Who shared the same cot and the same pram and the same bath with you? Who murmured and gurgled and kicked with you before you could talk? Who—'

'I get the picture. You needn't take me step by step through their entire lives.'

'Why not?' There was something about the way he was standing that suddenly infuriated me; he was altogether too upper-class, too smug and self-satisfied. 'All right, I won't. Just as long as you don't dare tell me you understand what she's going through. Not one of us can have more than the vaguest idea of what she's going through. She and Selena were two neglected little girls – they were sent away to school when they were eight years old – who shared everything throughout the whole of their disturbed lives.'

Why had all my grief and anger been directed at Laurie Bridgewater? Francesca and Paul were the guilty parents who hadn't wished to understand how much their daughters had to depend on each other while they led their own selfish lives. And for my part, I hadn't tried to understand how isolated and lonely they were; I'd been taken in by the act they put on and had ignored them as much as possible. Even I was far more guilty than Laurie Bridgewater.

'Do you want me to go?' he asked.

I nodded my head. 'I have to protect Annabel. She doesn't want to see you. Ring again when the funeral's over.'

Laurie looked as though he couldn't believe he was being dismissed. It had obviously never happened to him before. I wanted to ask him about his life, his background, longed to know what had made him so self-assured, so certain of his welcome in the world. If he'd showed any signs of being hurt and miserable, I might have weakened towards him, but he only showed signs of surprise.

'Can't I even come to the funeral?'

'I'm afraid not.'

'Can you give me Francesca's telephone number?'

'I'm afraid not. I never ring her.'

By this time I was getting a buzz out of being bitchy. I'd never before found the secret of it. I'd once managed to be icily polite to a critic who only the previous week had rubbished a performance of mine.

'I hope you'll let Annabel know that I think she's behaving very childishly.'

As I followed him to the door, I suddenly remembered that he'd decided to break off his relationship with Annabel when she'd made the decision not to have the abortion. 'He didn't want to be held back,' she'd told me, as though that was perfectly understandable and forgiveable.

I wasn't prepared to be understanding or forgiving. 'You made a decision that your work was more important to you than Annabel,' I said, quietly and rather venomously. 'And I think you should stick to that. After what she's been through, she deserves a partner who's at least whole-hearted about her.'

He avoided my eyes as he got into his car, but drove away, his back straight, his face as composed as ever.

When he'd gone, I phoned Lewis Owen but got no reply, which I told myself might be a good sign. If Annabel had called for him and persuaded him to go with her to Cwmllys,

185

it would show that she wasn't as disturbed as she'd seemed when she left the house. I tried to relax.

When the phone rang at midday, I hoped it would be Annabel, but it was Paul. 'You sound worried,' he said. 'What's happened now?'

I told him about the visit from Laurie and how Annabel had refused to stay in to meet him.

'I'm sorry she's being so difficult,' he said. 'I hope Laurie wasn't offended. Francesca thinks he's exactly right for poor Annabel. Did she tell you that she was at school with his father's sisters? Is he still there? Could I have a word with him? I suppose I should try to pour oil on troubled waters.'

'No, he's already gone. I sent him away.'

There was a long silence. 'You're not yourself, Kate, are you? I'm so sorry. I'm so sorry about everything. I think I ought to come down today to be with Annabel. I can at least do that much to ease the pressure on you. And I'll telephone Laurie to ask him to drive Francesca down on Friday.'

'That wouldn't be a good idea, Paul. I've told Laurie that he's not to come to the funeral. You may come today, of course, but you'll have to make other arrangements for Francesca.'

Another long silence. 'I'll see you this evening,' he said then.

For the first time, I felt a spasm of dislike for Paul. He lacked understanding, couldn't make connections. Francesca was welcome to him.

And as I relinquished Paul, I had a moment's intense longing for Rhydian. The thought of his strong, farmer's body, his half-smile and his storm-dark eyes which could become so tender and pleading, left me weak with desire, my breath catching in my throat. But then again the knowledge, even more blinding than before, that I couldn't have him and had no right to disturb his life. I'd leave immediately after the funeral, coming back to sort out the things I needed only a few days before I had to hand over to George Williams.

It then occurred to me that I should contact George Williams to assure him that I bore him no ill-will, and since I didn't know exactly where he lived and didn't have his telephone number, I phoned Maggie Davies to ask her help. 'Don't call at his sister's whatever you do,' she said. 'She'd only be abusive and upset you. You leave it to me. George will be out the back. Yes, I can see him hoeing the onions. I'll have a word with him and tell him to meet you at the Gardener's in half an hour. You'll be able to have a nice quiet chat in the Lounge Bar with his sister none the wiser. I'd get him to come up there to see you only it'll do you good to have the walk. You were looking a bit peaky this morning and no wonder.'

I set out at once, knowing she was right and that the walk would invigorate me.

The valley was already showing signs of autumn, bronze and copper lighting up all the tired shades of green. The tender yellow-green of spring had long gone, but I could still visualise the young green of the beeches, with the red campions in the hedges and the swathes of bluebells in Gelly Woods. I suppose I was fifteen and quivering in my own spring, before I realised how beautiful this place was; before that I'd taken it as much for granted as night and day. I remember standing at this bend in the road reciting pages of *Tintern Abbey* very soulfully, 'And I have felt a presence that disturbs me with the joy of elevated thought,' and wishing, almost praying, that someone, preferably a handsome young man, would come along and hear me. 'I came across a young girl in this isolated valley in Wales and she seemed the very spirit of the place. I'll never forget her.'

No, it never happened. The nearest thing was when a workman in a dirty white van stopped and asked if I was all right. 'Only you looked as though you was in pain,' the driver, middle-aged and paunchy, said. I gave him my disdainful look. It was the time I was doing a Saturday-afternoon drama class and Miss Elvira Morgan – singing and

187

diction – who taught us, was a great advocate of flashing eyes and exaggerated turns of the head. Dear Miss Morgan, small and fluffy as a dormouse, had once had ambitions to be an opera singer, but had given it all up, probably not before time, to come home to nurse her widowed mother and had finished up with a weekday nursery class and seven teenage girls attending elocution classes, fifty pence a week, on a Saturday afternoon.

It was sunny but the wind from the sea was cold. I was pleased that I'd persuaded Annabel to take my jacket.

There was no one in the Lounge Bar when I arrived, but George Williams arrived a few minutes later. 'I'm so pleased you could come,' I said. 'What are you drinking?'

I got him the half he asked for and half a lager for me. 'How do you feel about Arthur?' I asked him as I got back to the table. 'Are you happy about looking after him or will I have to take him with me to London? Are you fond of cats?'

'She was very fond of Arthur.' His eyes were so heavy with misery, he couldn't seem to lift them.

'But what about you?'

'I like Arthur well enough. But I don't know that he likes me. He used to go out when I came to call.'

'He didn't like me at first, but he's come round. They make the best of things; cats.'

George took a long drink of beer, looking at me as he did so. 'It's not what she would want,' he said. 'I know it's legal, Mr Richards told me all that. But it's not what she would want.'

I couldn't help smiling. 'Of course it is. She made the will. She was going to marry you, George.'

'Aye. But it didn't happen. Oh aye, it may be legal, but it's not right. Nobody thinks it's right.'

'*I* think it's right. I had a bit of a shock at first, I admit that, but as soon as I'd had time to think about it, I knew it was right. I'm happy to think you'll be there looking after the house, instead of it being left empty most of the time.'

'No, no,' he mumbled sorrowfully to himself, 'it's not right, not right at all.'

'George, let's talk about Arthur. That's the only decision we've got to make. The decision about the house has already been made and I'm sure you'll be able to accept it, given time.'

'I'll walk up there every day to feed the cat, keep the house aired, tidy up the garden, trim the hedge, but I can't promise anything else.'

'All right, we'll leave it at that. The furniture will be there for you anyway, and the bedclothes, the dishes, the pots and pans, and in a little while you may feel like lighting a fire and making yourself at home. Because it *is* your home, George. Will you have the other half?'

'No, thank you.'

What a dear man he was. I nearly bent to kiss him as I rose to go, but stopped myself in time, realising that it would utterly confound him. I left him staring into his empty glass. I had the feeling that he'd never get over my mother's death.

It was two o'clock when I got home. There was still no sign of Annabel.

# Chapter Nineteen

My agent phoned in the afternoon with the offer of a job.

'And I do think you should take it,' she said. 'I'm not trying to tell you it's a marvellous part, it isn't, but you appear in all eight episodes so of course the money's good. It's a Catherine Cookson-type serial, very meaty, and it's scheduled for the Sunday night ITV slot, starting in February. You don't even have to audition, you've got the part if you want it. The director knows your work, he was the assistant on the Dickens serial you did in '95. Terence McGrath. Do you remember him? He's very keen you do it. The part? Well, I suppose it could be described as the rather downtrodden mother of the heroine.'

'That sounds exciting,' I said in a morose voice, 'and very like the part I'm playing in real life. When does it start rehearsing? The pre-filming in the middle of October? Oh, I suppose I'd better take it. It will probably be only a few miserable lines in every episode and possibly some quiet snivelling, but I could do with the money. And I presume no one's offering me Cleopatra.'

'Not at the moment,' she said carefully. Agents have to be very diplomatic. All their clients have huge, easily bruised egos.

'So I'll let you have the contract,' she continued, relief oozing from her voice because I was being sensible for once. 'Can you spell out your address for me?'

'Send it to Camberwell,' I said. 'I'll be back at the end of the week.'

As I put the phone down, I felt that at least something had been decided. I was going back to London, back to work.

For a time I felt quietly elated, everything seeming safe again. My mother's death had dislocated me and Selena's suicide had thrown me even further off balance, but now I had glimpsed order and sanity once more. In my Camberwell setting I was a different person, fairly rational most of the time, far less emotional. There was something about this house which made me less sure of myself, more connected to the person I used to be, connected to my mother and my little wild grandmother who was considered psychic and used to have 'turns'. When I stood in the garden here or walked down the lane to the village, I was a different person breathing a different air. This was 'home', yes, but I suddenly realised that 'home' isn't necessarily, or even usually, where one lives, but where one dreams of. And dreams can trip a person up. I felt safer in London which might be vast and terrifying, but which usually kept itself to itself.

I sat puzzling about my life; all that had happened to me since I'd left here for university almost a quarter of a century ago

As a student I was greedy for life, determined, I suppose, to make up for the deprivations of my childhood. At that time, sexual freedom was new and potent; I craved the heady excitement of sex, but in my early twenties, my affairs rarely lasted longer than a few months and none of them was particularly important. After this, two longer-lasting relationships with some real pain at the ending of each. Later still, life with Paul, a relationship based on companionship and trust, and because sex was relatively unimportant, one I considered altogether more mature.

And then Rhydian. A blaze of passion, a huge, throbbing excitement I'd never known before as well as far more depth

192

of feeling. How could it be otherwise, since he was part of the dark love which comes from the accident of 'home', part of my earliest memories, bound up with all my hopes and fears, as near and known as my own flesh. For all that he was a first-cousin-once-removed, the relationship seemed closer than incest. 'I *am* Heathcliff.' I remember breathing out those words in a student production of *Wuthering Heights*, revelling in the sound of them but without much idea of what they meant. They made perfect sense to me now. Before Rhydian, nothing counted. 'If ever any beauty I did see, Which I desired and got, 'twas but a dream of thee.' Someone has always said it before.

Student days. If only Rhydian and I had met at that time, when we were both free. If only he'd happened to be in Cardiff for a rugby match and had bumped into me in one of the crowded bars at the Angel. For a moment I indulged my fantasy, even recalling the midnight-blue fake-fur coat I wore in those days, a dress barely covering the crotch, spiky hair – strawberry-blonde with screaming pink highlights. We'd be already thigh to thigh because of the crush in the bar and I'd looked up and recognised him. What might it have led to?

Except that I scorned rugby types in those days, and on that Saturday afternoon would probably have been queuing up for a student ticket for some pre-West-End production at the New.

I left home before he and I had a chance of meeting.

Of course I could have stayed in Wales; there were plenty of opportunities in radio and television, particularly for Welsh-speaking actors. But I chose to turn my back on my home. I chose London: more opportunities, more freedom, more excitement. That's the person I was – superficial, vain, ambitious. I made that choice; it was no use moaning about it now.

You make a choice and then Life gives you the part and you have to play it. A Welsh actor, but a Welsh actor in

London. Not that I ever felt an exile. I left that to the 'professional' Welshmen.

I remember being chided by a scriptwriter called Meic Hywel because I called myself Kate Rivers. 'I call myself Kate Rivers because it happens to be my name,' I told him. 'Would I be any more Welsh if I called myself Catrin or Cati?' He seemed to think so. 'I'm Welsh because I feel Welsh. I don't know whether I'm "pure" Welsh – who does? – but I feel Welsh. And I happen to believe that English people who settle in Wales and take an interest in Wales are Welsh too, if they feel Welsh. And feelings are sometimes fleeting and in any case surely too nebulous to be politicised. So any nationalism is screwy from the start it seems to me. It only breeds hatred, it seems to me.'

'Nonsense,' he said, looking at me with undiluted hatred.

I'd played one of Lloyd George's glittering young mistresses in that play. If they were casting it today, I'd be the poor neglected wife. I always feel for actors who've played a famously successful Juliet and who end up playing the nurse. I auditioned for Juliet once but didn't get it. I auditioned for Rosalind once and got Celia. I was often on the brink of success. That could be my epitaph.

I began to feel worried about Annabel. Surely she realised I would have got rid of Laurie by this time. What had happened to her?

I phoned Lewis Owen, but he hadn't seen or heard of her all day.

'She went off quite early without anything to eat and I'm getting really worried about her. She's taken my car, otherwise I'd be out looking for her. She was in a bit of a state when she left. She said she was going back to Cwmllys, but it's gone five now. To tell you the truth, I rather hoped she was with you.'

'No, I teach in Abernon Comprehensive all day Wednesday, and I've only just got back. Look, I'll cycle down

194

to Cwmllys, it'll only take twenty minutes, and I'll phone you from the kiosk there. What's your number? I'll write it down on my hand. Don't worry about her, she's just lost all sense of time. You do down there, don't you? Try not to worry.'

'Thank you, Lewis,' I said, but he'd already put the phone down.

It was six before he phoned and when he did his voice was cold and jerky. 'Your car is here,' he said, 'parked exactly where it was yesterday, but no sign of her, though I've walked all round the headland. She might have walked up Bryncelyn way. She's probably quite safe, but I've taken it upon myself to phone Sergeant Edwards in town.'

'Isn't it a bit soon to phone the police?' I felt an icy hand squeezing my heart.

'Edwards didn't think so. Not when he heard about her sister. He's going to drive round Bryncelyn and Morfa making enquiries, and he's already notified the coastguard. We'll soon hear something. Try not to worry.'

Try not to worry? When even the police were worried! I was suddenly frantic. What could I do? I phoned Rhydian, I couldn't help myself.

I felt it would be Grace who'd answer, and it was. 'I'm so sorry I haven't been in touch,' she said, before I had a chance to say a word. 'I was devastated to hear about your mother's will. Absolutely *devastated*. And Edwina felt the same. And we'd been hoping to have you living down here for six months or so every year. And then to hear about your little step-daughter. Oh, what a tragedy. I'd have been over there with you in a minute, except Rhydian was adamant, *adamant*, that your other little step-daughter wasn't in a fit state for company.'

'That's who I'm ringing you about, Grace.' She was such a kind, warm person. It made my guilt so much worse. 'Annabel, my other step-daughter. She's missing. The police are searching for her but she's taken my car, so, you see, I'm helpless.'

195

A moment's silence. I could almost hear her thinking. 'Right,' she said, 'Rhydian's in the shower. I'll give him a sandwich to eat in the car and he'll be over with you in no time. Now, try not to worry. A mother can't help it, I know that, but . . . here's Rhydian now. I'll let you go.'

Rhydian. For a moment I wished he was my cousin and not my lover. I cried with a mixture of guilt and desire as I waited for him.

Sergeant Edwards arrived at the door at the same moment as he did. I let them in together. Rhydian put his arm around me. 'This is my cousin, Rhydian Jones. Sergeant Edwards.' They shook hands.

'We need to know her exact state of mind,' Edwards said. 'I was told about her twin sister. Would she be feeling suicidal? Should we be looking for a body?'

'Have you looked for a heap of clothes on the rocks?' Rhydian asked. 'If there's no heap of clothes, there'll be no body.'

'The young chap walked all round the headland and saw nothing.'

'Who was that?' Rhydian asked me.

'The minister, Lewis Owen. I asked him to go and look for her.' They both looked at me oddly. 'She had a very bad night last night and got furious because her boyfriend, her *ex*-boyfriend, was insisting on coming down to see her. She rushed out of the house, it was about eleven, taking my car and begging me to get rid of him. Which I did. And I expected her back early afternoon at the latest.'

We heard another car driving up the lane. 'Oh God, this will be her father,' I said. I felt Rhydian's arm tighten round my shoulder.

I let Paul in. 'I'm afraid Annabel is missing,' I said. 'She didn't come back from her walk and I'm getting worried about her.'

'But I think we'll soon find her safe and well,' Sergeant Edwards said. 'She doesn't sound to me like a suicide case.

I'm off and I hope to let you have some good news very soon.'

As a rule, I'm not over-fond of policemen, but I looked at Sergeant Edwards with real love. 'Thank you.'

'I've got the strongest feeling that Laurie Bridgewater will have found her by this time,' Paul said. 'He's a very capable young man; he'll have tracked her down and taken her to some restaurant to calm her. He can't be expected to know that you've got into a panic because she's been away a few hours. They'll turn up together very soon, you shall see.'

I looked hard at Paul and didn't like what I saw. 'Make yourself a cup of tea,' I said, 'you know where things are. My cousin Rhydian is going to drive me round looking for her.'

'Oh, but that's my job, surely,' Paul said.

'No, I know the area,' Rhydian said. 'It's my job.'

He and I left. He still had his arm around me.


'She's two months' pregnant, she's been sick several mornings, she sleeps very badly. She's not physically capable of walking up Bryncelyn. Lewis Owen doesn't realise how frail she is. She ate like a horse last night when we were at the Indian restaurant in Abernon, so he thinks she's some sort of Amazon. Oh Rhydian, I'm so afraid she's been abducted by some pervert. And please don't say that there aren't any perverts in Cwmllys.'

'I wasn't going to. The place is probably buzzing with them. I just think it's a bit more likely that she's had some sort of accident, sprained ankle or something. Lewis Owen was probably rushing after her instead of searching properly. We'll search properly – I've brought my lambing torch. And there'll be a moon later.' He parked his car at the side of mine. 'Hold my hand. The quicker we get to the cliffs, the quicker we'll find her.'

Everything was silver, the sea and the sky – a strange phosphorescent light left over from the setting sun.

'Oh, it's high tide,' Rhydian said, slowing down and sounding completely deflated.

'What difference does that make? Tell me. For God's sake, don't keep things to yourself. Don't try to protect me.'

'My little theory's destroyed, that's all. When you said she wasn't much of a hiker, I thought she might have walked on the beach, turned into the cave and been trapped by the tide. But the timing's wrong.'

'When would it have started to turn? Even a trickle in the cave might have frightened her. She's not used to our tides. They always had holidays in Crete. She could still be sitting on one of those projecting rocks halfway up the cave. What can we do?'

'We can't do anything about that for at least an hour, but we can walk on the cliff and shine the torch and shout for her. After all, we don't know that she's in the cave.'

'Why isn't the coastguard here?' My voice broke and Rhydian stopped and put his arms tightly around me.

'He's got a huge area to cover, but he will come.'

We started to walk up the cliff path and almost immediately someone shouted at us from the beach. 'I think it's Lewis Owen,' I said. We waited for him to catch up with us.

'I called in at the Ship in Morfa,' he said 'but no one had caught sight of her. What are we going to do now?'

'My cousin Rhydian thought she might have gone into the cave, but it's high tide, so we can't do anything about it at the moment.'

'I can. I'm a swimmer,' Lewis said. 'No, I mean a good swimmer. No, I mean *good*. Brought up in New Quay, man. Nō, I'm going to go in. Great idea.'

'I can swim, too, lad, but the currents are strong round here. And I mean *strong*. Not like New Quay. I'd be all for you risking your life if we *knew* she was in there, but we don't. It was only a hunch of mine, lad. Well, if you're going in, I'll come with you.'

'At your age? No, you won't. I'm not taking that responsibility.'

'I think we should wait for the coastguard. If she is alive in there she can hold on a bit longer, can't she?' My voice was doing things I didn't know it could.

Both men were getting undressed so I started getting undressed as well. 'I'm bloody terrified of the water, and I'm not a good swimmer, but if you two go in, I'm going in too. She's my step-daughter.'

'Put your clothes back on this minute,' Rhydian said. 'I promise only to go as far as the mouth of the cave. I'll leave the heroics to the lad, but at least I'll be there to take over if he brings her out. If she *is* in there.'

I watched them wading out, their bodies silvered in the strange light, watched them plunging into the sea and then watched their two heads in the water until I could no longer see anything but sea.

I should never have contacted Rhydian, I realise that, he's fifty with three children and another on the way, and what if he's drowned? What if Annabel turns up safe and sound, and Rhydian – and Lewis – are drowned because of my panic? What if Paul turns out to be right; what if Laurie found Annabel and persuaded her to go off somewhere with him? It will be all my fault. Two good men drowned because of me. 'And she gave a great sigh and with that broke her heart. And a four-sided grave was built for her at the side of the Alaw.' Was that Branwen? Or Rhianonn? My tears are for all of us.

'Kate! Kate! She's safe. She's back in the cottage.' It was Paul, running across the strip of sand by the rocks, agitated and out of breath.

'Oh my God. Rhydian and Lewis are swimming into the cave looking for her and it's highly dangerous.'

Without a second's hesitation, Paul pulled off his clothes and threw them at my feet with the pile already there. Everyone brave but me. I shone Rhydian's torch to light up

199

Paul's path to the sea. The tide was already turning. 'She lost the car keys,' he shouted back at me before being swallowed up by the sea.

Annabel was safe and sound in the house. She'd lost the keys of my car. Why had none of us been thinking of ordinary, small events? I was thankful, of course, for her safety, but my heart was still thumping with fear. I prayed to the God I didn't believe in to bring the three men back safely.

'She's safe. She's safe.' I could hear Paul's voice behind the sea's clamour.

'She's safe. She's OK. Come out of there, lad.' Rhydian's voice, fainter and farther away.

And then the coastguard's Land Rover trundling over the pebbles towards where I was standing with the torch. 'She's safe,' I shouted at him as soon as he'd slammed the door and was walking towards me. 'The men are still out there, but I've just heard that she's safe.'

He took it in his stride, obviously used to, and perhaps even welcoming false alarms. 'Well, they'll be fine. Lucky the autumn storms haven't started. It's calm as a pond out there tonight.' He shone his searchlight towards the headland. Calm? The waves, strong and regular, were making shuddery, moaning noises which made me feel sea-sick. I closed my eyes.

'Can you see them?'

'Yes, I see them. Looks as though they're having a bit of a swim around.'

'How many do you see?

'There's two of them, if not more.'

'There should be three. One of them was going to swim into the cave. Is he out? I can't bear to keep watching.'

'Bloody idiot, swimming into that cave at high tide. What the hell was he thinking of? Stupid fool.'

Who was he calling a stupid fool? 'It's our minister, Lewis Owen from Glanrhyd. He was trying to save my step-daughter.'

200

'Bloody idiot! Tell him to save souls on dry land from now on . . . Jesus, he's made it! Well done, boy! Jesus! Aye, they're making for shore now. I'll get some blankets from the van.'

And then I had three naked men around me, all in the highest spirits, proud of themselves, pleased to be on dry land again. 'By God, he can swim,' Rhydian was saying, as he tried to dry himself with his shirt. 'Got no shoulders to speak of, but he's cunning with those currents. Doesn't fight them, that's the secret.'

'Nothing in the way of currents round here,' the coastguard said. 'I had no worries on that score or I'd have been in myself. Didn't you hear about the inquest on the man drowned in Cwmllys? "Died of exhaustion while trying to commit suicide." You're no heroes, none of you.'

I was the only one who accepted his offer of a blanket.

'I've got some brandy up in the house,' Paul said as soon as he was dressed. 'I hope you can all come back for a drink.'

'Thank you,' Lewis said. 'I'd love to come. Will my bike fit in the car?'

'Another time perhaps,' the coastguard said. 'I'll see you in the pub sometime.'

'Another time,' Rhydian echoed. 'I've got some paper-work tonight.'

Paul turned towards me, waiting for me to walk to the car with him and Lewis.

'I'm staying here for a while with Rhydian. Give Annabel my love.'

# Chapter Twenty

When the others had left, Rhydian and I sat close together on a low outcrop of rock, the noisy slap and suck of the sea in our ears.

'Are you going to stay here with me?' he asked, after several minutes. And after another few moments, answered his own question. 'No, you're going to leave me, I know that.'

The uncaring ocean surged around us. 'We met too late,' I said. 'You've got too much to lose.'

I opened his jacket and his shirt and put my face against his chest, listening to the beat of his heart and smelling the sea on his skin. I thought of all the poets in the world who'd striven to put the race of their blood into simple, sincere words. Millions of words; letters, odes, sonnets. What could I say? I love you. I love you true. I licked my index finger and wrote it on his heart.

'Did you understand that?' I asked him.

'I don't understand anything. I waited years. Not for you, but for someone like you, someone who could make me feel as you do. And now it's too late. I can't leave my farm and my family.'

'I waited years, too. There's never been anyone else. The others, all the others, were only substitutes.'

'In the future, I'll think this is a dream. Tonight seems like a dream. I wish I didn't have to wake. But tomorrow

I'll be up at half six as usual and it will be as though this never happened.'

'It won't be like that for me. I'll remember it and carry it about with me.'

'We've had so little time. Less than two weeks.'

'When did you realise you loved me?'

'The moment you opened the door that first night. You reminded me of the skinny little girl who'd cried so much at my mother's funeral. And you looked up at me and smiled. And that was it.'

'Do you think Grace suspects anything?'

'I don't think so . . . No, I'm sure she doesn't. Though Bleddyn said he knew as soon as he saw us together. And yet, what does he know about love? According to him, he fell in love with Helga, Siwan's mother, because she'd been able to solve some mathematical problem which had defeated him.'

We were talking together so sadly and gently, kissing and touching each other sadly and gently as though we were an old married couple with the urgency of sex long behind us.

The great moments are so few in a lifetime's toil and boredom, but surely their memory would shed a fleeting radiance. Surely I'd never sit by the sea again without feeling the lovely calm of this moment. Words like infidelity, forbidden love, treachery counted for nothing in this enveloping calm.

Yet, even as they were thought of, they exerted their power. 'I suppose you'd better take me home,' I said. 'Grace will be expecting you back.'

Holding each other so tightly that our bones crunched together, we stumbled over the wet stones to the car. There was no real sadness that night, only a memory of shared danger and an awareness of love flowing like a tune in the blood.

\*

204

When I got home, Paul, Annabel and Lewis were playing Scrabble at the living-room table. For a while I watched them through the uncurtained window. (Paul and I used to play Scrabble with my mother. She usually won because she insisted on using Welsh words as well as English, many of them invented to use up whatever letters she happened to have left.)

I knew it was going to be a difficult evening and wished I could creep up to bed without having to discuss mundane matters and make plans. I didn't want to hear Paul singing Laurie's praises, didn't want to hear him trying to be understanding about Lewis, didn't want him talking about Francesca. And I wasn't prepared for even a mention of the future. All I wanted was to go to bed and think about Rhydian, going over all he'd said, hearing his soft intent voice in my head.

The game came to an end, Paul seeming to be the winner. Lewis got to his feet as though pleased it was over. I went in as he was saying goodbye. 'I'm glad I caught you,' I said. 'You've been so kind. I hope they've given you something to eat.'

'I've had a great evening,' Lewis said.

'We had tinned mushroom soup and cheese on toast,' Annabel said. 'Lewis cooked us cheese on toast. The crusts were black, and it was really good.'

Paul said nothing, but when Annabel took Lewis to the door, he offered to run him home. 'No thank you,' Lewis said. 'It's a lovely evening. I'd rather walk.'

'Do you believe in love at first sight?' Annabel asked us as soon as he'd left.

'Annabel, you're not yourself,' Paul said. 'You know perfectly well that you're in a highly-wrought and highly emotional state. Please try not to get involved in something you'll regret later. Lewis is a perfectly decent boy, I'm not denying that, but I'm quite certain he's the type who takes things very seriously, definitely not the type to

205

indulge in a light-hearted affair. Don't you agree with me, Kate?'

'Yes, Paul, I do agree that Lewis is the sort who takes things seriously. And yes, Annabel, I do believe in love at first sight. And now I'm going to have a bath and then I'm going to bed. I'm very tired and I've been worried sick. No, Annabel, don't apologise. It wasn't your fault but mine. I never considered any explanation that didn't involve fatal accident or rape.'

'Do you really care about me, then?' Annabel asked, sounding awed and completely astonished.

'Yes, I really think I do.'

I lay in the bath until the water was quite cold. When I'd dried myself and put on my dressing-gown, I felt as weak and helpless as I'd ever felt in my life. Worn out by emotion. Had I had anything to eat during the day? I couldn't remember.

'You'll have to sleep on the sofa,' I told Paul. 'There are blankets and pillows in the airing-cupboard.'

'I thought it would be all right to sleep with you,' he said. 'We're not exactly strangers, are we?'

'No, we're not strangers. And we're both pretty disturbed and in need of comfort at the moment. That's why we could get caught up in something we'd regret later, something which would make things even more complicated than they are already. Goodnight, Paul. Goodnight, Annabel.'

I slept soundly, but woke before dawn. Soon after seven-thirty I could hear Paul moving about downstairs so I got up, realising that we needed to talk. I knew, and he probably knew, that life with Francesca wasn't going to be easy. I wanted him to know that he and I could still be friends.

I pulled on trousers and sweater, the only clothes I had with me apart from my Gucci suit, and went downstairs. 'Paul, I need to talk to you,' I said. 'Annabel won't be up for at least a couple of hours, so we won't be disturbed. I'll make some coffee. How are you?'

'You don't want to know.'

'I do.'

'I'm off to Salzburg on Monday. The Japanese assignment didn't come off, my assistant tied up the Spanish thing, so I'm grabbing this one. Only a few days' work. Not very interesting. But at least something to occupy my mind.'

'Good. I'm starting work too in a couple of weeks. A crap job, but better than nothing, I suppose.'

We looked hard at each other. Our conversation had echoes of so many others.

'I don't know how I'm going to live without you,' Paul said. 'Francesca will probably be back with Mark by the end of the year.'

'Only I think this one was a Matthew, love. And you don't know that. She's going through a great ordeal. Nothing has really touched her before. This tragedy may completely alter her.'

'It may completely alter me, too.'

'Not in the same way.'

'Anyway, what about Annabel? She seems really off her trolley. She's completely lost it, hasn't she?'

'There's no coffee. Damn. I remember now, I asked Laurie to call in for some on his way here, but he couldn't even manage that. Tea all right?'

'Fine.'

I made a pot of tea and carried it into the living room. It was the last of my mother's tea. Carradine – her favourite. She always insisted it was Welsh tea.

'Why in God's name has she turned against Laurie? Such an eligible young chap. Solid. Dependable. And likeable, too.'

'I'm going to leave Laurie out of it, if you don't mind.' I poured out the tea. 'I want to talk about Annabel. You've been caught up in your own suffering, so you haven't given Annabel as much thought as I have.'

'I have, believe me. She's lost more than anyone. Her other half. I realise that.'

'And of course there's also Miranda Lottaby.'

'Who?'

'The girl who died of drugs.'

'Are you saying Annabel was responsible for that? I thought—'

'No, as a matter of fact she wasn't. But she could have been. And since Selena's death, I think that's been on her mind a great deal. How that poor girl's family has suffered.'

'Are you sure? That doesn't sound like Annabel. She seemed able to dismiss all that.'

'No. I found some cuttings from the local paper under her pillow when I was straightening her bed. "Parents Weep at Bedside" – that sort of thing. Miranda wasn't a particular friend of hers, but she feels that Selena thought she was implicated in her death, and that it may have triggered her suicide. So you see, she feels guilty as hell – as well as heartbroken. That's why she wants a new persona. That's why she's turned to me. In her mind, I was her complete opposite – sensible, dull, worthy. That's why the funeral is being held here. It's the opposite of every-thing she's known. When her grandfather died, the funeral was a very smart affair, everyone in designer black and the Oratory full of white lilies. You told me that. You thought it over the top and I suppose she and Selena were far more scathing about it. So she's insisted on Horeb Chapel, Glanrhyd, with no guests, no flowers.'

Paul listened in grave silence. 'Are you sure of all this?' he asked at last.

I took a deep breath and exhaled slowly. 'No, I'm not sure of anything. I'm just feeling my way through the maze.'

'So that could be why she's turned against Laurie?'

'I think she's turned against Laurie because she found him wanting. But she'll tell you about that. Though perhaps not today.'

Paul studied my face as though I were a map. 'What a wonderfully sane person you are,' he said.

'Sane? Since I've been home I've had a passionate affair with my cousin Rhydian who has a wife and three young children. I should have told you about it when you told me about Francesca, but I simply didn't have the bottle.'

Another long silence. 'I thought you two were rather more than friends,' he said at last. 'Well, I can understand it. You've had two deaths to cope with in less than a week.' He seemed to be making an effort to keep his voice steady.

'It started before I knew about Selena. He and his wife called round on my second evening here.'

'It doesn't mean anything,' Paul said, as though to comfort me.

'It means everything, believe me.'

He poured me another cup of tea, again as though to comfort me. I could feel tears, hot and salty, on my cheeks. Could I possibly live without Rhydian? When we'd decided last night to renounce each other, it had seemed a grand, uplifting gesture, but what did I have left? A blank, my Lord. I blinked away my tears and took another sip of tea. 'Thank God Annabel was safe,' I said. 'What if she'd been found dead as well?'

'I didn't realise you and Annabel were so close.'

'Neither did I.' I took a deep breath. 'Since this seems a day for confessions, I may as well tell you that I had an abortion just over three years ago. I'd touched on the possibility of our having a baby, but it was all too obvious that you weren't in favour and I wasn't brave enough to go through with it on my own.'

'Oh, God. So I let you down then as well. Yes, I remember how nervous I felt when you mentioned it. Terrified of yet more commitment. What a coward I was.'

'You told the truth. I suppose you'd have come round if I'd said it was definite, but I didn't. Just took an easier option. Or one I thought was easier.'

'Oh God, what a mess it all seems.'

'I'm telling you so that you understand about Annabel. Perhaps that's why I feel as I do towards her. When legally I'm not even her step-mother.'

'What's going to happen to her? Who the hell is this Lewis she seems to have fallen in love with?'

'Hasn't she told you? He's the new minister of Horeb. He was sitting on the cliffs in Cwmllys, quietly reading some worthy book, when, lo, his life changed.'

'Don't make light of it.'

'I'm not. At the moment, I think it's important to both of them. I've no idea what will happen in the future, but I do know that he's more of a man than you take him for. Of course, Annabel thinks he's a pre-Raphaelite angel.'

'God help us.'

'And he does seem to have a touch of the angel about him. Even I can recognise that.'

# Chapter Twenty-One

'I was late coming back because I fell asleep. Yes, in that little sheltered spot just off the cliff path where we first met Lewis. Well, you remember what a terrible night I'd had, all those dreams. Anyway, I fell asleep and it was nearly four o'clock when I woke up. And when I got back to the car I discovered I'd lost the fuckin' keys. I didn't know your phone number and there wasn't a directory in the kiosk, so what could I do but walk? And you know how I hate walking. And when I'd walked about a mile, I got to this junction and this signpost and I must have taken the wrong turning. I didn't even know the name of this village; all I could remember was that it was unpronounceable. But both the names seemed the same jumble of consonants and of course I chose the wrong road.'

'Never mind, you got here in the end. And all in one piece.'

'I had a lift eventually. Two rather portly middle-aged men on holiday. In shorts. You know how I hate men in shorts. I wouldn't have accepted a lift from them except that I was absolutely desperate. And of course I wasn't able to tell them where I wanted to go. All I could remember was Horeb. I told them I wanted to go to a village where there was a red-brick chapel called Horeb. So we drove round for well over an hour looking for the right place. They smelt of sweat, but we got quite friendly in the end. They were chiropodists from Manchester.'

'They might have abducted you.'

'They might have given me some plasters for my blisters, but would you believe, they didn't have any. They said *they* wore suitable footware.'

'But they did eventually find the house.'

'We did eventually find Horeb and I got out there to call on Lewis. But he wasn't in.'

'Well, you know why that was. He was on your trail. But you managed to find your way back here on your own?'

'No, it was pitch dark by this time, so I dropped into the pub. And the postwoman was there with her mother-in-law and they bought me a beer and a shrimp-and-salad sandwich. And when I told them I wanted to live down here, they said there was a living-in job going at the something-something hotel on the something-something road. And the post-woman, Lorna, is taking me there at half-past one today when she finishes work. And then her husband, Cliff, came in and he drove me back here in his van. And Paul was already here. And, well, you know the rest. Where's Paul now?'

'He went for a walk up the hill. I don't know what he's going to think about you trying for a job at the Maes Garw Hotel.'

'Don't you? I do. He's going to be one hundred per cent against. What about you?'

'Sixty to seventy per cent against. I'm glad you've found something you want to do, but I don't think you're strong enough. Hotel work is very hard. I did it as a student so I know. And you're pregnant, remember.'

'I may only stay for a few months.'

'Lewis being the attraction, I suppose.'

She came over to where I was sitting and hugged me so hard I nearly lost my breath. 'What a pity you can't stay as well,' she said.

'I'll miss you. But you can always come to live with me in Camberwell if things don't work out.'

212

'Yes, I was counting on that. Perhaps I'll be quite good at cooking and things after working at the hotel for a while. That is, if I get the job. Do I look like a second chef?'

I didn't have to answer that question because Paul appeared at the window. 'I've been down to look at the cemetery,' he said, as he came in. 'It's a beautiful spot, overlooking the whole sweep of the valley with the mountains in the distance. I know it's probably sentimental and foolish, but I'll always get a measure of comfort to think of her being there. Would you like to come to see it, Annabel?'

I held my breath, waiting for the storm of angry tears. But she only blinked and took a deep breath. 'Lewis is taking me there at four o'clock this afternoon when he comes back from his hospital visit. He said we'd go round and read the words on all the gravestones. Some of them are incredibly moving, he says. There's one of five small children who all died in eighteen-something within a month of one another. Probably of malnutrition. He says he'll have to think about that when he has to say something about Selena. We thought "Brightness falls from the air" would be lovely words for her gravestone.'

Paul and I nodded our heads in agreement but neither of us could speak. After a few moments' silence, Paul went to the kitchen and we could hear him blowing his nose. 'I'm enormously proud of you,' he told Annabel when he got back. 'I don't know where you get your strength from but it's certainly not from me or your mother.' He stopped abruptly, on the point of breaking down, but after a moment was able to continue. 'I'm going back to London now so that I'll be able to drive Francesca down tomorrow. With the . . . the hearse following behind. We'll see you at the chapel at two.'

He kissed us both and left. That day I felt very tender towards him. It might not be the sort of love I felt for Rhydian, but it was love all the same.

*

213

Annabel got the job. She didn't pretend to have had any experience, but said she'd spent all her holidays in Crete and knew quite a lot about foreign food – though not that she actually knew how to cook it. No, she hadn't had any experience, not hands-on experience, though she'd eaten at many famous restaurants. She'd then said how much she loved the hotel and the village, and that she knew she could be happy there. Perhaps they'd had problems keeping young staff in the past, because that seemed to clinch it. They offered her the job, starting in a month's time, at two hundred pounds a week, all found.

'So now I've got to learn how to cook,' she said mournfully. 'I think it's going to be mostly breakfasts and puddings. Fried eggs are damnably difficult, Lewis says.'

She didn't mention her visit to the cemetery and neither did I.


The morning of the funeral was grey and stormy, the Indian summer well and truly over. It was only a week since my mother's funeral and I hadn't yet managed to come to terms with that, and now I had another ordeal to face. I felt immensely sorry for myself; it was only the need to support Annabel that kept me going.

'Nasty old day,' Lorna said when she called, 'but it will be bright this evening, you shall see. My mother-in-law and I were thinking of turning in to the chapel this afternoon unless you'd rather we didn't. We both took to your little step-daughter and so did Cliff. She hasn't got up yet? Well, that's all for the best, isn't it. Let her sleep. Only there's a letter here for her. Miss Annabel Farringdon. Lovely name . . . George Williams thought he might come as well. Out of respect for your mother, I suppose. I hope Lewis Owen will have one of his better days. You'd be surprised how deep he can be sometimes. Now, you won't go and forget us, will you, when you're back in London? Oh no, you'll come down to see Annabel, won't you? They say it's very nice in Maes

Garw under the new management. Even though breakfast is extra. Tell you what, you pay for your room, they charge plenty mind, and come and have breakfast with me and Cliff. We do ourselves proud at the weekend.'

Though still absorbing the rhythm of her sentences, I'd stopped listening to what she was actually saying. I excused myself. 'I'm trying to decide whether to keep Annabel's letter until after the funeral,' I told her. 'I've got the feeling it might be from an ex-boyfriend who could be trying to upset her.'

'She's twenty-one,' Lorna said, getting to her feet, 'and already as upset as can be. For goodness' sake, don't try to play God.'

'Lorna, will you mind if I ring you up from time to time to ask your advice about various things?'

She laughed. 'You do that,' she said.

I gave Annabel the letter as soon as she got downstairs. 'From Laurie,' she said savagely. 'Offering to marry me, would you believe. Prepared to put his career prospects on hold for a year or two. How very noble. Excuse me while I go to the bathroom to throw up.'

'How long does this bloody morning sickness go on?' she asked me when she got back to the living room.

'It's not so severe after the first couple of months,' I said cheerily. I'd read that somewhere.

For a time she sat at the table sipping some hot water, seeming almost too quiet and composed. She had a harrowing day in front of her.

I could hardly believe that she intended staying in Glanrhyd. I'd miss her so much. I'd imagined her living with me in Camberwell where I could look after her. What was wrong with my hormones? I was her ex-step-mother, not her mother.

'Can I get you a cup of tea?' I asked her.

'No, thanks. Not at the moment.'

God, I had to get out of the habit of offering everyone cups of tea. I was beginning to sound middle-aged. Come off it, I *was* middle-aged, at least half my life behind me. And I was going back to London to live alone in a four-bedroomed family house.

Arthur jumped onto my lap and dug his claws into me. It seemed like affection, rough love. Oh, I'd take him with me! Why not? Why shouldn't I settle down and become the stereotype spinster with a cat for company? Perhaps I could write a scintillating television script, set in the twenties, for a grumpy middle-aged detective who lived alone with her cat and had spiffing adventures. I'd have a trilby hat to set me apart from all the other female sleuths and possibly a wooden leg. It was a pity I didn't know any criminals. I knew *of* several, but had never taken the trouble to cultivate any of them. Another bad career move.

'Would you like baked beans on toast?' Annabel asked me after a long silence.

I knew we should have a large nourishing meal before the ordeal of the funeral service, but these days Annabel couldn't eat much until evening and I didn't feel at all like cooking or eating. 'Just one piece,' I said feebly. All I wanted was for the day to be over.

Annabel brought in the beans and two bottles of Coke. Her mood had darkened again. 'I think Selena may have killed herself because she knew I was going to have an abortion,' she said, her voice thin and trembling. 'Perhaps she wanted to make me think again.'

The idea of such self-sacrifice frightened me. 'Annabel, don't torment yourself. She'd been working too hard, she was deeply troubled and confused about various aspects of her life, perhaps about yours too, I won't deny that, and Francesca's sleeping pills just happened to be there. It was a hideous tragedy, but trying to invent some logical explanation for something which was in all probability completely illogical is just self-indulgence.'

216

She became calm. 'Lewis said something very like that,' she said.

The reading was from the Book of Isaiah, incomprehensible, but like Beckett's monologues, shot through with what was perhaps a thread of hope. There was a long organ voluntary instead of a hymn, Mr Cynrig Ellis the organist possibly trying to persuade us of the pressing need for a new organ.

The sermon was short: how tragedy called forth love, not original perhaps, but deeply felt. How there was always a huge crowd of eager volunteers at the pit head when there'd been a horrific accident underground, how lifeboat men were always at hand to launch their little boat into a hideously perilous sea. Love was not necessarily life-threatening but always dangerous. Christ's message was that we must live dangerously, love courageously. Lewis was so pale that I realised he was finding it almost impossible to continue.

He stopped abruptly, announcing that Annabel wanted to say a few words about her sister.

'Selena and I were always together. We were identical twins so people thought we had identical minds but we didn't. She was gentle and thoughtful and I was brash and thoughtless. Now I have to live without her. And that has to be my act of courage. Please cherish her memory.'

Then Lewis looked towards the organ, Mr Ellis struggled with some Bach and then we went out into the rain.

Either by accident or design, the committal at the grave was in Welsh. I glanced over at Francesca to see what she thought of it, but her face was so distorted by fierce grief that I felt guilty to be spying on her. Paul had her and Annabel, one on each side, in a tight grip. I was pleased about that. More or less.

Maggie Davies and Lorna were both dabbing at their eyes as we walked from the cemetery. George Williams said nothing but when we reached the gate, shook my hand for a

217

long time, perhaps not trusting himself to speak. I invited them to join us at the Maes Garw Hotel for afternoon tea, but they declined, though I could see that Maggie was sorely tempted.

We drove there in two cars, Annabel with her parents in one and Lewis and I in the other. 'You did well,' I said. 'I don't want to talk about it,' he said. 'And please don't patronise me.' He seemed nervous and surly, but I was prepared to forgive him. 'You did well,' I said again.

Both cars arrived at the hotel together. Why exactly was I there? I wished I'd gone home.

'You mustn't hate me,' Francesca said, taking my arm and squeezing it as we walked up the steps to the front door. I couldn't think how to reply, so I didn't.

We were ushered into a large, opulently furnished but rather chilly sitting room. As a student, I used to clean the seven guest bedrooms, but wasn't considered either experienced or mature enough to have any dealings with the lounge and the dining room with their antique furniture and their brass and crystal ornaments. Paul ordered a pot of tea and toasted tea-cakes, but Francesca called the waiter back, demanding brandy and insisting on having the fire lit. 'I don't hate you,' I told her and we smiled at each other in brief reconciliation.

The log fire in the wide inglenook fireplace was soon blazing away, the tea and tea-cakes were good, the brandy was soul-warming; we sipped it as though it was life itself.

'Shall I tell them or will you?' Lewis asked.

Annabel raised her eyes from him, looked towards us and cleared her throat. 'I'm eleven weeks' pregnant,' she said. 'An accident, of course. Yes, Laurie was the father, but it could have been anyone. What I mean is, I was never in love with him or anything like that. Absolutely not. But I've fallen in love with Lewis, isn't it extraordinary. I didn't think it would ever happen to me but it has.' Her clear grey eyes were suddenly luminous with tears and

218

love. 'And he understands me better than anyone else because, you see, he was a twin himself and he's felt lonely and incomplete ever since his twin brother died at two years old.'

We looked at them with wonder. It was like something out of Shakespeare. Shakespeare was obsessed by twins; he had fathered twins himself, so knew about their magical affinity.

'And I've asked her to marry me,' Lewis said, 'and she's agreed to it. And it must be as soon as possible, if that's all right with you all. You see, in my position, I don't want to wait until everyone is gossiping about us. We think it's best to give as little offence as we can.'

I broke the stunned silence. 'The courage of love,' I said. 'Let's drink to that.'

Paul rallied and repeated, 'The courage of love.'

Annabel came over from the sofa where she'd been sitting with Lewis and kissed her parents and me. Francesca seemed to wake from a trance. 'And I suppose the wedding will be here, too,' she said, sounding pathetic but resigned.

'Do you really hate it here?' I asked her.

'Oh no, the chapel is beautiful.'

'It is, isn't it? And I was a member for years without ever noticing it.'

'All the same, what I'd like is a wedding at St Botulph's,' Annabel said. And probably only I knew how much that peace-offering to her mother was costing her.

Francesca came to life again. 'Oh, darling! But what about the people here? Oh, but we can lay on a coach – or two coaches – to bring them up, can't we, Paul?' She looked at Lewis as though seeing him for the first time and managing to convey, yes, you'll do very nicely, in her glance. 'Of course, Lewis must decide everything. It's very important that his congregation doesn't turn against them.'

'With Maggie Davies on their side, who will dare turn against them?' I said.

# Chapter Twenty-Two

Now it's just over three weeks later. I was hoping, by this time, to have found some sort of calm, but here I am in the middle of a huge, raging excitement.

I left Wales the day after Selena's funeral, Paul, Francesca and Annabel having already gone the previous evening. At about seven o'clock, a sad hour on a sad day, Lewis called on me to apologise for his surly behaviour in the funeral car. 'I had so much on my mind,' he said. 'But now I'm really happy.'

One part of me wanted to warn him that he wasn't going to have an easy life with Annabel, but I concluded that he already knew that. 'I came up thinking you might be lonely,' he said. 'Annabel told me about Paul and her mother getting back together. And that must be very difficult for you.'

'Yes, I shall miss Paul. He's a decent man who tries to do his best for everyone. You'll get on well with him. Francesca has treated him badly in the past and will probably do so again in the future. But perhaps not. I'm afraid I'm not very charitable towards Francesca.'

'You're doing fine, it seems to me. Annabel thinks so, anyway.'

My eyes prickled with tears. Annabel seemed like an exotic butterfly who'd landed briefly on my shoulder and then flown away again in a butterfly's zig-zag fashion. She'd never need me again.

Lewis noticed my distress. 'What's this wedding going to be like, then?' he asked.

'Have you ever watched any of the royal weddings on the telly?'

'No.'

'Just as well. Do you ever have those dreams when you have to do something very difficult and nerve-racking and you've completely forgotten to prepare for it?'

'Oh, very often. An important exam when I realise I've been swotting up the wrong subject.'

'And I'm usually on stage in a play I haven't rehearsed. Well, it won't be as bad as that. Not quite. Have you told your parents about it?'

'Yes. A wedding in London. They think it's very posh. You will be there, won't you?'

'Of course.'

'Can you give me your phone number so I can ring if I have a problem.'

I wrote it down and handed it to him. 'You'll have lots of problems, love, but at least you won't have to worry about how much it's all going to cost. Francesca can be depended on to cough up for everything.'

'Going to be an expensive do, then?'

'No. Twenty grand ought to cover it.'

'You're joking, aren't you? Tell me you're joking.'

'I'm joking. She'll probably decide to cut down on certain of the more vulgar extravagances because of Selena's death. You know what I mean – she'll probably decide to get the dresses for her and Annabel in Harrods rather than in Paris, arrange the reception at a small five-star Knightsbridge hotel rather than in the Ritz . . . Listen, it's going to be OK. And even if it isn't, Lewis, it's only a day out of your life.'

'Thanks. And if I need any more cheering up, I'll give you a bell.'

I kissed him when he left. After all, he was almost my step-son-in-law.

Rhydian phoned that night. He was angry when I said I was leaving in the morning, saying it was too sudden, too brutally sudden, altogether too cruel. I had to remind him about the decision he'd made in Cwmllys. He said that was the sea talking. It was the exhilaration of the swim, the discovery that he wasn't entirely without courage, the gratitude for Annabel's safety, the need, he supposed, to appease the gods. That night, he'd felt a largeness of spirit which was entirely false. His voice broke. He insisted that he was a weak man who needed me in his life. We owed it to ourselves, he said, to fight for a little mercy, a little happiness.

I was too fraught to say anything. I couldn't see any happiness for me, with him or without. He begged me to let him phone me in London. I begged him not to contact me for at least a month. Things had happened too fast, I said, and we needed a cooling-off period. Did we? I put the phone down. I was shaking with misery.

Far too unhappy to go to bed, I sat on my mother's sofa with Arthur on my lap, thinking about her sad life. Only a few days ago I'd been determined that mine was going to be different, that I was going to fight for my share of the world. That night, I had no fight left in me. It was almost three o'clock before I even had the energy to get myself upstairs.

The journey back to London was a nightmare. I'd remembered to let George Williams know that I'd had a change of heart about Arthur; he'd found me a wonderfully strong cardboard box for the journey and I'd made it everything a travelling cat could ask for; air-holes in the lid, a cushion covered by a smart tartan travelling rug, a new cat-nip mouse. I talked to him, sang to him, recited poetry to him, he yowled back at me without pause, except for brief periods when he seemed to be hurtling himself about or

223

feverishly scratching the box to pieces. I drove for 235 miles, without daring to stop for a snack or a pee.

When I got back, I could hardly believe that the house was still standing, hadn't even been burgled, was in fact beautifully clean, the late afternoon sun patterning the walls and the carpet, the central heating breathing gently in the background. My spirits rose.

I carried in the snarling cardboard box, leaving it unopened in the sitting room while I filled two new plastic trays with the cat litter I'd bought in a pet shop in Abernon, filled a new stainless steel bowl with water and another with cat food. Then, after making sure that every door and window was tightly fastened, I opened the box and retreated to an armchair. I expected Arthur to emerge looking angry, worn and threadbare. He seemed in tip-top condition, looked around him as though fairly satisfied, then, ignoring the food, the water and the cat litter, jumped up onto my lap. I was a cat owner. 'I'm not going to get stupid about you, Arthur,' I told him, as I fondled his almost transparent white ears. The large, round eyes he turned towards me were the colour of young wheat.

The next day was cold and windy, the sky a pewter grey. In spite of the fact that Arthur had used the two litter trays and eaten a hearty breakfast, my heart was leaden as the sky. I had almost two weeks before I started work, the most I could hope for in the interim was a costume fitting. For my various shabby blouses, long droopy skirts, aprons, down-at heel button boots and possibly a brown Sunday coat with a bit of rabbit fur round the collar.

Annabel rang me at midday to say she'd enrolled for a two-week Cordon Bleu cookery course which Francesca thought was in preparation for the entertaining she intended to do at the Manse. They'd already managed to book the wedding for three weeks' time, though they'd had to accept a Friday afternoon because Saturdays were completely full until after Christmas. She was going to wear Francesca's wedding dress, ivory silk oversewn with seed pearls, which only needed a little letting-out. Francesca was going to see to all the other arrangements and wanted to know how many guests I wanted to bring. I'd have to get hold of a handsome escort from somewhere. I tried to think of a distinguished-looking, silver-haired actor who'd a) own a decent dinner suit and b) could be depended on not to giggle or get drunk. I couldn't think of one. What a pity I didn't know John Thaw. Annabel then said she had to rush. And put the phone down.

The thought of John Thaw brought Joanna Morton back into my mind, the woman I'd met briefly on the train a week ago. She'd seemed so strong and sympathetic; we'd had a few moments of real communion. She'd given me her card, asked me to ring her. I decided to phone and invite her to lunch.

She wasn't in but I left my name and number on her answerphone.

I felt a desperate need for company. I had friends, I told myself, but they were people I met at work and at parties, people who talked about plays, acting and actors, occasionally about agents, directors, theatres, then about plays and acting and actors again. I came to the sad conclusion that I had no real all-purpose, all-weather friend except Paul. He might have lacked something as a lover, but had always been a good friend.

All that day, I waited to hear from Joanna Morton. She didn't ring.

Arthur was still behaving immaculately, taking in his new surroundings without once demanding to go out. A pamphlet I'd picked up at the pet shop informed me that I had to keep him in for two weeks, that cats had been known to walk the entire breadth of England to get back to their original home. Arthur seemed untroubled by homesickness; ready to settle for luxury cat food, central heating, a clean, comfortable bed and frequently changed cat litter. We got through the weekend.

At half past nine on Monday morning, before she'd even started on the hoovering, Mrs Heathfield, my help, announced that she could no longer work for me as she was allergic to cats. She rolled up her overall, put it back into her bag and said she was sorry. Very sorry.

I insisted that people could only be allergic to long-haired, pedigree cats, but at this, she sneezed several times and then started to have palpitations, so that I had to accept her tearful goodbyes. Of course her tears may have been due to the allergy, but I gave her the benefit of the doubt and a month's wages. She'd been so thoroughly dependable for so many years – ever since we'd bought the house, in fact – that I was near tears too. 'I may have to take you for a little drive to the nearest motorway, Arthur,' I told him when she'd left. Oh God, I was turning into a woman who talked to her cat. 'Only kidding, Arthur.'

Feeling that things couldn't be much worse, I decided to pack some of Paul's belongings, starting with his clothes. Several items looked grubby and in need of ironing, but I folded them neatly – actors are always good at packing, they've had to do so much of it – and filled two of our largest suitcases, writing PLEASE RETURN THIS on the label of the slightly less battered. The sad business of sorting out and dividing up had begun.

The phone rang and it was Paul inviting me out to lunch. I was longing to go, but told him I was too busy; it wouldn't do for him to realise how lonely I was. In spite of all my weaknesses and failings, I could cross my heart and say I wanted him to be happy. And not feeling guilty about me.

No one else phoned. Still no word from Joanna Morton. I had too much pride to ring her again.

The whole of that week passed without incident, without company, one day dropping into night as silently and sadly as leaves falling. I walked briskly to the nearest shops to buy cat food and instant meals and small brown loaves, and

226

hurried back to Arthur who'd started greeting me with a deep and I think affectionate crooning sound in his throat, something between a purr and a growl. Sometimes I talked to him in English, sometimes in Welsh; he seemed to have a perfect understanding of both. He didn't respond to music, classical or pop, but would often keep one sleepy eye on television programmes. He settled down far better than I did. I missed Wales; the silence, the voices in the silence, the views from the windows and doors, the hint of sea in the wind. I missed Annabel's company. I missed Rhydian almost unbearably.

I spent part of the next two weeks in a village in Cumbria, where the television serial was to be set and where they were pre-filming some of the outdoor scenes. The hotel I stayed at was pleasant enough, the surrounding countryside breath-taking; immense hills and huge tracts of moorland. But the other actors there were far too young, I couldn't keep up with the amount they drank in the bar after supper nor with their talk which was all jest and jargon like people in American sit-coms. I'd felt middle-aged ever since my mother's death, now I felt I'd been catapulted into a situation where I had to be on my guard not to look bewildered nor ask questions nor talk in grown-up sentences.

Annabel was staying at the house in my absence, looking after Arthur. I phoned every day to check on them. One evening I was terrified to hear that she'd bought him a harness and lead and taken him for a walk round the garden. 'But he is safely back in the house now?' 'I've already said so. Twice. Would you like to speak to him?'

I was pleased to get home. Annabel had made a very impressive spinach-and-mushroom roulade for supper. She'd also learnt how to make choux pastry, she told me, but still hadn't mastered fried eggs. She loved Lewis, but didn't want to talk about the wedding. She still cried every night about Selena. She hugged me before she left and asked me to cross my fingers for her. I said I would.

Arthur ignored me that evening and the whole of the next day.

The next time Paul phoned he seemed very subdued and asked when he could call to collect some of his things. I told him to come later that day, invited him to bring Francesca with him, but was relieved when he said she was, as usual, far too busy.

When he arrived at the house we'd shared for almost ten years, he was pale and tense, unwilling to look at me, unable to decide what packing to do first, unable to start on anything. I pretended not to notice, but felt pleased that it was he and not I who'd decided on the break-up. After a while I got him to sit down with a coffee and gradually he managed to relax.

He said the wedding preparations were going well, that Annabel was managing to keep a check on Francesca's excesses. 'So it's going to be fairly low-key?' I asked. At which we smiled ruefully at each other.

Francesca had spent the previous day with one of the organists of Westminster Abbey, an uncle, as it happened, of one of her clients, deciding on the right size pipe-organ for Horeb. Paul said she'd described the chapel as 'an architectural gem, just a little bigger than my drawing room'. It was to be in place in time for Christmas and I was to go with them for the presentation ceremony. It was difficult to hate Francesca. I decided I wasn't going to try any longer.

Paul didn't get much packing done that day, but we both realised that the most harrowing part was over.

'Did you see the obituary in this morning's *Times*?' he asked me as he was leaving. 'That German professor you met on the train – Dr Joanna something.'

I sat down heavily in the nearest chair. 'I can't believe it. I've been trying to get in touch with her.'

'I recognised her photograph. Sad. She was only forty-three. An embolism in the brain. I'll get you the paper from the car.'

228

I hurried Paul away so that I could be alone. A third death. I felt sick and faint. It shouldn't be affecting me as much as it was. I hardly knew her; we'd only spoken for a few minutes. But I'd wanted her as a friend, felt she *was* a friend. And suddenly she was dead. And exactly my age. I studied her photograph, read an account of her life, her scholastic achievements, all the while shivering with fear and shock.

I wanted Rhydian, needed him. Life was too short for scruples. When the month was up and he phoned, I'd beg him to come to me. I don't mean for ever, I still didn't intend to break up his marriage, but he could surely visit Bleddyn for the occasional weekend and spend some time with me. Because I needed him. I needed him. I needed him as a bird needed the sky. I wasn't going to give him up. Not entirely.

About a week after this and a few days before Annabel's wedding, I woke up one morning suddenly realising that my period was late and that I might, that I just conceivably might . . . be pregnant. Until then, the possibility of such a thing had never occurred to me. As soon as it did, I was almost sick with excitement, realising that it was the one thing in the world which would make me really, deeply, truly happy. I felt it was my last chance and my best chance. To have deliberately set out to have a baby would have been selfish and irresponsible, I accepted that, but the possibility had never crossed my mind. If I was pregnant it was by some divine chance.

A brisk walk to the nearest chemist's. A pregnancy test, the kit with the most fool-proof instructions. A slow walk back trying not to think how I'd feel if the result was negative. I felt as nervous about the outcome as a woman who'd been having infertility treatment for years, as though all my life I'd been denied an inalienable right.

Yes, I was pregnant. *Yes*. And I felt as though I'd won the lottery prize. The big one. And much more besides.

Much, much more. I was deliriously, insanely happy. Oh, if only it was a little girl. Or a little boy. I didn't really mind which.

Oh, I was going to be so careful. I was going to cook myself proper meals and drink gallons of milk and take proper exercise. And go to classes for breathing and relaxation and to clinics for advice about nipples.

I knew it would be difficult. But when, from the age of three, had my life *not* been difficult? I was obviously partial to difficult. If I'd wanted an easy life I wouldn't have become an actor, for a start. OK, I was old to have a first baby, but I didn't care; I was healthy and anyway feeling younger by the minute. I had a colleague who, pregnant in her early thirties, had been annoyed to be classified as an 'elderly primigravida'. They could call me whatever they chose. I'd be forty-four by the time my baby was born but it suddenly seemed a marvellous age in every way. I was strong and determined, I had money and a fairly decent career and a family house with a cat. And I was going to have a baby with the only man I'd ever truly and passionately loved. That seemed a miracle in itself. Of course I wanted to tell him, but I didn't intend to at the moment. Eventually he'd have to know, but that would be when the stardust had settled. Yes, of course I'd manage to see him now and again. He was a part of my life and I was a part of his. Our affair had had a beautiful inevitability and would have a beautiful outcome. All day, my mind was full of shining words: baby, having a baby, birth, birth-pains, baby-love, love-child, cradle, nursery, lullaby, hope, hope for the future, woman, mother, fulfilment, destiny. The word destiny seemed to absolve me from much of the blame. Adultery was a hard word, but destiny was kind and forgiving.

Life was wonderful at times and this was one of the wonderful times.

\*

That evening, still ecstatic, I had a phone call from a young director, Isabel Alexander, who'd been assisting at the Young Vic when I'd played Varya in *Cherry Orchard*. She'd become an assistant director at the Manchester Exchange and had been asked to direct a *Hamlet* there in March and was contacting me to see whether I'd be interested in playing Gertrude.

Gertrude? I'd be thrilled to play Gertrude. It was a stunning part. It would be such a great challenge after the months of being the meek little nobody in the less than wonderful, what am I talking about, I mean the *pitifully poor* television serial which was limping on until the end of February. March. It fitted in beautifully. It couldn't possibly be more . . .

Except that I'd be gorgeously and wondrously five months' pregnant by March.

'I'm so pleased that you're enthusiastic,' Isabel was saying. 'You were my first choice. You've got such a presence. You're so bold and sexy. But so vulnerable, as well. You're exactly . . .'

Interrupting someone who's in the middle of singing my praises is usually the last thing I think of, but this time I did. 'There's just one problem,' I said. 'I'm pregnant. And I'll be about five months' pregnant by March . . . But I daresay a loose, dress in some heavy, regal velvet would conceal it perfectly. Perhaps I shouldn't even have mentioned it. Only, you see, I'm longing to tell someone. It's my first baby. And I've only today found out.'

Isabel hid any surprise she may have been feeling. 'I'm glad you did tell me. Congratulations. And you'll be fine. I can't see there'll be any problem . . . Anyway, why shouldn't Gertrude be pregnant? If she was, wouldn't that make Hamlet's jealousy even more understandable? And, hey, by the closet scene, we could pad you up so that you were looking really heavily pregnant, which would be a cunning way to show the passing of time. And which would give an added poignancy to Hamlet's treatment of her in that scene. Wouldn't it? What do you think? Oh God, I think we could be on to something. Don't you?'

'I'll be thrilled to play Gertrude. That's all I can think of at the moment.'

'I wonder if a pregnant Gertrude has ever been a feature of any production? I suppose so. You can't really do anything new with Shakespeare, can you?'

'I don't think it's strictly necessary. But on the other hand, it might give the critics something to chew over. Have you got a Hamlet?'

'I think so. Robin Furnival. He was marvellous in *Darnley* – did you see it? They're already calling him the new Ewan McGregor. Did you see the notice in the *Guardian?* An absolute rave.'

'And what about Claudius?

'No, I haven't got a Claudius yet. Of course, John Thaw would be my first choice. He did a lot of Shakespeare, you know. In the RSC – '84 I think. I've contacted his agent. I suppose he could be in between television serials. What do you think?'

'We could be lucky. I'd certainly like to work with him.'


I shivered again as I thought of Joanna Morton who was dead. And my mother, her sky-blue wedding suit still hanging in the wardrobe. And little Selena, whom I hadn't taken the trouble to get to know properly. But they passed like shadows across the sun of my joy. My intake of breath seemed to reach down to my womb. Already, I felt heavy with child.

I played Beethoven's *Choral* very loudly. *Freude. Freude. Freude.* And afterwards, as I cooked myself some eggs, I thought about Rhydian and his family; my Auntie Jane, so steadfast and loyal and Uncle Ted, a bit of a rogue, perhaps, but handsome and very likeable. And I suddenly remembered my mother telling me that Uncle Ted's grandfather had burned down tollgates in his youth and in old age become a famous poacher. In Wales, we're proud of our ancestors, particularly the rebels and eccentrics. Perhaps my child's great-grandchildren would one day boast about me: a middle-aged actor – and not a bad actor, either, in fact her Gertrude was said to be rather fine – who decided she wanted a baby. In her middle forties. Why didn't she walk across the Sahara, climb Everest, book a passage to the moon? Crazy or what? No husband, no partner, no lover in evidence – and that, apparently, quite unusual back in the twentieth century. And they say she never regretted it, that she revelled in all the pleasure and worry and work, grew fat on it.

I played the *Choral* again. *Joy. Joy.* It was the best day of the first half of my life.

# Visit the Piatkus website!

Piatkus publishes a wide range of exciting fiction and non-fiction, including books on health, mind body & spirit, sex, self-help, cookery, biography and the paranormal. If you want to:

* read descriptions of our popular titles

* buy our books over the internet

* take advantage of our special offers

* enter our monthly competition

* learn more about your favourite Piatkus authors

## visit our website at:

## www.piatkus.co.uk